The Heart of the Lightkeeper's Daughter

The Sea Crest Lighthouse Series
Book One

Carolyn Court

Esther,

I hope you

Enjoy this story!

Carolyn

Court

First Edition Design Publishing
Sarasota, Florida USA

The Heart of the Lightkeeper's Daughter
Copyright ©2019 Carolyn Court

ISBN 978-1506-908-10-6 AMZ PBK
ISBN 978-1506-908-02-1 TRADE PBK
ISBN 978-1506-908-03-8 EBK
ISBN 978-1506-908-26-7 AUDIO

LCCN 2019937852

May 2019

Published and Distributed by
First Edition Design Publishing, Inc.
P.O. Box 17646, Sarasota, FL 34276-3217
www.firsteditiondesignpublishing.com

Cover Art: Consuelo Parra and Model: Kuoma-stock.deviantart

Library of Congress Cataloging-in-Publication Data
Court, Carolyn.
The Heart of the Lightkeeper's Daughter, Series Book One, The Sea Crest Lighthouse Series
/ written by Carolyn Court.
    p. cm.
  ISBN 978-1506-908-10-6 AMZ PBK
  ISBN 978-1506-908-02-1 TR PBK
  ISBN 978-1506-908-03-8 EBK
  ISBN 978-1506-908-26-7 AUDIO

FICTION / Romance / Suspense . 2. / Contemporary. 3. / General.

T3744

10 9 8 7 6 5 4 3 2 1

In memory of my loving mother,

Evelyn Courtright.

Mom wrote numerous warm and wonderful poems, that were most often, faith-filled and insightful words of wisdom. She also had a talent for highlighting humorous situations with a lighthearted positive twist.

I'm grateful that I had the privilege of spending a meaningful period in my life to pause and share a journey with her. I read all of her poems to her often and we shared the chapters of this book as I finished each one. I will always treasure our precious time together.

Chapter 1

Kate couldn't breathe. She grabbed her chest as her legs buckled beneath her.

No one had ever said it would be like this.

She cried out in pain as her knees hit the pavement. With tears streaming down her face, she opened her clenched fist and tried to focus her eyes on the voucher.

What were those numbers? Yes. It's my birthday plus my house number. These are the numbers I play every week.

She stared sleepily at her ticket as she woke up and her eyes focused on the sheet of notepaper she loosely held in her hand. Bit by bit, she realized, she was actually looking at a list of ideas she had been compiling for a meeting this afternoon.

Wow, she thought. *What an exciting dream. That was probably the closest I'll ever come to winning the lottery. Maybe if I'm quick, I can fall back asleep and pick up where I left off.*

However, with her heart still pounding a mile-a-minute, Kate was far too elated and keyed up for that to happen. Instead, she began to fantasize about what it would mean to win the lottery. With her limited observations, she supposed that, *when most people daydream about winning the lottery, they usually pick one of three basic arguments to rationalize why they deserve to be that one lucky winner. These justifications for un-earned riches range from living a life of total luxury after all of our hard work and tough breaks, to the other extreme, which involves a level of benevolence that only the likes of Mother Theresa could achieve.*

In our minds and with nothing to lose, these are the most popular options.

Number 1: This is what we really want, but we would never say out loud. You can quit your job and enjoy every luxury you can dream of for the rest of your life.

Number 2: You can share your winnings with family and friends. You might still be able to quit your job, but you will need to be a little more careful with your money. Okay, that sounds much better.

Number 3: You can share your winnings with those less fortunate and hope it brings some good into the world. That teeters on the very edge of the beauty contestants' most frequent answer with their wish for World Peace. (Oh ... come on.)

Now, Kate took a giant leap back to reality and acknowledged that, *most people in this world, will not, in fact, win the lottery or anything else.*

Coast Guard Captain, Kate Walsh rose from the recliner in the keeper's cottage, studied her list and as she scanned it, she murmured to herself, "I know I can't give the proceeds of a winning lottery ticket to anyone. However, I know my friends and I can make a positive improvement in the lives of the people in the Sea Crest area, by doing anonymous acts of kindness."

She was smiling at the thought of meeting with her co-conspirators, this afternoon, as her mother entered from the side door of the keeper's cottage.

"Hi, Kate. How did your Search and Rescue Training go with the recruits, this morning?"

"It went fine. In fact, they are a terrific group. I'm trying to put a project together which will combine the helicopter with other air/sea vehicles."

"That sounds like very useful knowledge for them to learn," agreed her mom, as she put down the papers, she had carried in.

"I've just met with your dad and the safety engineers to assess the storm damage to our lighthouse and the walkway that leads out to the tower. It looks like our lighthouse sustained only slight cosmetic damage, although the walkway, and the jetty that supports it, needs total reconstruction. However, we're lucky the damage wasn't worse."

Her mother crossed to the window, adjusted the plantation shutters and gazed at the tower which was surrounded by crashing waves and crumpled debris. "We need to finalize our repair options and costs, to assess how much money we'll need to raise at the Sea Crest Festival this weekend. By the way, were you able to train and certify the extra American Red Cross lifeguards you'll need for the beach?"

"Yes! The final classes were completed last week. Plus, many available Coast Guard trainees have volunteered to help out."

"I love it that you chose to follow in the footsteps of your dad and grandfather."

"Well I love that our family has been the Coast Guard lightkeepers here at Sea Crest for three generations. That's what we know and who we are," laughed Kate as she hugged her.

"Well, I couldn't be prouder," replied her Mom.

"Oh, in a few minutes I'll be heading out for my Mah Jongg game."

Meanwhile, across town, Kate's best friend Maggie, was finishing up her judo practice, in her back yard. She executed the clean and precise movements of the drill with grace and power until her eyebrows perked up.

Yes, the swaying of the branches along the top of the hedge mysteriously stops every time I finish a move.

Maggie brought her hands and arms up to pose in a fighting stance.

What or who is that? With every action I make, the rocking of the leaves increases and it's coming closer.

With one more move, she somersaulted over and pulled a pistol off a chaise lounge as she drew down on the intruder.

She found herself face to face with a Great Dane. Maggie froze in place, as she carefully withdrew her out-stretched arm, laid the gun on the grass and gently ask, "Where did you come from?"

The huge dog seemed curious but showed no fear as it came closer.

Maggie laughed at herself and wondered what the dog thought of this absurd behavior, *I'll bet you haven't seen anyone else display judo, gymnastics or pulled a gun on you before.*

She extended the back of her hand toward the dog as it came forward for a lick, and a friend was made. She smiled as she praised the dog in a calm voice, "Okay, good dog, good dog."

This time the Great Dane sat down and looked at her.

I've never seen a Great Dane up close and personal, like this before, she acknowledged to herself, chuckling at her amusing understatement.

"Yes, you have a clean, almost sleek, shiny black coat and you look magnificent," she murmured softly.

The large dog looked expectantly at her and voiced a small whine, as Maggie continued to look the dog over for any clues as to why this mysterious dog had arrived in her back yard. She only discovered that this was a female dog, but had no collar or identification tag of any kind.

"Who do you belong to?" Maggie whispered.

Maggie rose and walked with caution toward the back door of her home. When she said, "Stay," the dog immediately stopped and sat down again. The dog remained sitting until Maggie directed, "Okay, Sweetie, come on. I have to set the tiles up for a Mah Jongg game."

The dog promptly got up and hurried along behind Maggie as she went through the French doors into her home. The Great Dane followed her into the kitchen, and when Maggie stopped at the table, she sat down and put her paw out. Maggie laughed as she patted the head of this surprising dog.

Maggie gave her a dish of water and then proceeded to open and shut various cupboard doors as she said, "Let me check if I have anything at all you can eat. I used to have some treats and food for Kate's dog in here."

"First, you must promise not to tell anyone what's hidden in here," Maggie disclosed with a secretive whisper. She slowly opened the double glass doors to the nearby china hutch but the delicate lace curtains were hanging inside of each door, which hid the contents from the dog's view.

"Just as I expected," she said as she peeked her head inside. "I have no food edible for dogs or humans."

"Well, don't give up hope. My best friend, Kate, is coming over for a meeting of our Mah Jongg Club. I'll call and ask her to bring over some treats for you."

She looked down at the dog as she closed the doors to hide the mysterious contents.

"You'll have an opportunity to see this later. In fact, three of my very good friends are due here any minute. They are joining me this afternoon to finalize our plans regarding a couple of pending situations. Our Mah Jongg Club is actually a cover to plan our Anonymous Acts of Kindness, projects," she explained as she clicked the beautiful doors shut.

"Right now, however, we'll move on to Plan B, and contact Kate."

She could not stop smiling as she put a call into her best friend. "Hi, Kate. I wanted to catch you before you left to come over."

"Great timing. I've got one foot out the door. What do you need?"

Maggie always held the Mah Jongg games at her Sea Crest cottage, and Kate was not only her best friend but also a fierce competitor in the game they both had learned to love. Since Kate was a Coast Guard Search and Rescue Helicopter Pilot, the times for the game, always had to be flexible and revolve around her schedule.

"You'll never guess who just sneaked up on me in the back yard and surprised me. I actually drew my pistol. Nevertheless, they didn't even stand down."

"What? Who would dare do that to you, and why are you so nonchalant about it?"

"It's nobody you know," Maggie haughtily replied.

"Well, does he know you're an FBI Special Agent?"

"I don't think *she* will be impressed one bit by that fact. She is, however, very hungry. Do you think you could bring her some dog food and treats when you come?"

"Very funny," laughed Kate. "How on earth did you manage to end up with a dog?"

"She found me. I was practicing my judo and I saw movement along the bushes in the back. I immediately primed to stop the intruder and out walked this beautiful dog. I never dreamed a Great Dane was this big."

"A Great Dane? You can't be serious. I wonder who she belongs to!"

"I have no idea. She has no dog collar or identification."

"Wow, I wonder why."

"She seems sociable and well behaved. She must belong to a visitor to the Sea Crest Lighthouse or someone that came for the festival this weekend. Oh..." cooed Maggie. "Oh Kate... she just put her paw out, and it is huge."

"This I've got to see. I'll be right there. I think the dog will be much more impressed with me, though. I'll have food."

"Okay, but don't ring the doorbell. I want her to stay calm."

"Fine. I'll be there in five minutes. If her owner shows up, don't let them leave until I see this dog."

Maggie, Kate and two of their other close friends, Mary Beth and Grace, were meeting this afternoon to play one of their frequent Mah Jongg games. Maggie had learned of the ancient Chinese game during her international travels. She found it so fascinating and fun that she bought an American version, with beautiful colorful tiles and decorated wooden racks. The foursome was soon playing at least once a week.

At first, they'd meet to play innocent games of Mah Jongg. However, each time they got together, they found themselves talking about the many challenges that people were facing in the Sea Crest area. That developed into their efforts to help solve various problems secretly.

A short time after her unexpected call from Maggie, Kate arrived at the house and waited at the front door as Mary Beth and Grace, parked their cars. "You'll never guess who's visiting with Maggie this afternoon," she said with a laugh. "We need to be quiet when we go in, so we don't disturb them."

Mary Beth was shocked. "What do you mean? When was the last time you quietly entered the residence of an FBI Special Agent without knocking?"

Kate slowly opened the door, and there stood Maggie with an enormous black dog as big as a miniature pony. She invited them in with great warmth, so the dog would know they *came in peace*.

Mary Beth and Grace were flabbergasted as they clutched each other's arms in alarm. They both started talking at once. "What on earth?" "My goodness, is that a dog?"

Kate laughed out loud as she sailed forward and gave the dog a treat. As she handed the rest of the food to Maggie, she heard her two friends remark, "Kate, you're going to pay for setting us up."

"I'm shamelessly trying to score points," she said. "I can't believe this dog just showed up in your backyard."

"Well, she did," beamed Maggie. "I'm going to call her Misha."

"Wait just a minute. You cannot give her a name. She's not even your dog," protested Kate.

"Of course, I can. I need to call her something, and she answers to Misha, so that's her name," explained Maggie, daring anyone to disagree.

Kate just shook her head at Maggie, as she said, "We'll talk about that later. Right now, we have to talk about one of our acts of kindness. I just ordered our Mah Jongg pizza. Before Alex gets here with our delivery, bring me up to date on what we planned for him.

"If I remember, since he is an outstanding Botany student, headed for college, we needed a way for him to 'accidentally' meet someone very special who could serve as a mentor for him."

Mary Beth chimed in, "Yes, we arranged for Alex to meet our recently retired, Botanist and Master Gardener, Mr. Brown. He needed his garden gate fixed. Now, who better to appear out of nowhere than Alex, our outstanding student and pizza boy?"

Grace smiled with delight as she agreed, "It's working out beautifully. Mary Beth and I left a note in Alex's car last night, while it was parked outside the pizzeria."

Mary Beth continued, "It had directions to: *call the 800 number and leave a message, to either accept or reject the surprise job to fix Professor Brown's broken garden gate. Take no money from Mr. Brown but keep the attached Universal Gift card as payment.*"

"He called our 800-number last night and accepted. Won't Alex be surprised to see the extensive garden and beautiful flowers that grow at Mr. Brown's home?" replied Grace.

"Better yet, won't Alex be surprised when he sees what stands behind this front door?" asked Kate with a laugh.

Alex had just parked his car in the circular driveway and was now proceeding up the walkway to deliver their pizza.

Moments later, the doorbell rang. Maggie stayed a couple of steps back, petting Misha, while Kate cautiously opened the door. None of the women had any idea how the dog would handle this new situation, but they were not disappointed.

Alex started to step inside, but he stopped short when he caught a glimpse of the huge dog. With his right foot still suspended in mid-air, he stumbled awkwardly backward, almost falling into the bushes. The pizza teetered precariously, balanced with his hands, arms, and even his knee, as he tried to keep from dropping it. He finally landed with both feet planted firmly on the floor.

"Gee, you have a dog," exclaimed Alex. "He sure is big. I've never seen a dog like this before."

"Well, Alex, he is a she, and her name is Misha," explained Maggie.

"And we're not certain if she'll be able to stay," Kate sternly added with a warning look at her friend.

"Oh, is she an FBI dog or something?" asked Alex. "I'm sure she'll be very effective."

"We don't know who she belongs to. We don't see any identification on her. Alex, could you keep a lookout for any news of someone missing a Great Dane dog like this?" asked Kate.

"Sure, but you'd be surprised at the number of people that drop their pets off somewhere if they get too big, or they can't take care of them anymore," said Alex. He shook his head as he laid the pizza on the counter.

"Do you mean they abandon them in a strange place?" asked Maggie with alarm.

"That's what one of my friends told me. His name is Matt, and he works part-time at the animal shelter. I'll ask him tomorrow in school if anyone has come in asking about a lost dog like this," he promised as he turned and left.

From the window, the women watched Alex's vehicle exit the driveway and wondered how on earth the dog had ended up in Sea Crest.

After a few minutes, Kate broke the silence, "Let's eat! This pizza looks delicious."

"I have a pitcher of pink lemonade in the refrigerator," offered Maggie.

"I'll get the napkins and paper plates," added Grace, as they settled around the table.

After a few minutes of small talk, things moved on to the anonymous acts that were in play. Once again, Maggie proudly opened the double doors to the nearby china hutch. Misha promptly moved over to stand beside her, curious to see what was behind the lace curtains.

Maggie laughed as she told Misha, "See, I told you there were no treats in here."

Kate stepped around the corner to give Misha another dog biscuit and the dog curled up at Maggie's feet.

The women now surveyed the extensive storyboards hanging inside, which displayed newspaper clippings, notes, and pictures of almost every person in town. This masterpiece revealed the oldest citizens right down to the newborn babies. It was a montage of drawings, stick figures, various numbers, letters and question marks made with magic markers, as well as a variety of sticky notes, lighthouse pictures, and little maps. This research had taken weeks to compile.

Over the next hour or so, they laid out details of their plans in progress. Each of the women had specific responsibilities to complete as they worked together to accomplish their latest secret acts of kindness.

Maggie stated, "My top priority is to check on the progress of buying the Chambers' beach house property. It's an ideal location to set up coastal surveillance as a combined partnership between the FBI and the Coast Guard, to investigate and prohibit smuggling and impede the drug problems along this coastal area.

"We think the beach house, more like a mansion, on the hill overlooking the Sea Crest Lighthouse, would be ideal, if it's priced right. I understand the elderly owner, who has not used it for years, recently died. Since the relatives have not even visited here for years, we assumed that they might be happy to sell."

"We did reach out to the family through our attorney, to try to locate any known family," added Mary Beth. "Now we just have to wait."

After some additional discussion, Grace said, "Well, I guess I'm up next and it looks like we're on the same page. In my effort to research any history that involves Sea Crest, I ran across some information that might shed some light on things. I plan to attend a storage unit auction in Rosemont tomorrow morning. I was surprised to see two units listed under the name of Chambers."

Grace flipped through the papers on her clipboard, until she found the details she'd been searching for. As her hands came to a stop, she continued, "Here they are. I plan to buy both units, #2041 and #2042, on the outside chance that the owners are the same Chambers that own the beach house."

"Do we have enough money?" Kate asked.

"Yes. The research grant provided sufficient funds to purchase both units if they don't cost too much. I was thinking, since Mrs. Chambers recently died, that may account for the fact that no one had kept up the rental payments on these units. I'm sure money is no object for *our* Chambers family."

Now that their plan of action for the next few days was set in place; the women could turn their competitive talents to their favorite game.

Kate looked at the thirteen Mah Jongg tiles on her rack as she thought, *Okay, let's see what I've got here. Two flowers, two north winds, one east wind, an assortment of mostly even numbers and one joker make up my entire hand. These tiles don't represent a favorable chance of working into a winning Mah Jongg hand for me, but I'll see what I can do, when we begin to play.*

Misha stood up and could easily view the entire game as she walked around the table. She was extremely interested in these little tiles and carefully poked her head in and out, to investigate the various hands, but didn't disturb anything. "That's right, Misha. You let me know what they've got," laughed Maggie.

Each of the women was adept at taking a mediocre hand and producing a winning Mah Jongg, depending on a little luck and a lot of flexibility. Kate was feeling pretty good as she silently prepared, *one of my most valuable keys to victory is my ability to change my plan, if my original idea dissolves, as the game progresses. I'll figure out what other viable options will still work with the tiles I have left.*

Once the player's possibilities have decreased to the point of no conceivable way to win, they needed to play defensively and make sure that no one else can win either. These friends had gotten surprisingly skillful at this, all the while looking innocent and angelic, as if they did not mean to derail anyone else and prevent them from winning.

At last..., an Air/Sea Rescue Helicopter Pilot, an FBI Special Agent, a Realtor, and a Historical Ancestry Researcher sat down to play Mah Jongg.

What could possibly go wrong?

Unfortunately, they were about to find out that the plans they put in place today would have far-reaching ramifications. They would, in fact, wreak total havoc on the Sea Crest community. The surprises they were soon to discover, would turn their world upside down, and prove that nothing was, as it seemed.

Chapter 2

Meanwhile, halfway around the world in London, Michael Jensen, a renowned architect, specializing in lighthouse repair and restoration, was delivering the keynote speech at the annual meeting of the International Summit for Disaster Preparedness and Recovery.

Jensen was a founding member and leading participant in this European think tank and annual get together of some of the brightest minds in the field.

"Welcome. Good to see all of you again this year," Michael began. "The main topics under discussion will continue to be our focus on ways to prevent the loss of human life in disaster situations. I am sure you all are aware of the vital role such things as water purification, medical assistance, and economic revitalization play in this effort. The primary subject today is safe shelters.

"One of our primary goals is to concentrate on prevention," he explained. "The impact of these natural disasters will be reduced a great deal once these precautionary measures are underway. When a catastrophe does occur, this will enable us to speed up the recovery time and stabilization of the hardest hit areas.

"Next, I'd like to share the status of the safe shelters that my team has been perfecting since our mid-year session."

He smiled as he stepped forward and prepared to show off his pet project.

"Many of you have contributed to developing the emergency shelter model, and we would like to bring everyone up to date on our finished product. Those presenters, who developed the protocol and nuances of this unusual project, please join me up here on the stage. We want to show what we were able to accomplish when we worked together.

"Now, we want to demonstrate how easy and quick we can snap these simple pieces together to assemble our modular shelters."

As his team gathered around and got ready, he laughed as he instructed, "That's right, I want someone to time us." He pointed to a colleague in the front row, who was holding his watch in the air.

"Okay, go!" he called out, as he flagged the start by waving his arm.

"I'll describe a few of the features as they build," Michael said.

"The basic kit includes a pile of 8 large, flat, modular squares. Each one is approximately 6 inches thick and extremely lightweight. What you can't tell from your seats is that these are actually stronger than a concrete block.

"Now please watch while we join and lock these sections together at a 90-degree angle. With one effortless click these two modules now create two waterproof and insulated walls, which can withstand 120 MPH winds."

The team showed off the lightweight secure bond to the audience by picking it up and easily moving it around.

Michael continued, "Next we will connect two more walls to form a giant box. We have now built a square, which is the basis of our shelter.

"This structure is adaptable to expand to various living quarters, as needed. For example: if we secure these four corners above ground onto the pile stilts which are included, it will stabilize and keep this refuge safe during various weather events."

The team demonstrated how easy it was to bond the two sections together.

"Please notice that one of the sides has a hinged opening embedded into the wall. This will serve as a doorway."

The team opened and shut the movable section for the audience to see.

"Now we will add two of the special sheets that have pre-attached solar panels, to the top. They create a rooftop," Michael proudly finished.

He felt his phone start to vibrate in his pocket. He reached for it, recognized the caller's phone number, and promptly ignored it.

Hearing the spontaneous clapping of hands, he turned his attention back to the audience and announced, "I'll now hand this demonstration over to the solar panel, the water purifier and the wind power experts so they can show how this shelter functions."

As the team members came forward, Michael stepped back, behind the stage and took his phone out. He was annoyed as he looked at the screen and glared at his uptight brother's number.

Oh! What does he want now? Well, I guess I have no choice but to answer it.

As he reluctantly connected, he promptly heard a barrage of irritating threats. Michael tried to defend himself from this exasperating call, "Yes, I know. Look, I told you I would do what I can."

That apparently was not good enough for his irate brother.

"Okay, I'm sorry, James," Michael explained. "You don't have to yell, for heaven's sake. I said I'd do it."

"Listen! I never promised I would be on that earlier flight, but I will try to get on the very next flight."

"Well, just give me a chance to write it all down. Okay, the storage sale is tomorrow, in a town called Rosemont? Units #2041 and #2042. Man, I don't know why you can't take care of this yourself."

This was met with such an eruption of objections until finally Michael had heard enough. He practically yelled into the phone, "Listen, I am in the middle of an important conference, and I cannot leave until noon."

He quickly followed up with a firm, "Look, I have to go. I'll do the best I can. Goodbye!"

Michael was extremely frustrated as he ended the call. *This is crazy. I can't seem to extricate myself from the ridiculous assignment that I'm expected to carry out.*

He put a smile on his face as he walked around to the front of the audience. He joined in the applause with heartfelt pride and invited everyone in the audience to come up and check out the shelter.

"By the way," he added. "The lifespan of each of these units is approximately twenty years. Depending on the number of panels you connect, it can accommodate a family of four to eight people. The attachable bathroom panels, running water and electricity are also included to make the shelter self-sufficient, as well as safe.

"We have reached out to various manufacturing businesses, as well as numerous humanitarians, to help advance our disaster relief efforts. Philanthropic endeavors from across the globe have been extraordinary."

Michael finished with the sobering acknowledgment, "This shelter idea, started one year ago and kept moving forward until one day, *it all just clicked.*"

Everyone laughed and celebrated the success of the new creative structures.

Michael thanked everyone who worked on the project and handed over the conference to the next presenter.

Within two hours, Mr. Michael Jensen had boarded a flight to New York City. He was dreading the job he'd been conned into doing after he landed.

Chapter 3

"This is not good," groaned Grace as she tried to get out of bed the morning after the meeting of the Mah Jongg Club. Every bone in her body ached. Yes, every single one.

"Ok slowly. Let's try that again. This better not be the flu that's been going around. I cannot be sick today." Grace needed to get up and dressed, get to Rosemont, and purchase the contents of the storage units thought to belong to the Chambers family.

I can do this, she thought as she put on jeans, two sweaters, a big scarf over her head and another one around her neck. The day was gloomy but she donned sunglasses to cover her swollen eyes, gingerly walked to her car and drove to Kate's for help.

It was a sniveling, red-eyed, disheveled Grace who weakly climbed the front steps of the lighthouse keeper's cottage, and presented herself at Kate's door fifteen minutes later.

When Kate opened the door, she took one look at Grace and cried out, "What happened to you? You look awful. You need to go back home and get into bed."

"But I'm supposed to buy the Chambers' units at the storage sale," she said sneezing. "I don't feel like I should drive."

"You have no business going anywhere. I'll make a deal with you, okay? You go back home, and I will buy the storage units. Give me all the details I'll need to know."

Grace gladly handed over an envelope of cash required to bid on units, directions, time of the sale and the identifying numbers of the units. Now Kate was ready to buy.

"This change of plans will fit perfectly for a Coast Guard project I've been trying to set up," said Kate as Grace backed out of the driveway.

She had been looking for an opportunity to do a training  exercise for her students with various combined vehicles. She planned to use the Coast Guard Rescue Helicopter for air. The US Navy HU-16 Albatross, the amphibious air/seaplane was going to be used for the sea, the land, and the air. The trucks would cover any additional land portions of the project. "This will work out great," exclaimed Kate.

Kate had her two flying students, Ryan and Dylan, meet her as previously planned, but requested they wear casual street clothes when they joined her. They flew her nine-passenger Rescue Helicopter up the coast and landed in Rosemont without a problem.

They took a truck from the little airport and soon the three arrived at the storage location.

Kate said, "Okay, we've got about an hour before the actual auction starts, but we need to sign up in the office and pay an upfront fee. We don't have much time; we need to get familiar with everything real fast. We also need to find out which units were owned by the Chambers. We don't want the other bidders to suspect how interested we are in these two units."

"I've never been to one of these sales before," Ryan stated as he looked around. He was excited to be included in this training exercise and he was thrilled that his flying skills had maneuvered the helicopter flawlessly.

"This should be fascinating," he finished with a smile.

Dylan would fly the return trip to Sea Crest after the sale. "What do you want us to do?" he asked. As an after-thought he asked, "Can we bid on something?"

Kate laughed, "That's a splendid idea. Bid, but *Do Not Buy* anything. Gauge what you think the bidders are going to offer, then try to blend in with the other people. It's a way to distract everyone else from the real reason we're here today."

"The Chambers' units are #2041 and #2042. They are in the climate-controlled building," Kate explained.

"I have money that should more than cover, the typical cost of the units. I also have three extra combination locks to put on the units after we buy them. Later we'll use the truck and load the contents of what we bought."

They walked toward the small gathering of people who were waiting for the auction to begin. There were many different types of people, some wearing very casual clothes, some single shoppers, some in pairs, maybe friends and maybe family. Kate and the two pilots in training blended in with the other people who were attending the storage locker sale today.

The auctioneer addressed the crowd in a loud voice, "Good morning everyone. We're going to start the auction right on time."

Several people responded eagerly, "Good," "Yeah," "OK."

He continued, "The rules are simple. No one can go inside the units, only look from the outside. You have to pay with cash. If you don't have the money in your pocket today, don't bid." He concluded with the last few rules as he walked to the first unit.

His assistant cut off the lock and opened the first doorway. "Right this way folks. Keep the lines moving."

Thus, the auction began. The units had an impressive array of things. Some had personal belongings; some had toys and Christmas decorations with fake trees.

One unit had what looked like the contents of an entire card shop that had gone out of business; not just a lot of merchandise but sales racks, a glass-topped display case, a cash register and a safe. The buyers were loudly bidding against each other for that unit.

Kate even bid a couple of times on that unit to cover up that she was, in fact, there to buy the Chambers' units. The auction moved along very quickly.

The two Chambers' units came up individually for sale. A couple of people seemed interested, but nobody could get a good look at anything inside. The units had big boxes towards the front, hiding what was behind them. Several people put in bids, but it was obvious they were bidding blind.

Kate waited for a short time before she started bidding herself because she did not want to look too eager. She joined in and replayed her previous style of not being too concerned if she was successful or not. When she finally placed the winning bid, she was relieved. Her luck held out, and she got the second Chambers' unit for a reasonable price also.

After the auction ended, the flight students arrived with the amphibious vehicle to help, and they soon had everything packed up.

They unpacked the truck onto the Navy HU-16 Albatross, and the team headed for Sea Crest.

Everything had come off without a hitch; however, Kate soon discovered that they were not the only interested party in the Chambers' storage units.

Chapter 4

The other interested person had boarded a plane at the London Heathrow Airport last night. Yesterday's inclement weather had created havoc with the departure of hundreds of planes in the entire area. These flights could not be diverted to London Gatwick Airport or other nearby airports because they were all caught in the same weather situation. The delays and cancellations had been escalating all day long.

As a result, Michael Jensen's flight to New York City was completely overbooked. It was packed with tired, unhappy, stressed out passengers who were crammed into the one and only flight for the entire day. The plane sat on the runway for hours in a very long line behind many other aircraft, waiting for clearance to take off.

When, at last this passenger arrived at the New York City airport, he went directly to the car rental area. The agent looked up his reservation and relayed the sad news regarding his red sports convertible. It had, in fact, been rented out to someone else. As a last resort, Michael Jensen accepted the keys to the one remaining vehicle on the lot, which unfortunately turned out to be a very sub-compact older model car.

He tried to fit his legs into the small car, which proved to be extremely uncomfortable and very cramped, as he drove to Rosemont. However, his problems didn't end there. He had trouble finding the storage place that was auctioning off the Chambers' belongings.

Michael hurried into the storage company's front office only to find the manager finalizing the results of the sale with the auctioneer. Luckily, the auctioneer had left the clipboard on the counter when he went to answer a phone call. Michael had been

 able to see the name and phone number of the buyer. Kate Walsh, from Sea Crest, had purchased both of the Chambers' units. He quickly jotted down her phone number and the amount she had paid for each unit. He turned around and left before the auctioneer returned.

Much later that day, when Kate got home from her training adventure, she had a message on her phone.

"Hello, I understand you purchased the property from two storage units this morning. I'd like to acquire their contents. I am sure I can make it worth your while. In fact, I would be happy to help you out with what you would consider a good deal," Michael explained in a self-important voice.

"Depending on what I see, I might take both units off your hands," he said. "Maybe I'll even go as high as twice the money you paid. Call me when you get this message, Michael."

Kate did not like the attitude and arrogance that she detected from his tone. He left a phone number where she could contact him. The area code was from New York City.

How could he have gotten my name and phone number? Did the storage company give out your private information to just anyone?

She was flabbergasted at the audacity of this guy. *Does he think he can just call me up and get our stuff? Well, we'll see about that, buddy.*

Kate called Grace, "Hi, how are you feeling?"

Grace said, "I'm doing much better, thanks. I appreciate you going to the auction for me, today. How much did you end up paying for each unit? Did you see any value in the contents yet?"

Kate explained all about the auction and her training exercise.

"My students came through with flying colors, and the mission was a success. I do, however, have a few questions for you."

"Okay," replied Grace.

"I was somewhat surprised to find a phone message when I got home today. It was from some guy named Michael who says he wanted to buy the contents from at least one of the storage units from today's sale. He would even pay me twice as much as I paid for it at the auction. I did not like his attitude one little bit. When he left his phone number where I was supposed to call him, the area code was from New York City."

Kate continued, "Is it normal for someone to follow up and get the name and contact information of the buyer that got a particular unit?" She was starting to get rather fired up.

"I mean, how could he have gotten my name and phone number in the first place? Did the storage company give out your private information to just anyone?"

CAROLYN COURT

"No, I've never known that to happen.," Grace answered. "However, many of the regular buyers know each other. Sometimes they will deal back and forth while they are emptying their lockers. One buyer might have a second-hand shop and need particular items that another customer has gotten, and sometimes the one who just bought the locker is eager to sell things on the spot to a ready buyer."

"Oh sure, I can certainly understand that."

Next Grace asked, "Did anyone try to outbid you?"

"No," Kate answered. "I think I would have noticed. We had a few bidders interested. None of us could see past the first couple of large boxes, and nothing unusual was visible. The other bidders didn't seem too interested after the first few bids, so they dropped out."

Grace suddenly thought she had a logical explanation. "Maybe Michael figured you were pretty and wanted to go out with you," she suggested. "Although, on second thought, it's not usually a place to pick up an attractive blond, especially if you had a couple of guys with you."

"I'm telling you, Grace, this guy's message sounded like he was very aggravated. He did not sound like he was interested in dating me. I would like to know what the connection is with these specific storage units. The auctioneer does not announce who owns the items, so I am not sure if Michael knows they were both the Chambers' units. I think I should call him back and see what I can find out about him."

Grace agreed, "Yes, but be very careful. Afterward, let me know everything he says."

Chapter 5

Kate planned what she would say to Michael before she dialed his number. For starters, she was going to see what Michael was up to and turn the tables on him. Kate dialed the New York City number he had left.

Michael picked up the phone right away as if he was waiting for her call. "Hello, Michael Jensen speaking," he said abruptly.

"This is Kate," she answered, in an equally sharp tone. "I'm returning your call regarding the storage lockers I acquired today."

He thought he detected an attitude. He decided he better take charge of this phone call and make it clear just who was in control. "Yes, I'm prepared to buy those units, I believe their numbers were #2041 & #2042."

He resented having to talk with her, but he wanted this terrible mistake fixed as soon as possible. He usually had people to handle extraneous or trivial situations that came up in his life. He now needed to straighten out this family issue where someone was trying to steal the storage unit contents, of all things. Michael was getting ready to make a deal with this person and lay out just how it was all going to go down.

"I'd like to know how you got my name and phone number," Kate demanded.

What was that? thought Michael. *She sounded like a street fighter.* He pictured her sitting on the back of a Harley with a seriously tough looking boyfriend. *This is certainly not good.*

"It was on the clipboard at the front desk of the office," Michael responded.

Kate was very peeved as she demanded, "Why did you pick out my two units? Did you think because I'm a woman, I'd be easy to take advantage of?"

Wow, this is going off the tracks fast, thought Michael. *I'd better change tactics in a hurry.*

He answered in a very sincere tone, "Of course not. One of my friends thought they saw something that I'd be interested in and told me you'd bought both units. He doesn't know which one it's in, so I thought I'd do you a favor and buy both of them from you."

That last remark didn't sit well with Kate at all as she retaliated, "What do you mean you thought you'd do me a favor? What do you have in mind?"

He did not want her to know his real reason, so he made up something that he thought should satisfy someone who would usually spend his or her time buying and going through someone else's trash. He tried to hide the disdain he felt for the likes of her as he offered, "Well, I'm willing to pay twice what you paid for them. How does that sound?"

Kate tried to calm down as she thought, *Grace said to see what he's up to, so I'd better string him along for a while.*

She swallowed her pride and agreed, "Well, that sounds more like it." She was very suspicious and decided to have Maggie run a check on him to see if he had a record or anything. To buy time, she agreed to meet with him, but she set a time and place out in the open with lots of people around.

Kate had an idea. "I can meet with you tomorrow around 3 P.M. on the beach by the Sea Crest Lighthouse." She would be finishing one of her surfing classes at 2:30 P.M. That would give her time to change and make sure some of her friends were around.

"What did you say your name is again?" she asked as if she needed to write it down to remember it.

"My name is Michael Jensen," he said proudly. That name certainly meant something, and he was aghast when she asked him to spell it.

Kate almost laughed out loud when he slowly spelled, "J E N S E N."

She just couldn't resist, as she asked, "Mike, did you say, J E N F as in Frank, E N?"

Michael impatiently replied, "No that's S, as in Sam, E N."

"Oh, that's better; I thought your name was Mike JENFEN. Now, this doesn't sound nearly as funny." Kate was enjoying insulting this jerk. Now she needed to get in one last jab. "By the way, don't be late," she demanded as she slammed the phone down.

Michael stared at the phone in his hand. "I can't believe she hung up on me."

Kate, on the other hand, was very satisfied with the whole call. However, she did set the safety plan for the next day in motion.

I'll have no problem identifying any stranger who was seen in the vicinity of the beach beside the Sea Crest Lighthouse, especially if he looks as shady as this guy sounded.

She called Maggie and explained, "Hi, I need a favor."

"Ask away," laughed Maggie. "Misha and I are just looking at the newspaper's Lost and Found section."

Kate jumped in with, "How is the search for her owner coming along? Any luck yet?"

"Well, at this point, I'm looking for *Good Luck*, which would equate to Misha getting to stay with me for good."

"That's what I figured, but please prepare yourself for the reality that her owners may want her back," warned Kate.

"I'm trying, but my heart isn't in it. I visited the animal shelter today and talked with Alex's friend, Matt. He said no one has called or shown up looking for a Great Dane. He verified what Alex told us about the problem of Great Danes growing so large while they are still only puppies. If new owners are not aware of this, they often don't want to keep a huge dog that acts like a puppy."

"Wow, that's so sad."

"Yes, it is. But I'm selfishly hoping that the previous owners DO NOT show up."

"I know. Misha is a beautiful, sweet dog. I hope you get to keep her."

"Thanks. Now what did you call me about?" asked Maggie.

"I bought both of the Chambers' storage units today. Grace was sick, so I went."

"Yeah, I got a call from her this morning after you left," replied Maggie with concern. "How's she doing?"

"I think she's feeling much better this afternoon. However, when I got home around noon, I had a strange message on my answering machine from some guy with a New York City phone number who wants to buy all the stuff. Grace and I thought I should call him back to see what he's up to. He sounded like a real loser, but I have agreed to meet him tomorrow, at the beach by the lighthouse at 3 P.M. I was wondering if you could run a background check on a Michael Jensen. Thanks. Call me if you get anything on him. Bye."

Next Kate called Grace to fill her in. "I'm meeting Mike tomorrow at 3 P.M. at the beach, after the surfing lessons. I asked Maggie to run a check on him."

Grace was very concerned, "Look, I'll have a couple of our friends show up tomorrow afternoon and keep this stranger under surveillance while you talk to him."

"Great. Thanks," Kate said as she hung up.

Chapter 6

Meanwhile, Michael was making plans of his own for tomorrow's meeting at 3 P.M. He was astounded that Kate had the nerve to hang up on him.

Who does she think she is? More important, who does she think I am?

He couldn't let it go, as his indignation continued, *by the way, don't be late?* Nobody talks to me like that.

He did not want to drive all the way down to Sea Crest when he didn't even know if she'd let him buy anything from the sale. He decided to take matters into his own hands.

He was fuming as he blatantly affirmed, *I'm certainly not used to calling up strange women who picked through the garbage, that people abandon, in storage lockers. Who on earth does that?*

I simply can't imagine what would justify that kind of behavior. Well, I'm not going to let her have the upper hand. If I have to meet on her turf, at least I'm going to be prepared.

He went to the nearest car rental location to turn in his old clunker. But, when he saw their sporty inventory, Michael decided to rent a sporty Porsche convertible instead. Now, he would get a good night's sleep and start fresh, first thing in the morning. He planned to arrive early and check out the whole area. He also made reservations at a Sea Crest Inn for tomorrow evening. They mentioned that they had a very nice seafood restaurant next door and asked if he wanted to make reservations for dinner. It sure sounded good to him. He decided he might as well turn this wild goose chase into a lovely evening.

He called his brother, James, and started, "Well, that didn't work out very well, did it? Why didn't you go down before it went to auction and pick up all that stuff?"

Classic brother-to-brother, shifting the blame, followed for several minutes.

James was peeved at this line of questioning and assured Michael that, "it was impossible" and "I can't do everything" and "by the way, you were due back here over a month ago" and finally, "this is your fault, and you can just fix it."

Michael was quick to respond, "My bridge project in London had significant delays. Most of my contracts, as an architect have complications and hidden issues to solve once work begins. I followed with my safety shelter project that we unveiled yesterday at The International Summit for Disaster Preparedness and Recovery. I never expected or promised to be back on any particular date. You know that."

Finally, as they ran out of excuses, the squabbling ended. James said apologetically, "Look, Michael, I'm sorry. I should not have blamed you for the slip-up. It is entirely my fault." He did not want his little brother to know the real reason he dreaded returning to that area. It was entirely too painful to experience again.

He asked solemnly, "Could you please do me a big favor and try to buy the stuff back?"

Michael readily agreed, partially because he had already arranged to do just that. "Sure, I need a little Rest and Relaxation anyway. This should be a piece of cake. I will call you when I get Grandma's stuff."

"Thanks," replied a very relieved James.

The following morning was beautiful. Michael was well rested, refreshed and looking forward to the drive. He put the top down on his rented convertible and followed the coastline road for miles. Taking the scenic route had certainly lived up to its name. He was so relaxed that he was almost sorry when he reached his destination. It was just after 1 P.M. when he pulled alongside the beautiful beach and saw the majestic Sea Crest Lighthouse.

Now that is breathtaking, he thought, as he parked the car and took in the surf and the sea air. It was a splendid day. He suddenly pulled off his shoes and socks and strolled barefooted onto the sand. He felt all the built-up tension melt away. It had been a long time since he had felt this relaxed. His meeting was a couple of hours away, and he decided to enjoy the refreshing feeling that had come over him.

He rolled up his sleeves and unbuttoned the top few buttons on his shirt. He suddenly noticed that he felt starved and he decided to try out the Snack Shack on the beach.

"Hi, I'd like a hot dog with everything on it." He looked at the menu board. "Plus, a large order of fries and a Coke," he added, to top it off. Michael could not even remember the last time he had eaten a hot dog.

He smiled, as he reflected, *it's funny how I seem to be so busy, that I sometimes forget to enjoy the simple things in life.*

When he got his order, Michael decided to sit down on a nearby bench and watch the waves crash against the beach, while it was so pleasant. *Ah, this is a perfect day,* he thought.

Chapter 7

Michael spotted a group of teenaged girls on the beach area closest to the Sea Crest Lighthouse. It looked like they were waxing surfboards. It was evident that the girl with a large, wide brim, floppy hat, and a long shirt was more or less, in charge. She seemed to be going from one girl to the next, checking on their progress.

Michael had never been on a surfboard. He thought that; *even to consider going out on the waves, was very dangerous for the little group.*

As he watched, the girls put down their surfboards and gathered around the one that was in charge. They were all listening intently and following her arm motions like paddling freestyle strokes on a surfboard. Next, they spread out and began to cup their hands and push back as much of the imaginary water as possible.

Boy, this was quite a beautiful workout. Michael felt like he was watching an intricate ballet, led by a nimble magical princess. He could not have dreamed up something this spectacular if he had tried.

The leader took off her floppy hat, to reveal her silky blond hair pulled back into a long braid. Wisps of feathery, fine, hair danced around her face as the loosely twisted braid fell out and floated down her back.

Next, she unbuttoned that long shirt which fell off her shoulders and dropped onto the sand. This simple act revealed the brightest red swimsuit Michael had ever seen; along with an incredible dark, flawless tan.

Wow. Does she live on this beach? What a knockout. She looks like she just stepped off the set of 'Bay Watch.'

His immediate reaction scared the wits out of him. It is not as if he had been in a monastery for the past six months.

The 'knockout' in question knew the minute he sat down on the bench. She also knew that he would be watching her. "This is going to be fun. I'm going to take full advantage of this situation."

Michael stood out like a sore thumb on this beach. Kate, on the other hand, knew everyone on the beach today. She was purposely going to make him pay for being so rude and arrogant. She took great pleasure in seeing him almost choke on his hot dog as she let her shirt slowly drop onto the sand. This was ironic on so many levels.

She gracefully bent down and attached the leash from her surfboard to the ankle of her back foot.

Yes, she thought. *I've pointed my toes at just the right angle.*

She picked up the surfboard and turned toward the ocean. She mentally measured the waves and the water. Next, she carried her board into the ocean and proceeded to walk out until the water reached hip height. Kate laid her board down in the water and hopped on. She paddled out, with the other girls in tow, using that cupped hand's freestyle motion.

Once they were all safely ready, she directed them as they each caught their wave to ride in. All the students headed to shore, while their amazing young teacher waited for the perfect wave.

Michael was so captivated by her at this point that he could hardly breathe in anticipation of seeing her rising out of the water, like Venus emerging from the sea.

Good grief, what is happening to me?

The expectation of watching her beautiful body riding that surfboard was almost unbearable.

Kate saw her perfect wave, and as she caught it, she said to herself, "*It's Show Time.*"

She had never demonstrated to students, what she was famous for, but the gloves were coming off for the snob on the bench. She had won surfing championships with this next move. Her boost off the wave into an aerial was perfect, as her board took off from the lip of the wave and traveled back to the face of the wave. Next, she used a couple of cutbacks to change direction while streaking ahead of the curl of the wave, followed by an astonishing turn back towards the breaking part of the wave.

That was one flawless performance, she thought excitedly, as she rode it home, with the natural grace and skill of a professional. *Yes, that was marvelous!*

Michael had risen to his feet and moved toward her, in stunning admiration, as if drawn to the awesome surfer. *Wow. Who is she? How did she do that?*

He suddenly realized it was almost 3 P.M.

Oh no. It's getting late. I am not prepared to deal with the storage locker lady. What a nightmare.

He looked back at the beautiful surfing mermaid just in time to see her step into and pull up a pair of cut off blue jean shorts. Next, she pulled a white tank top over her magnificent red swimsuit.

Now I must be dreaming. It looks like she is walking straight toward me. I can't believe my luck. Maybe I'm dreaming.

Kate, on the other hand, thought she might be the one that was dreaming. She had not planned on Michael being this handsome, mind you, only in a laid-back kind of way. The fact that she had been unable to see him very clearly, except for quick glances, made her unprepared for her startling reaction to him. She suddenly felt flushed as a pleasant feeling and tingling sensation swept over her, from head to toe.

This was not the plan, she regretfully thought. *Why was I showing off for this guy? What must he think of that ridiculous exhibition?*

To make matters even worse; currently, she was only a few steps from him. She felt mortified as the voice, in her head, offered, *Well, I might as well follow-through and try to salvage what little dignity I have left.*

Finally, thought Michael, *she's right in front of me.*

With a beautiful smile, she took the last step forward and extended her hand as she said, "Hello. You must be Michael. I'm Kate."

Chapter 8

Michael felt like he had just been sucker-punched in the stomach. He had not seen that coming. He blinked and tried to clear his head.

The man was literally speechless, but his mind was going a mile a minute.

What is she trying to pull on me? She has probably used this beautiful mermaid ploy on many other unsuspecting guys to get them to let their guard down. Well, it is not going to work on me. I am a very successful man. I've traveled all over the world. And lest we forget, I've had plenty of chances with beautiful women, let me tell you. These ladies view me as a handsome eligible bachelor. They don't resort to trickery, he insisted with his thoughts bubbling over. *Well, a few had, but that wasn't to steal my family's contents from a storage unit.*

Michael felt blindsided, and as he tried to gain control of this shocking turn of events, he grew increasingly infuriated.

Nobody plays me for a fool. I'm going to fight fire with fire.

That is when he realized that he was still holding her hand. His palm was now sweating profusely. He quickly yanked his hand away. He tried to speak, and a croaking sound came out, "Ah..." He went red with embarrassment.

He tried to talk again, and this time something did come out, and he was back on his game. "I'm glad you could take a few minutes from your playtime, to meet with me."

As Kate's mouth opened in protest, he continued, "I won't take up much of your time, and then you can get back to your fun day at the beach."

Kate was flabbergasted. She was giving valuable lessons, not having a Playtime at the beach. "I was conducting surfing lessons for a few of the high school girls," she responded hotly. "They get school credit for safe surfing, in water sports."

"Well isn't that nice," he said sarcastically, as he rolled his eyes. "They get credit for playing in the water. Must be nice. However, I'm not here to discuss the games of the spoiled kids of today and those who encourage their behavior."

Kate was furious. *How dare he insult my class of students and question my efforts to teach them.*

The sound of her phone interrupted her response. She glanced down, and as she recognized the call was from the Coast Guard Emergency Situation Center, she answered it immediately, "Hello, Kate speaking."

The dispatch operator, responded, "Glad we could reach you, Kate. We just received a mayday, distress call from a vessel that has lost power. They are taking on water at a fast rate. We need to deploy a Search and Rescue Mission, STAT."

She understood and promptly agreed, "I'll be right there. I'm on my way."

"We need your unit, plus the medical team if you can make that happen." the person continued.

"Yes, get together some of the available guys. I'm on my way."

Kate suddenly remembered Michael, who was standing there just waiting to start up with her again. *Well, I will have to deal with this idiot later.*

As she turned and began running, she yelled over her shoulder to him, "I have to go. I'll call you tomorrow."

Michael was flabbergasted, as he yelled back to her, "You can't just leave. What about the storage units?" His comment sounded ridiculous even to Michael, as he heard himself say it. *How did this happen? Have I now been reduced to yelling, at a complete stranger, that she can't just leave?"*

Who did she think she was? Michael had just been dumped in the middle of the beach in response to a suspicious phone call.

He knew the drill. He had used it from time to time himself. Have a friend call you when you were in the middle of a meeting or a date. They make up some excuse to offer you, and you have an opportunity to leave. Why did he bring 'a date' into this? He was never going to take the likes of her on a date. Michael continued to fume over her quick exit. Now he was sure this had been set up ahead of time as a simple way to leave if she did not want him to get the storage unit contents.

Well if she thinks she can get away with this, she can just think again.

Michael stomped over to a bench where he had left his shoes and socks. He struggled to put them on because there was too much sand on his feet. This small act of unsuccessfully wrestling to get his foot into his sand-filled shoe, struck a disturbing chord inside him, so compelling that he immediately rose to his feet.

Something was very wrong.

He unexpectedly broke out in a cold sweat, and he abruptly felt as if he was going to throw up. Somehow, this reminded him of something, but he just could not put his finger on it.

What just happened to me? I feel terrible.

Michael looked out past The Sea Crest Lighthouse at the ocean waves as they reached the shore. The rhythmic sound was somehow soothing, and he gradually felt the calm and peacefulness that he had experienced upon his arrival this afternoon.

He decided to head on over to the Sea Crest Inn. He felt much better now, as he picked up his offending shoes and socks.

He checked in and discovered that his second-floor suite was perfect. He had a fantastic view of the lighthouse as well as a breathtaking panoramic view of the ocean. He opened the French doors and stepped out to his balcony.

The Sea Crest Inn had, *No Vacancy*, due to the Festival. In fact, the lodging capacity for the entire coastal area was overbooked and had a waitlist for any additional rooms. Michael felt fortunate to have been able to reserve this special suite, with no prior knowledge of the Festival.

Michael watched the waves rolling back and forth down the beach, but he couldn't get his thoughts past, *the beautiful mermaid in that spectacular red swimsuit. Granted, she changed into my deplorable enemy, right before my eyes. Still, that gifted water nymph is the most desirable woman I've ever had the pleasure of meeting.*

Alas, she left me all alone on the beach. I wonder who she was going to meet? What a strange, exciting, bizarre episode that proved to be.

Chapter 9

Later, Michael started to feel hungry. *I think I'll see if the food is as good as was promised, at The Sea Crest Restaurant.*

As he stepped into the elegant dining room, the maître d' greeted him with a smile. "May I help you, sir?"

"Yes, I have a reservation. Michael Jensen."

"Yes, Sir. Follow me, please," he said with a warm and welcoming smile.

Michael immediately felt right at home. Not that Michael was 'at home' very often. The decor was very tasteful, and there was even someone playing softly at the Grand Piano. It was almost magical to hear those familiar melodies. How pleasant.

Michael felt very comfortable and famished. He decided, *I am not going to even think about HER.*

His table was next to the window with a breathtaking view of the ocean and the lighthouse. It looked like a postcard. It must be the fresh sea air, but Michael felt starved. He gave the waiter his drink order and proceeded to look over the menu. When the waiter returned, he took a sip of his drink. "It's very good, thank you."

"Fine, are you ready to order?"

"Everything on the menu looks good. Let me see, I think I will have Surf and Turf; Lobster Tail with Center-cut New York Strip Steak, medium rare. I'll start with a Classic Caesar Salad."

"Very Good, Sir"

He heard the patrons at a nearby table talking about some Air/Sea Rescue that was going on this evening. It was, somehow related to the Sea Crest coastline.

A couple of minutes later, the waiter returned with the Caesar Salad. It looked very inviting, and he intended to eat it immediately, but he paused and laid his fork softly on the table when he overheard the conversation of the couple again.

Michael glanced over to see a very attractive woman with beautiful rich auburn red hair. Her resemblance to Maureen O'Hara was uncanny.

34

The woman was certainly concerned as she explained the dire situation. "The SOS was a sailing vessel that had lost power and was taking on water. The distress call indicated that it's a family with a couple of kids onboard."

"Well, did they have life jackets on?" asked the man with her.

"Yes, Joe, they all have life jackets on, but two are children, and they don't know how to swim," she replied sadly, as she shook her head. She could not understand it. "Why would any parent be irresponsible enough to take a child out on a boat if they don't know how to swim? Even more unbelievable that they would take two kids out there, who must be so scared."

Michael overheard this. That last arresting remark was what did it.

Michael felt a chill go down his back. He was experiencing that peculiar feeling again. His feelings seemed to be spiraling further and further down into a dark, sad place. His apparent concern for these children, who were virtual strangers, was suddenly making him sick with fear. Questions came flooding into his mind. *Where were their parents? I hope their mother is okay. Maybe she is already dead. Oh No. Now, what if their father dies too? That would be terrible.* His hopeless sorrow felt almost unbearable.

Michael felt like he was experiencing a full-blown Panic Attack. Not knowing what else to do, he was ready to escape to the bathroom to get control of his feelings when the woman added a remark, which made everything seem all right again.

"Well, at least the Coast Guard with the Air/Sea Rescue Team has just arrived on the scene."

Wow, thought the very confused Michael. *That's better. Maybe I should sit here for a minute.* The pit in his stomach was slowly disappearing as he solemnly imagined, *I'll bet those kids will be okay now.*

"Great," the man at the next table answered. "I hear that the Rescue Helicopter they use is a true lifesaver. Every second will count in genuine life and death situations like this."

A waiter, who had noticed that Michael had not started to eat anything, appeared at his table and inquired, "Sir? Is there something else I can offer you as a substitute for your Caesar salad? Our chef makes a delicious Cobb Salad or perhaps a Chef Salad."

Michael was quick to acknowledge, "No, this is fine. I'm sorry, I've just been distracted by the beautiful sunset."

He smiled as he took his first forkful of crisp lettuce. Then, just for good measure, he added one comment that is more heartfelt. "This is truly a beautiful evening."

That positive validation seemed to have the desired effect. The waiter smiled and nodded knowingly, as he withdrew.

Michael was proud of himself for handling that little snafu. He was feeling much better now. This feeling, however, was about to take a sudden unexpected turn.

The woman at the nearby table announced, "Kate's been training the new Coast Guard trainees for a few weeks now."

Michael immediately reacted, *Kate?* He repeated that caustic name in his head. *Kate? That name is like scraping your fingernails over a chalkboard.*

The woman continued, "I heard she had two of them flying the Sea/Plane yesterday on a practice mission. She even had various land-based vehicles coordinate with the Coast Guard boats to evaluate how well they all worked together. The whole project went very well. She was relieved that her last-minute change of plans for the day proved to be the best possible test of her trainees."

The man across from her agreed, "Maggie, that's wonderful. I know how hard she's been working on combining her teaching for the Coast Guard and her free Water Safety Classes for the public."

Michael felt like chiming in with the following News Flash: *Maggie, that's enough about Kate. Please do not mention the name again while I'm trying to eat.*

He would like to announce, *Your Kate may be all about Coast Guard trainees and conducting great missions and using her powers only for good...,Blah, Blah, Blah..., but my Kate is the complete opposite. She's tricky, underhanded and rude. She also likes to look through other people's garbage-filled storage units, and when she finds a good one, she wants to steal it from unsuspecting relatives of the newly deceased.*

Kate! Michael thought as he persisted with his non-stop grievance, *that is the last name I want to hear tonight. I distinctly promised myself that I was not going to think of her. I certainly don't want to sit here and listen to my dinner table neighbors, Joe and Maggie, discuss* the *virtues of someone they know, named Kate.*

She had sounded like a wonderful person. It's downright maddening.

Just as Michael was finishing his scathing mental tantrum about Kate, he noticed that the couple had finished their meal and they were leaving.

Well, that's lucky. I won't have to overhear the couple talking about Kate anymore. However, Michael soon found that once he started, he could not stop thinking about Kate.

Chapter 10

Michael finished his meal and left the restaurant. He strolled along the beach towards The Sea Crest Inn, on the beautiful moonlight pathway. He knew that over the next few nights, due to the full moon, the high tide would bring *spring tides*, which are extraordinarily high. Michael was involved with several lighthouse projects as an architect and these monthly tidal ranges always needed to be factored into the plan.

The Coast Guard's Helicopter Pad with a large red cross painted on it, was located on the beach next to the Sea Crest Lighthouse. He watched the Emergency Medical Squad, which had two ambulances stationed nearby. They were in constant communication with the Search and Rescue Team while preparing to help with casualties as they arrived.

He heard the pulsating swish, swish, swish of the blades before he saw it. The Coast Guard Rescue Helicopter proceeded to land on the helicopter pad. One of the ambulances with the Emergency Medical Team met the helicopter. They unloaded two injured people on stretchers. One had an adult, as well as what looked like a child.

Another stretcher held an adult, who was tightly holding onto the hand of a child who was walking beside them. They were both transferred to the second waiting ambulance.

Many people were gathering around to help. They wanted to know about the condition of the family that had been rescued.

Michael looked on with concern for these people, and he had real admiration for the Coast Guard Team that had saved them. He watched the Pilot-in-Command climb out of the helicopter, holding a clipboard and conversing with the other rescuers.

Boy, thought Michael. *You've got to be an incredibly skilled expert with a steady hand and nerves of steel, to pilot one of those rescue helicopters, which need to hover stationary over the water, often in violent, stormy weather. It's simply amazing. The family from that boat can be thankful that this*

excellent US Coast Guard team had been able to get to them in time."

The pilot nodded affirmatively and handed off the clipboard to another crew member who now took control of the helicopter.

Everyone around it, backed away as the blades began to circle rapidly. The rescue team backed off the pad area and stepped onto the beach. The helicopter rose slowly from the pad and headed north. *It is sobering to be here, observing this heroic rescue.*

As he looked down once more, he saw the couple from the restaurant. It seemed like this Maggie person was approaching the Coast Guard pilot. They were both looking out, over the ocean, as the pilot reached up and took off the helmet. A long blond braid fell to her shoulders.

No, it can't be! thought Michael. She was turning back around, as she unzipped the top of her jumpsuit and a very familiar white tank top appeared.

What on earth is happening? That's Kate. Michael's jaw dropped wide open with surprise and shock. *Don't tell me my Kate is a Coast Guard Helicopter Pilot.*

Michael felt the rug being yanked out from under him.

Kate? Michael still could not believe his eyes. *This can't be possible.*

My Kate, is their Kate? Both of his worlds had just collided. Meanwhile, it looked like Kate was calmly conducting business as usual. She and Maggie walked slowly along as people came forward to talk to her and asked her questions about the rescue efforts.

Michael was almost numb as he walked the rest of the way to the Sea Crest Inn. He entered the beautiful lobby, waved acknowledgment to the desk clerk and continued to his room. He stepped out onto the balcony, but this time, it gave him no peace. He gazed out toward the rescue group. For a moment, he thought he saw Kate look up towards him. It appeared like some guy was talking with her and he had his hand on her shoulder. They ended up walking to the lighthouse keeper's cottage, and they went inside; together.

Michael sadly retreated into his room. He sat down in a nearby, comfortable chair. It was all too much to comprehend. When he had thought about Kate since she had run off and left him yelling on the beach, (and he had thought of her plenty), he had thought she was out partying with the available guys she was getting together.

He felt extremely conflicted.

How could Kate be a professional Coast Guard Helicopter Pilot? How could she coordinate a mission for Coast Guard trainees yesterday? I thought she was at the storage unit sale. Furthermore, I cannot imagine her going through someone else's garbage.

Could she possibly be the same Kate who headed up a water safety program here at Sea Crest Beach? Well, that might explain why she was teaching that surfing class today. Finally, did she have any idea what she looked like in that red swimsuit?

Well, one thing is for sure. Michael Jensen was not leaving Sea Crest until he had the answers to these questions.

(He had all but forgotten that he was in fact, really here to get the contents from his grandmother's storage unit.)

Chapter 11

Meanwhile across town, there was someone who had not forgotten about the contents of his grandmother's storage unit. Grace was finally able to search through some of the boxes. What she found was truly incredible.

The boxes held some of the most valuable treasures she had ever seen. She carefully unwrapped the tissue paper from an object that she was holding in her hand. It revealed a beautiful antique Kaleidoscope. The colored glass, with the multiple mirrors, had been made of the best glass that was available in the early 1800s.

A small chain attached a tag. It read: *Patented (GB 4136) granted in 1817.*

Treatise on the Kaleidoscope by David Brewster

There was also a handwritten note:

To my great friend, Sir Michael Chambers,

Best wishes to you on your voyage to America. Enjoy my gift and remember the value of the flat Fresnel lens that I wholeheartedly endorse for use all lighthouses. I believe that over time, they will save many lives by protecting vessels against shipwrecks.

God's Blessings to You,

Sir David Brewster.

This discovery was just the beginning. It seemed that each thing that Grace inspected was of tremendous value. The information acquired from the Chambers' storage units answered many questions about the history of the Sea Crest Lighthouse.

Grace picked up the phone and called her friends for an emergency Mah Jongg Club meeting for 11:00 tomorrow.

Chapter 12

Kate had spent her whole life devoted to safety and saving lives. She was genuinely compassionate and caring through and through.

However, you certainly would not know it, by the behavior she had exhibited over the past couple of days. She met a man who had brought out the worst side of her. A side she never even knew she had.

It's not like I've never been around guys before, she thought. *Good grief, the Coast Guard and Search and Rescue Team, was full of them. I can work with and get along with all of them, no problem.*

Just what is it about this guy that justifies my horrible behavior towards him, she wondered. She continued to try making sense of why he was driving her absolutely, nuts.

Kate seemed almost obsessed with him. She thought about him all the time. *Okay, try to think of his good qualities,* she told herself.

Well, he was extremely good-looking, in a very casual, everyday sort of way. At this point in her thinking, she became sidetracked, imagining him in different ways; *like in a tuxedo or maybe tennis shorts. Better yet, how about a bright red lifeguard swimsuit.*

She had first met him at the beach where she had been shamelessly showing off her surfing skills, in front of him, because she knew he was watching her. But when she got up close enough to see him, then she felt like a fool. In fact, her heart skipped a beat, when she walked up the beach, stopped in front of him and introduced herself.

Why did I have to do that anyway? she thought. *Oh yeah, now I remember. I resented his arrogance. In fact, he was talking down to me, and I didn't like it one bit.*

Well this hotshot, with a New York City phone number, was going to pay me twice what I had paid for the storage unit contents. How dare he? Now she was beginning to warm up to the subject and she had valid reasons to justify her behavior.

Who did he think he was? Yes, it was all coming back to her now.

Kate was completely baffled by her reaction to him.

I've had plenty of men try to win me over, and they were always very respectful of me. Many were in awe of my superior talents and skills in the Coast Guard. They would never treat me with that arrogant attitude, (I will look over the storage contents and buy both of them if I think they have got good enough stuff.) They would never treat me with disrespect, (criticizing my surfing lessons). Never yell at me on the beach and never tell me, You just can't leave.

Kate thought back to the rescue at sea of the two children and the Mom and Dad last night. *I swear I saw Michael on the balcony of the Sea Crest Inn. I guess that he didn't leave town after their blow up on the beach. I think he looked down and saw me at the landing pad. He appeared to be sad and tired.*

Kate wondered, *why does this matter to me anyway? He pushed all my buttons, and when I was around him, I acted downright terrible. Exactly what is it about him that caused me to spend most of the night thinking about him?*

Well, he'll be gone soon, and I won't have to deal with this guy anymore. I don't need to go out with a man who was so rude and uncaring.

Wow, who said anything about dating, how did that subject come up? Well, I certainly don't need someone like Michael.

She stopped to think about it; *I am currently surrounded by 'Yes' men who pretty much do anything I say. They rarely, if ever, even bring up another idea, but simply agree to do what I ask.*

She had certainly never thought about that before.

However, when I do get ready to settle down, what am I looking for in a husband?

Chapter 13

The next morning when Kate got up, she made a conscious decision to have a very positive outlook. She had spent the entire night, tossing and turning, agonizing about the handsome jerk on the beach. Now, this must stop.

After all, the Mah Jongg Club was meeting with Grace this morning, to look at the contents of the Chambers' storage units. Depending on the results, she would call Michael and let him know if he could buy the contents or not. Why he seemed so eager to do this was a mystery to her, but that would end their involvement with each other. Kate would never see Michael again. She felt strangely conflicted at this thought.

Well, I'm not going to feel sad. I intend to have a lovely day, and I am not going to waste my time thinking about Michael J E N S E N.

"Hey Connor," she called to her brother. "Want to go up to the top of the lighthouse?"

"Sure do," He answered. "I've just been waiting for you to get up. You'd think that managing your Coast Guard Search and Rescue Team was hard work. However, when I watched as you maneuvered that helicopter last night, you made it look like it was a piece of cake."

"You'll never know how responsible I feel when I think about having someone else's life in my hands."

"By the way, you did a bang-up job last night. Do you ever do any follow up in the cases involving kids?"

"We don't, but I think the parents or adults that are involved would certainly get help for them. It's got to be traumatic for them to go through a scary, life or death situation."

Kate had seen it all.

Connor thought that over and said, "You know, just having that

helpless feeling that you have no control and it's going to be bad. Those kids last night are going to have nightmares for a long, long time. It's a shame."

"We can always hope they remember the positive ending. There had been no loss of life, and the adults should recover completely over time."

"I sure hope they keep that in mind," he said thoughtfully. Connor followed up on a much happier note, "Hey Sis, let's climb to the top and look around. I've already taken a thermos of hot coffee up there."

Kate and Connor often marveled at how lucky they had been to get to live here in the keeper's cottage. The lighthouse had been like a second home to them. Of course, the Sea Crest Lighthouse was in a populated area, and they had lots of friends and family around.

They climbed to the top and walked around the catwalk before they stopped to rest their coffee cups on the wrought iron railing, as they'd done a thousand times before. The sea breeze swirled around their faces as they gazed out over the shoreline and out to sea.

Connor exclaimed, "What a view." It was a beautiful morning, and it didn't get any better than this.

Kate agreed, "I feel so grateful that this lighthouse is not only part of our life, but we've gotten to live here our entire lives. Who else can be this lucky?"

"I don't know. I always feel so peaceful and centered when I'm up high in the sky, like this," smiled Kate.

"Boy, I know what you mean," replied her brother, quietly. "I don't think I'll ever be happy living anywhere else, after this. I often find myself wondering about the future. You know what I mean?"

"I think so," said Kate softly. "Yes, I understand completely."

As Connor looked out over the ocean, he said, "I hope I marry, someone wonderful, who will enjoy the great life we've built here at this lighthouse."

After a few minutes, Connor asked, "Do you ever think about what kind of husband you hope to marry?"

Well, Kate had struggled with this very question last night. In fact, she had fallen asleep trying to come up with a very well, thought-out list of necessary attributes, which her future husband would need to possess.

"I'll need someone with spirit, as well as passion. But I do not want a *Yes* man. I need a man who knows what he believes and why it's important to him," stated Kate. She continued with confidence, "He doesn't back down but can change his opinion if new information supports it. He won't be rigid."

Connor joined in immediately with, "He'll need a great sense of humor, like someone who laughs easily and loves deeply."

"I want someone who won't try to change me. I worked hard to become exactly who I am. I intend to continue to improve and learn new things, but I like who I am," declared Kate.

As Connor chuckled, she continued, "someone who has a sense of responsibility."

"A good moral compass."

"It's also important to have someone who is tender and has some vulnerability because they feel and care so much."

"And finally, I want someone like our dad, who'd be a loving father to our children," she said. "We have the best dad in the world."

"We sure do." Connor agreed. "By the way, it sounds like you have it all figured out. Do you have anyone particular in mind for the job?"

"Of course not, but I want to figure out what kind of guy I'd like to fall in love with, so I don't fall for the wrong one."

They both laughed at that, but Kate was not laughing on the inside. She was afraid that might be a very distinct possibility.

With that out of the way and off his mind, Connor continued, "It would feel strange to move out of the keeper's cottage. Maybe they'll let us stay here even after we get married."

"I don't think I've ever even thought about that particular issue," laughed Kate.

A phone call from Grace interrupted her train of thought. "Hey, Kate. What are you doing right now?"

"Oh, I'm up here on top of the lighthouse having coffee with Connor."

"Well, you'll never guess what I just uncovered from the storage units. It was probably something from your family. I've never seen one, and I've never heard you talk about it."

"Well, what is it?" Kate impatiently asked.

"It's a surprise. Come on over and bring Connor with you. It involves both of you. I know we're getting together later, but if you both could come over now, I've got some questions."

"Sure. We'll be right over."

Kate turned to Connor as she explained, "I picked up the contents of a couple of storage units for Grace, and she's got something special to show us."

"Great, let's go," replied her brother.

Chapter 14

By the time Kate and Connor arrived, Grace had coffee ready for them.

"First, I want to know," started Grace, "Do you two ever remember your family talking about a Lighthouse Traveling Library Box? They used to have them a long time ago, and they rotated from one lighthouse to another."

"No," they both said at the same time.

"We've had three generations of our family at this same lighthouse, and I've never seen one," stated Connor.

"Well, get a load of this," announced Grace. With a flourish, almost like a magician, she pulled the tablecloth off from a large weathered trunk. "Ta-da. Does this look at all familiar?"

When they both silently stared in wonder at the great chest, she continued, "This is one of the Lighthouse Traveling Library Boxes that started circulating between various lightkeepers in the 1870s."

"Kate, do you remember ever seeing or hearing about them?"

"No, I don't know that I ever saw one, but I think our grandpa might have been familiar with them. He once recalled that they had games like Dominoes and interesting books they could read, like 'The Adventures of Tom Sawyer' and 'Huckleberry Finn,'" Kate replied. "He'd said that they had to be careful with the things in the big wooden box because they were portable and they'd trade them with other lighthouses. It was very exciting. I guess I have heard about them before, but I haven't thought about that for years."

"Well, you'll now have a chance to see a real one," Grace said excitedly. "Can you believe there was one in the Chambers' storage units? It has this paper with it, and it lists the contents."

 Connor took the paper from her and read, *"Beginning in the 1870s, the Lighthouse Service put together small portable libraries for lighthouse keepers and their families.*

These libraries would include about 50 books in a wooden trunk."

"Look at this list of what this library trunk contained," Grace said.

MATERIALS: (in this trunk)

Coffee Grinder, Coffee Pot, Dominoes, Climbing Bear, Handkerchief Doll, Toy Soldiers, Jacob's ladder game

The Adventures of Huckleberry Finn book, Games and Songs of American Children book, and a Sears, Roebuck and Co. Catalog."

"Isn't that wild?" asked Grace.

Kate and Connor wondered why their family had not reminisced about this fantastic piece of the Walsh family's life, as multiple generations, of Sea Crest Lighthouse keepers.

"I'm sure I never heard my dad mention anything about a box of books with unique toys and games in it," said Connor. "However, both Dad and Grandpa were excellent at Dominoes, and they were both, very well read."

Kate added thoughtfully, "But I've never seen many of the books they've read, around our keeper's cottage, either."

Connor was also trying to figure out, "How in the world did this Portable Traveling Library Box get into the Chambers' storage unit? They were never lighthouse keepers, were they?"

Grace answered, "We don't think so. We've never known for sure if there was any connection was between the Chambers and the Sea Crest Lighthouse."

"In fact, that's one of the important reasons why we wanted to buy these particular storage unit contents," she continued. "If they are the same Chambers family that spent summers at the beach house, here in Sea Crest, their belongings might hold the answers to our town's history."

"It certainly looks like it must be the same family," stated Connor slowly.

"Oh, Maggie is here," said Grace as she looked out the window. "Mary Beth is pulling up right behind her."

"I've got to get going," explained Connor. "I'm helping Patrick hang the Sea Crest Festival banner across Main Street later, and I've got a few errands to run this morning."

"Okay," said Kate. "Can you pick me back up in about an hour?"

"Sure," answered Connor as he left.

Chapter 15

Maggie and Mary Beth came inside as Connor was leaving.

"Hey, Connor. How are you?" asked Maggie.

"Fine. I'm on my way to prepare some of the things for the Sea Crest Festival this weekend. Is your mom going to make her pies this year?"

"Sure. In fact, I believe she's helping some Girl Scouts qualify for their Baking Badge this morning. She's going to let each of them make their very own blueberry pie for the festival. Since they are helping with a Fund-Raising Project, it will count towards a Girl Scout Journey Certificate."

"That's great. My friend Patrick and I are hoping to take a break this afternoon and drop in on them. We're hoping they will let us taste test the pies."

"Well, good luck with that idea," Maggie laughed. "I'll see you later."

"Bye for now. I'll drop back to pick up Kate in about an hour."

As Connor left, Kate immediately started telling Maggie and Mary Beth about the Portable Traveling Lighthouse Library Box. They carefully lifted the lid and opened it up. They gazed at the contents with the realization of what this unique collection would have meant to the lighthouse keeper and their family. They each wondered why they had never even heard about these library boxes before. It seemed incredible to them.

Chapter 16

At the Sea Crest Inn, Michael awoke with a sad, melancholy feeling of doom, which he'd been experiencing for most of the night.

He finally got out of bed and opened the door out onto the balcony. He felt a sense of peace as he gazed out over water and heard the rhythm of ocean waves pounding on the shore.

Maybe if I take a calming walk along the beach, I'll be able to get my mind off Kate. I need to think.

Of course, forgetting about Kate, was next to impossible. He changed into shorts and a shirt. He looked at his reflection in the mirror and wondered what Kate thought of his looks. He ran his hand through his hair a couple of times and then returned to the bathroom to brush his teeth.

At last, he figured he was ready. Ready for what, he wasn't exactly sure. However, as he stepped out of his room, he purposely left his phone in the room.

I do not want to answer a million questions if my brother calls. I don't have a believable defense for any of the strange things that keep happening to me, and I'm very frustrated with Kate's effect on me.

On the other hand, he wasn't even concerned about the fact that he hadn't bought back their grandmother's things yet.

He strolled down the beach to the water's edge. He watched the ebb and flow of the water across the sand, with its unbelievably hypnotic effect. He noticed the damage that the recent storm had done. A long walkway connected the lighthouse to the beach beside the keeper's cottage. It was above the jetty that jutted out into the ocean, and part of the walkway had broken down. It remained a lopsided old pile of debris which recently caused the pathway to collapse.

It did not appear that it will stay above the water at all times, depending on the tide. That would mean that the lighthouse would be unreachable during high tide and for the next few nights; there would be spring tides, which were even higher. Michael could understand why they wanted it repaired as soon as was humanly possible.

He glanced along the beach at the sight of the surfing lesson, which was still burning in his memory. His footsteps wandered knowingly to the spot where she had waxed the surfboard, where she dropped her big floppy hat in the sand. Where Kate's shirt slid off her shoulder, revealing her bright red swimsuit.

He felt an attraction that was almost scary. This was impossible. He knew he'd be leaving soon and he would never see Kate again.

He started to move away, to return to the path that was safer. Maybe he should return to his room. His walk took him past several huge planters along the boardwalk. Flowers overflowed, and the breeze carried a faint floral scent.

After walking the entire length of the beach and back, he returned to his suite at the inn. He quickly hurried into the bathroom, but as he bumped the edge of the nightstand, his phone fell off. It silently hit the side of the bed, bounced off the leg of the nightstand again and finally landed on the floor. The momentum caused it to end up hidden, way under the bed, up by the headboard.

By this time, Michael was turning on the shower in the bathroom and didn't hear any of the rebounding noise. In fact, he was completely unaware of this little mishap altogether.

Now, the only thing that seemed to get his attention was Kate.

Chapter 17

The Mah Jongg Club was eagerly awaiting news of what Grace had found in the storage units, and they will not be disappointed. As she carried a fresh carafe of coffee into the room and set it on the table, her face was flushed with anticipation.

"What did you call about, Grace?" asked Maggie.

She quickly replied, "You'll never believe it."

"Hurry and tell us. The suspense is killing us," exclaimed Mary Beth.

Grace did not even know where to begin. "I can't believe it myself," she spoke with so much feeling that she struggled to get it out. "I mean, I never expected ever to be able to hold anything this precious in my hands."

"What on earth did you find," asked Kate? "I didn't get a chance to see any of the contents yet."

Grace cleared her throat, took a deep calming breath and began seriously. "Before we begin, I must explain how shocked I am." She put her hand on her chest like her heart was about to burst, as she emotionally searched for the words to express how huge this news was.

Finally, she whispered almost prayerfully, "I don't know if we can rightfully keep what was in that unit. It belongs to the Chambers family. It is their flesh and blood."

"I'm sure we were never supposed to get this," she murmured as she slowly pulled an old tattered journal from her pocket.

"I honestly don't know why the family didn't take care of this unless they don't even know it exists."

"A couple of hours ago, I started to go through the things that were in the Chambers' two units. So far, everything I have unpacked is precious, noteworthy and valuable. Each thing is an heirloom or of enormous historical value. I mean everything. It's unbelievable to me."

She held the journal with both of her hands. "This is a personal journal, handwritten in the 1860s, by Sir Michael Chambers. He was

Captain of the Scottish Schooner named The Sea Crest that wrecked off of our coast."

"Wow, what a find," declared Kate.

Maggie added excitedly, "That might answer many of our questions about our history and our ancestry. What a surprising stroke of luck."

Grace continued with genuine amazement, "This journal has 171 pages, all carefully written. It is very readable and full of adventure and many amazing facts. I started reading this and thought I would rather go through it with you. It reads like a "Who's Who" of famous people and events of the day."

"Captain Chambers was a friend of David Brewster, who invented and patented the Kaleidoscope in 1817. David Brewster had also studied the Fresnel Lens, which the French physicist Augustine Fresnel, developed in 1822."

"The Sea Crest, shipwrecked off our coast here, and most of the crew were able to survive, due to Captain Chambers' safety program for all on board."

Maggie was floored. "You mean, *The Chambers*, the summer people, were here before we were?"

"I thought they didn't have any history or roots at Sea Crest," replied Kate. "They were just tourists who had an impressive beach house."

"I'm still trying to locate the abstract of title, for the chain of ownership, for their beach house property," explained Mary Beth.

"That's not all. Captain Chambers includes notes about water safety. An Irish architect was traveling with him on this voyage, and they disliked each other very much," said Grace. "They constantly argued about everything including the Captain's swimming lessons."

"What?" asked Kate. She had started a Water Safety Class here in present-day Sea Crest.

Grace searched for the appropriate pages and continued, "Listen to this. *Every member of the crew needs to learn to swim. These classes are a source of much strife between myself and an Irish architect of lighthouses who had been commissioned to build a lighthouse in America.*"

Kate was dumbfounded. "No way. How on earth, was he teaching swimming, from a ship at sea, no less? Was he throwing them into the ocean and having them practice? Sink or Swim? That is utterly absurd."

"No wonder the Irishman was objecting. That's crazy," agreed Maggie. "Did it say anything about Captain Chambers being Nuts? It's a miracle the crew didn't rebel and call for a mutiny."

Grace interrupted, "Let me find that part of the journal and maybe we'll see." She skimmed through several pages, muttering to herself, "Some of this is hard...oh, I see... Here we go. It seems that our Captain Chambers had met Alexander Parkes when he unveiled the first man-made plastic at the 1862 Great International Exhibition in London."

"That must be like The World's Fair, today," said Mary Beth. "So, this goes back to 1862? I guess our Captain was moving in all the right circles."

"Just wait," said Grace, as she continued. "He wrote; *the English chemist was granted the first of several patents on a plastic material he called Parkesine. Following this, in the 1860s, was celluloid, which was the first synthetic plastic material. This celluloid material was mold-able and waterproof. That's what I was most interested in, so I arranged to meet with him. After several discussions, I commissioned Alexander to design and produce a small swimming pool which could be put together and taken apart easily."*

"What on earth is he talking about?" laughed Kate.

"Hold on, Kate, he's not finished yet," Grace laughed, her eyes wet with tears.

The pieces interlock and click together, which seals the pieces with a close-fitting bond which will hold water. Rows of metal latches and buckles hold the seams together where the pieces meet, on the outside of the pool. They remind me of the metal rings that hold the barrel together.

Grace showed them the page, as she explained, "he made a little drawing of it on this page."

"Way to go, Michael," yelled Kate, with her full approval. They all cheered.

Mary Beth called out an additional, "Yeah, Michael, way to go."

Kate immediately felt herself shudder slightly, as an uneasy feeling pricked at her subconscious, but it didn't quite penetrate.

Grace held up her hand for quiet, "All right, calm down everyone."

She continued to read; *The side pieces are curved and will form a wall and complete a circle, as the pieces come together again. Additional large pieces click together to constitute the bottom with added latches to secure it. I think this will work very well for the onboard swimming pool.*

"Talk about ingenuity," Kate excitedly clapped her hands.

Maggie agreed heartily, "This guy is unbelievable."

Grace showed the ladies a pencil sketch of the pool in the journal labeled,

Portable Swimming Pool for Deck of Ship.
Fill the pool with rainwater,
or
Fill with buckets full of water from the ocean.
Goal: Everyone on board needs to know how to swim.
Safety Plan: They first need to learn to float.
*Everyone on board needs to ***** Learn to SWIM.*

This goal is met with harsh criticism from a stubborn Irish architect, Joseph Walsh, who is on-board. His Uncle, John Donahue, is a famous Irish lighthouse builder who also built several towers, in America in the early 1800s. *He usually built stone tower structures with a fixed white light that showed about eight miles, and he often included detached dwellings for keepers.*

"Whoa. Excuse me, but his last name is Walsh? That's my last name," exclaimed Kate. "Do you think there's a connection?"

"I have no idea. It's a common Irish name, and we'll research that as we go through this stuff. If he's related, we should be able to find a connection," said Grace. "Wouldn't that be ironic? This guy thinks swimming lessons are stupid. Your whole life is water safety."

The Mah Jongg ladies were all duly impressed with the irony of it.

"For the time being, let's continue with the journal and see what else we can learn about both of them," said Grace.

Now, Joseph Walsh thinks he's equally unique because he was commissioned to rebuild some lighthouses in America, which have been damaged or destroyed in the American Civil War.

They all stopped and just looked at each other in disbelief.

"What is he talking about?" Maggie asked. "Lighthouses damaged in the Civil War? I've never heard anything about that."

"Well," explained Grace, who knows a great deal about history. "There were many instances where lighthouses were damaged during the Revolutionary War also. Some of them have been repaired or replaced."

"What are you talking about?" asked Maggie. "Which ones were destroyed that far back?"

"Well, we know that the Boston Harbor Lighthouse was the first lighthouse built in America. That was in 1716. It was destroyed twice during the Revolutionary War. When the British forces occupied it, the American troops also attacked and burned it twice. However, British soldiers blew up the tower and destroyed all of it when they withdrew in 1776. It was reconstructed about seven years later, around 1783."

"Wow," Mary Beth marveled, "Is that the one that's still standing today? We visited it a couple of years ago."

Grace put her head to the side as she thought about it for a minute, then answered, "Well, not completely. Before the Civil War, the tower was rebuilt, to its present height, enabling its light to flash several more miles, out into the Atlantic Ocean. That's pretty much what you saw when you visited, Mary Beth."

Grace continued, "Before this time, many of the lighthouses along the coast of America had been built with wood. During the Civil War, both the North and the South were guilty of burning down lighthouses that would aid supply ships helping the other side."

The ladies were genuinely surprised to hear all of this information.

"I can't believe that we've lived here in the shadow of the Sea Crest Lighthouse our whole lives and we've never heard a word about this," complained Kate. "How many other things have we missed?"

Grace tried to explain. "I only know because I studied it in college. We go much deeper into various parts of American History and read books that you normally wouldn't even know about if you weren't studying for a degree."

"By the way," she continued, "Many light stations and towers were destroyed or disabled during the Civil War. For example, in some areas, the Union Navy took the lens out of the top or damaged them so they could not provide a warning for the approaching ships. The Confederates did the same things when it worked to their advantage. During that war, the Union's naval blockade had been especially helpful as many ships avoided the coast entirely. They knew they would shipwreck, due to lack of safety."

"Wow," said Kate, "I wonder if our Sea Crest Lighthouse has been damaged or replaced?"

"That would indeed account for all the shipwrecks off the coast," said Maggie. "I'm going to ask my dad about that. He's spent his whole life in this area."

"Yeah," Kate agreed. "Both of our fathers have had careers in the Coast Guard, and Maggie, your dad, and my mom are siblings, but I've never heard either of them talking about this? You'd think we'd know about it if this is the original Sea Crest Lighthouse or if this is a replacement, in part or whole."

While they were mulling that over, Grace returned to the journal and continued reading.

Well, he is arrogant and rude. He thinks the swimming lessons are ridiculous and ridicules at every turn. I cannot abide him.

"He's got to be referring to Joe," said Kate with a grin. "Yes, he sure sounds like he might be related to our family."

Grace turned the page and laughed, "Get a load of this. He has a couple of pages with random thoughts or remarks and another drawing."

"He lists:"

Procedures, necessary to survive, in the case of a shipwreck.

Practice Drills – What would each person do in the event of an Emergency?

****Work with Alexander Parke to design a flotation device of some kind.

"This had little stars in front of it," Grace explained.

Will each of the planks for the sides of the pool float?

Can these pieces double as a life-saving float if needed?

Can they carry supplies to shore if needed?

Shape the top curve at the correct angle, so they will float in water if unsnapped from the pool.

I have also ordered a waterproof container, in which to keep valuables. Since most of my life is at sea now, I like to be able to take things, which are important to me, on the ship.

If I experience a shipwreck, I hope to be able to recover this container.

Grace continued, "He then lists other thoughts that are on his mind."

I have a very arrogant lighthouse architect on board. If I ever shipwreck, I sincerely hope he knows how to swim, because I am not helping him. He refuses to take a lesson.

Grace turned several pages, which appear to be unrelated, then started again. "Let's see, towards the end of this journal; Captain Chambers sums up a few important things."

The Irish Architect thought that I was nuts for doing all this foolishness. However, when we shipwrecked, the Irishman was convinced this was a very, very prudent idea and approved the plan wholeheartedly.

We suffered no loss of life amongst the crew, and unbelievably, the arrogant Mr. Walsh already did know how to swim. I guess he just didn't think anyone else deserved to survive a shipwreck.

"He continues."

We worked together to put up shelters and ended up making a settlement here. Due to the pieces of the swimming pool, which floated, we were able to salvage much of the bounty and supplies from the shipwreck site. We named the settlement Sea Crest in honor of the Scottish Ship, which had brought us here.

Now, Joe and I joined forces. He had worked with Daniel Connors to build lighthouses in Ireland which had foundations made of solid granite. Structures made of brick, cast iron, and stone. He thought he could manage to create a similar design for a new lighthouse.

After we had been on land for a couple of weeks, a massive storm hit the coast. When the winds and waves subsided, it had left part of the Sea Crest ship uncovered, out in the water by the jagged rocks. Some of the compartments, which included both my and Joe's secluded rooms, were now accessible to enter.

The crew, as well as Joe and myself, took turns swimming out to the Sea Crest, to retrieve valuable things.

It turns out that Joe had sailed with several blueprints of various lighthouses that need to be improved when he rebuilt them. In fact, he had brought three powerful Fresnel lenses of the first order. That is the largest size made.

Joe decided he would help me build the best lighthouse possible and this location was ideal for the type he wanted to construct. By the time it was finished, (with the help of the crew,) I should add, it had turned out to be one of the best lighthouses built in America. We installed a powerful Fresnel lens, of the first order, in the Sea Crest Lighthouse.

Throughout this experience, Joe Walsh and I have become very best friends. We decided together that The Sea Crest Lighthouse will be an appropriate name.

Grace closed the Captain's journal and hugged it to her chest as she thoughtfully said, "these words from the past are the most valuable gifts we have ever found. We will have much to decide shortly."

The Mah Jongg Club members, each sat quietly, almost reverently, savored the miracle of this discovery.

Maggie's phone interrupted the silence. She answered, "Hi Joe, sure..., I can come over. I'm just five minutes away. I'll be right there."

She hurried out with a wave of her hand, "Well, something important has come up. I've got to meet with Joe, but I'll catch up later."

Chapter 18

"Maggie, this is what I've been waiting for," explained Joe, as he welcomed her into his office.

The attorney for the deceased, eyed her intently as he quietly handed over the last will for the elderly matriarch of the family he represented.

Joe Lawrence had known and admired Maggie for years. He had vacationed at the Sea Crest Lighthouse and Beach in college and liked the area so much that he decided to set up his law practice here.

Maggie assumed that her appointment today, was to consult, as an FBI detective, for some case. It was common for various law enforcement officials to meet with her when they needed her help. The most convenient and secure place for them to meet was usually in the boardroom at Joe's office.

This meeting, however, was not usual at all. To Maggie's surprise, what she was holding in her trembling hand was a document stating that she was inheriting a mansion. It was the grand old Victorian beach house, overlooking the Sea Crest Lighthouse and Beach, to be exact.

This news was so personally shocking and puzzling that her legs almost crumbled beneath her. "Why on earth would this wealthy widow, with lots of relatives, leave me 'anything' in her will? There is positively no connection between us."

"It was filed with her attorney in New York. I handled her family's business when they were here at Sea Crust. However, they haven't been around much the last few years, and I had no idea what was in her will," explained Joe.

Maggie was dumbfounded as she tried to understand. "I believe I met her one time, as a child, when Kate and I knocked on her door to sell Girl Scout cookies. I'm not even sure if it was this lady that we met that day."

They were summer people with a large Victorian beach house overlooking the Sea Crest Lighthouse and Beach.

"This sounds like she left this mansion to *Me!* Why?"

Chapter 19

Meanwhile, miles away, in a plush New York City attorney's office; that is precisely what the deceased matriarch's family wanted to know. James was receiving the very same shocking news and had the very same question. *Why?* He, however, had an opposite reaction.

"I don't believe it. This has to be a mistake," declared James.

"I just got information from the Realtor in Sea Crest. She offered to help the family in any way possible. She has an interested buyer if that's what we decide to do."

James was reeling. "First, we got the news that someone else had bought our family's storage unit's contents, and then we learn that our family's beach property has been left to a complete stranger."

He soon learned that was not all.

The family's attorney, Jeffrey Williams Esq., dealt the final blow. "The will also orders that the contents of the beach house, is to be left intact, and shall go to the same individual who got the beach house."

That statement was the absolute final straw, and James lost it. "This can't be right. We have lots of personal things left there."

The attorney continued calmly, "Your grandmother has removed the items that were to go to relatives and put them in storage."

What is happening? Something terrible is going on, and it started and ended at Sea Crest.

Indignantly, he addressed the attorney who had just delivered the stunning news, "Naturally we need to contest this horrible part of our grandmother's will, immediately. I would also like to know if you had any prior knowledge of this. Do you know why she would have done this?"

Their grandmother's longtime attorney tried to keep his temper intact as he replied in a heavy-hearted, serious tone. "Your grandmother had her reasons, and I believe she wanted you and Michael to understand and agree that she was right. She did leave instructions for both of you to obtain the contents of her storage units, three weeks before the reading of this will. It may seem like an odd place to keep the answers to your questions, but it would explain what was in her heart."

He then added, "It appears that your delay in checking on the storage units caused the lapse of payments, which resulted in the public auction sale of both units. Your grandmother certainly never planned for that to happen."

James was furious. "I need to get in touch with my brother, but you can start proceedings against these con artists right now. Why the very idea of someone preying on our poor defenseless grandmother. It's an outrage."

James' memories of the lighthouse and the surrounding area had been tainted by the only time he ever visited the Sea Crest area. That visit had caused him nightmares for years.

Chapter 20

Back in Joe's office, in Sea Crest, this was the first time he had ever seen her come completely unglued. The super FBI Special Agent, who was never shook-up over anything, was completely blown out of the water, on this one. Joe continued to marvel at Maggie's reaction as she tried to make sense of it all. He was well aware that the surviving Chambers family, had no idea that the beach house in Sea Crest, was being left to a complete stranger. He had a feeling that they would contest the will before sundown.

Joe tried to prepare Maggie for this. "Well, let's just sit tight. Moreover, please do not count on receiving the beach house. I seriously doubt that will happen. If it looks too good to be true, it probably isn't true. I'd say this is a classic example."

He watched her as she paced around the office, her auburn red hair flouncing loosely around her shoulders. This behavior had been going on for a while now. First, she would ask, *Why?* Then she would come up with some inspired reason that made no sense at all. "Maybe I was left on Mom & Dad's doorstep, and they never told me that the Chambers are my real parents."

"Why? Maybe it's a joke, you know, a prank. A few close friends know that I am working with Mary Beth to buy this property. Did they set this up to see if I'd fall for it?" Maggie planted her hands squarely on her hips as she slowly and deliberately, swaggered up to him. She looked him straight in the eyes, with the greenest, widest eyes he had ever seen. "Joe," she demanded as if she were interrogating him.

He swallowed hard, as she blasted, "Tell me the truth right now."

Joe tried to recover, as he said, "You know you really need to stamp your foot when you do that. It would certainly be a lot more effective."

Chapter 21

Within an hour, the other shoe had officially fallen. Joe had done business with Mrs. Chambers' attorney in New York a few times over the years, and he found Attorney Jeffrey Williams, a civil and reputable lawyer. A short time, after handing Maggie the last will and testament of Mrs. Chambers, the telephone call came.

We had certainly been expecting the call. The surprise was that Maggie had been named the beneficent, in the first place.

When he got to his office Jeffrey Williams Esq., was on hold. Joe picked up, "Hi Jeffrey; I've been expecting your call."

"Well, Joe, due to a mix-up in communication between their grandmother's wishes and them not picking up her things within the specified time, the brothers are irate," he explained. "The one that lives here in New York is officially contesting that part of the will."

"I understand. How do you want to proceed?"

"Have you notified the beneficiary? I know you were trying to set something up for this morning. How did that go?"

"Well, Jeff, it went as expected on this end also. She was absolutely floored. She can't believe it."

Jeff stated that they are contesting, "only that part which leaves the beach house and its contents to someone outside the family. They are not contesting the will in its entirety."

"Where does that leave my client?" continued Joe. "Do they have any of the grounds under which they can successfully change it?"

"No. I told him the legal grounds under which a will can be contested. I verified that the will was legitimate because:

#1- The will was signed, in accordance with state law.

#2 – Their grandmother was very competent at the time.

#3 – There was no undue influence.

#4 – There was no fraud."

"Next, I ask him which legal grounds they intended to use, and he answered that the *Outsider* was a con artist," replied Jeff.

"I told him I would draw up the papers, but it would take a few days. I wanted to give him some cooling off time. He also needs to contact his brother, who is in Europe."

Jeff did not disclose the fact that the grandsons still have not located the contents of Mrs. Chambers' storage unit, which was sold by mistake a few days ago. It contains the things from the Sea Crest Beach house that she bequeathed to them. It also explains *why* she did this, and Jeff is hoping they can understand her intentions when they go through the things, she did leave to them. Jeff thought this would fall under privileged information.

However, he did tell Joe, "I know exactly why she made her will as she did and I wholeheartedly agree."

"Do you think that will make a difference to them?" asked Joe.

"Yes, I've known them their whole lives. I took care of their mother's will when she died many years ago. I'm sure they feel very hurt and angry now, but when they find out what happened; I guarantee they'll happily consent."

"Well, I for one can't wait to see what happened to produce this surprising gift," proclaimed Joe. "It must have been something big."

"The biggest," remarked Jeff quietly. "You won't believe it."

Joe hung up the phone. He tried to figure out what the wisest thing to tell Maggie was. *Well, when in doubt, tell the truth. At least, I'll tell her as much as I can.*

Joe walked thoughtfully down the hallway to the conference room. As he opened the door, Maggie had thoroughly calmed down. She was sitting in a chair with complete composure.

"Well, it was just as we expected. The family is officially contesting the will. It is nothing against you personally. They simply don't understand *Why* either."

"I know," said Maggie softly. "It sure didn't sound right to me either. However, it was pretty exciting there for a while though." Maggie tried to chuckle, but it ended up with a false ring to it.

Joe walked over to her chair and sat down beside her. "Maggie," he said seriously, "I'm going to ask you to do something for me. I think it might be very, very important."

Maggie looked at him, she trusted him completely. "Okay, what is it?"

"I'm going to ask you not to say a word about this to anyone," Joe stated. "Now, I know that sounds strange, especially when you have a couple of great, close friends, but in this very unusual case, I think it's crucial to the outcome."

Maggie thought about that without saying a word, *Yeah* or *Nay*.

"Maggie, I've never encountered anything like this in my law practice before. This situation is my first. However, I have observed a whole lot about human nature and about how people view things. If the will holds up and you do, through some miracle, end up with something, I think it will make the difference about what the family can live with and what you feel good about," explained Joe quietly.

"Legally, of course, you're free to tell everyone you want and put any spin on it, you please," said Joe. "That's my legal spiel."

"However, my advice as a very dear friend, stands. Please don't tell anyone about this until we see what happens with the family."

Maggie thought about that for a minute, and then she gave a little smile and said, "Joe, I can see your point. Just because you have the right to do something, doesn't mean it's the right thing to do."

She folded her hands in her lap and said thoughtfully, "If I put myself in their place as if I'd been on the other end of that will, I'm sure I'd feel like the rug had been ripped out from under me. I'd certainly appreciate someone letting me either straighten things out or at least give me time to catch my breath and get my bearings again after I was so deeply hurt."

"Thank you, Joe," she finished, "I can certainly agree to not tell a soul about this."

Chapter 22

James had been furious when he left the attorney's office. As he tried to dial his brother Michael, he muttered a prepared excuse, "I had purposely left the job of picking up the contents of the storage units for you to handle."

If that didn't work, I could try: I know you were overseeing projects in London, but I thought you'd be back in plenty of time.

As he waited, the number connected to a voice mail again.

All right, that gives me a few more minutes to think of some reasonable justification for; why I didn't tell him the truth, that I didn't want to go anywhere near Sea Crest!

I also neglected to mention that we needed to pick the stuff up three months before the reading of the will.

James was getting thoroughly frustrated. He had not even heard from Michael for two days.

Where is he and where is all that stuff? It was easier to get a hold of him when he was in Europe.

Well, one thing is for sure: I am not going down to Sea Crest and straighten anything out. And here is the second thing for sure: Michael better hurry up and answer his phone.

As it turned out, Michael was nowhere near his phone. After he had walked the length of the beach and back, he went back to his suite at the inn. He ordered a pot of coffee and blueberry muffins from room service, but first, he wanted to get a long hot shower. He arranged to have it delivered in half an hour.

James called twice while Michael was in the shower. Both of those frantic calls went unanswered.

Michael's breakfast arrived, just on time. The room service waiter, wearing a name tag that read Harry, called, "Room service. Good afternoon, Sir."

"Hello," Michael answered. He directed Harry, "Please go ahead and set it up out on the balcony."

As Harry happily set up the coffee and muffins, he stated, "This is one of the best views in the whole world. It's another splendid day."

"It looks very picturesque. Is the lighthouse open for tours?"

"It used to be, but it sustained heavy damage from the last major storm. The walkway and the jetty, leading up to the lighthouse, need some repairs before it's safe for the general public, but it's still working and saving lives," Harry proudly informed him.

"Really? That's strange. I just saw another couple go right in and it looks like they were walking around the turret at the top, drinking cups of coffee," Michael said as he sunk his teeth into a delicious warm muffin.

"Oh," laughed Harry. "That's got to be Kate and her brother, Connor."

Michael reacted with a cough, and a sharp gasp, that sucked a blueberry right down his throat. He choked and gagged, as a big chunk of muffin plugged his throat and went down the wrong way. He struggled to catch his breath as the muffin broke apart and continued to obstruct his airway.

Harry started pounding on his back and shouting to Michael, asking if he could raise his arms and breathe. With a few tears in his eyes, Michael tried to nod, yes, that he was okay.

Finally, after more strangling tries, Michael was able to clear his air passageway and breathe. What a relief!

"Okay, I'm fine. Now what were you saying about the lighthouse tours?" asked Michael.

Harry continued, "Well, Kate won't let the general public go up in it until it's safe.

She is trying to raise money to secure the foundation of the Sea Crest Lighthouse. Yes, our Kate is all about safety."

"That's very commendable," answered Michael aloud. However, silently he sarcastically thought, *is there anything she can't do?*

"I brought you a paper," Harry said as he handed it to Michael.

"Thanks."

"There is the story, about last night's rescue. It's right on the front page with pictures of Kate," Harry pointed out proudly. "You probably saw the ending of it. The Coast Guard helicopter lands right over there on that big red cross."

Satisfied that he had done everything possible to make the guest happy, Harry added, "Let me know if you need anything. I'm here until four this afternoon when Kelly comes on." He started out the door.

"Thanks," said Michael as he gave him an ample tip. "I'm good for now."

What he truly wanted was to get a look at the inside of that lighthouse. The architect in him, couldn't pass up the opportunity to investigate that wonderful tower.

He sat down on the balcony to read his paper and have his coffee. He was not at all surprised to read a major story about the performance of Kate's numerous acts of heroism last night. He had mixed feelings and tried to decide how he could be so proud of her, while at the same time, she drove him crazy. It seemed like his emotions towards her were so ambivalent that it was hard to keep track.

Michael closed his eyes as he thought, *she looked like a stunning, surfing mermaid, with the Best Red Swimsuit, I've ever laid eyes on.*

He slammed his feet on the deck and sat bolt upright trying to change the memory into something deplorable.

There, that's better. Kate is horrible: a stealer of precious possessions, with no regard for the lovely grandmother who had left them for her grandsons.

Then, when I finally had her number and saw behind her disguise, (saw her for the thief that she was), she turned into a Superwoman, Coast Guard Search and Rescue Pilot, (of a Helicopter, no less). It is downright impossible to get an exact reading on her. She's an enigma. She's a confounding mystery.

Yes, Michael had been thinking about Kate for almost two whole days now. The realization suddenly crept into his consciousness.

This is going to take a lot of thought, and I'm secretly going to enjoy every minute of it. That scared the wits out of Michael, as he protested; *No, I must Not enjoy it.* He quickly changed to; *I'm dealing with a mysterious enchantress. No, that was even worse.*

He took a sip of coffee as he moved the offending newspaper aside and gazed out over the ocean. As the waves rolled in and danced along the sand, the rhythm of the tide seemed to have a pleasant, soothing effect on his disposition. In fact, he was wondering, *how I can possibly stop hoping to connect with Kate on any level?* when his opportunity to get a look at the inside of the lighthouse, presented itself.

Harry knocked on the door, calling out, "Hello, room service!"

Michael answered the door.

"Hi again. I was just told that Kate and her brother left flyers for the Sea Crest Festival at the front desk, earlier. They had to leave; however, they asked that we make sure each one of our guests received one of these."

Michael thanked him for the paper as he shut the door.

"Finally. This is the break I need," Michael exclaimed triumphantly, as he immediately planned his secret entry into the lighthouse. He had only brought a couple of shirts and pants with him. He had not intended to stay any longer than overnight. He was trying on and tossing his clothes all over the bed, the chair, and the room in general, trying to get just the right look.

No one will remember me if I can only blend in. He put on his sunglasses. *Of course, everyone here at the beach wears shades.*

He looked at his reflection in the mirror with satisfaction.

Now that's the special look I've been after. He was ready.

This entire hectic time, no thought of his phone had entered his mind. As a matter of fact, he never even missed his phone, which was remarkable because much of his life had been spent using his cell phone, conducting business, ordering blueprints, making and verifying changes on construction plans.

Michael seemed to be wrapped up in a new, exciting, secret-agent man type game, which was extremely out of character for him. He successfully managed to carry out his covert goal of leaving his room, unobserved. However, Michael had neglected to grab his room key.

Oh well, he thought. *No problem, I'll ask at the front desk when I return.*

It took him another few minutes to exit the Sea Crest Inn.

He looked very *blended* indeed, as he strolled over to the abandoned lighthouse. He wasn't sure who might still be in the cottage, so he tried to stay out of sight and be quiet as he approached the lighthouse door. He went from one tall obstacle to another barrier, zigzagging back and forth, as he tried to stay hidden. Michael was bordering more on the *suspicious* side than the *blended* side at this time..., but he made it.

He was surprised to find the lighthouse entryway unlocked. "Great," he whispered excitedly to himself. "This is going to be a piece of cake."

He ducked inside and immediately; an elated feeling came over him. "This is outrageous," he almost laughed out loud, at how absurd it was. Michael was secretly enjoying this chance to put one over on Kate by breaking her rules and getting inside her lighthouse. After all, she didn't own it.

Here I am, one of the most sought-after architectural minds in the business, resorting to sneaking into a lighthouse to check it out. It's so far-fetched and ridiculous that it fits right in with the rest of my bizarre visit to Sea Crest.

He pulled the door shut after himself.

Chapter 23

That was just about the time, Connor and Kate came sailing around the corner and pulled to a stop at the keeper's cottage.

Connor had just picked up Kate from Grace's house. On the way home, Kate and Connor had discussed their many questions regarding the Portable Traveling Library Box and wondered where it had been hiding all these years.

Kate reasoned, "That was probably delivered to the lighthouse, while our family was here."

"If that's true, how did it end up in the Chambers' storage unit?" asked Connor. "What's most extraordinary is how our family kept from talking about it?"

"I know, that's just plain laughable," answered Kate. "Our family talks about everything having to do with the lightkeeper's life."

"It's who we are, for heaven's sake," laughed Connor as they arrived back home. This phrase had been one of their favorite sayings for how they described their lineage of lightkeepers, here at Sea Crest.

"We'll get to the bottom of this mystery," laughed Kate as they entered their cottage.

"Well, no one is home to ask about it," said Kate as she looked around. "I'm supposed to go over to help Aunt Mary bake some blueberry pies for the picnic and festival this weekend." She went on to her bedroom and gathered some things to take.

Connor explained, "Yeah, I'm going over to help with the big banner that hangs across Main Street and says: 'Sea Crest Festival This Weekend.' See ya later."

Chapter 24

"Impressive," Michael marveled as his eyes swept over the inside of the tower. His hands felt everything as they went over the terrific workmanship that was before him. He was looking at some of the finest artisanship that he had ever seen. The spiral staircase curved gracefully along the inside of the wall, as it rose higher and higher, up the tall, 117-foot-high, tower. A beautifully scrolled railing of wrought iron lined the steps to prevent a fall as you climbed.

As he ascended, the tower wall had several built-in compartments utilized for various things, over the decades. A few were sealed and plastered over.

Windows were spaced evenly along three sides of the wall. A row placed about every fifteen feet of height between them as the tower rose. The thickness of the brick walls resulted in a deep window jamb, whose pockets contained an entire interior shutter. The design proved ideal for keeping the harsh weather out in all but the roughest storms. They provided not only privacy but also insulation or shade, especially when the elements started to bear down. Michael slowly opened the shutters. He could look far out to sea.

Michael discovered many surprises in this old lighthouse. He was amazed to see a superb dumbwaiter, which had a graceful scroll design in the wrought iron sides. It was large enough to carry supplies the size of a large laundry basket. When you slid your cargo into the compartment and closed the latch, you could transport it effortlessly from ground level to the top level.

This small freight elevator could carry coffee, bread, wine, and cheese to the top for a picnic when you felt like it. It had been, modernized with an electric motor, but it also retained its mechanical chains, which pulled it up or down, by winding the crank with a beautiful mahogany handle.

When you arrived at the top of all those stairs, there were two landings. The very top was the Optic or Light Floor, which held the

Fresnel light lens and equipment for the light beacon.

Below that was the old Service Room. That entire floor had been converted, over the years, to a very comfortable space, which had several modern conveniences.

As Michael stepped on to the beautiful mahogany floor, he marveled, "Isn't this nice? It's warm and cozy on the roughest of nights."

"I can't believe they have a Rumford fireplace up here." They were tall but not very deep, which allowed them to reflect most of the heat generated by burning wood, back into the room. These were very common in the early to mid-1800s, and this had been an excellent addition to this space.

Michael was impressed. He speculated to himself, as he investigated, *Wow. It's vented to the outside with a fireproof device that keeps it safe. Ah..., very nice indeed.*

There were a couple of comfortable chairs and a relaxing hammock with big pillows, which stretched across one side of the library wall. The wall had built-in shelves, which held several, leather-bound first edition books.

Michael also saw a small refrigerator, a coffee maker and other things to eat. The leftover muffins from this morning were also in a basket on a three-legged table. The setting was warm and hospitable.

As Michael walked around, he smiled and approved one more discovery. "Ah... this is great..., a very nice addition to make for a comfortable stay. I haven't seen these in ages. Two Murphy beds fold out of the walls to serve as beds when needed." It transformed the room, into something reminiscent of the much-loved sleeping porches that became popular in the 20th century. Many held the belief that the fresh air they provided bolstered immune systems.

The vintage touch, just tickled Michael as he whispered, "They've thought of everything."

You could exit the stairs by using the Dutch door to access this level, which had a catwalk around the outside of the lighthouse. It was located just below the top catwalk outside the light floor. The small freight elevator could stop at each of these levels.

There was a high-powered telescope with a tall tripod by one of the windows. Michael walked over to it to see what you could discover out at sea. When he opened the window near it, he noticed that it was made a little differently.

All ten windows on this level had been designed with special shutters that were made entirely different from the ones below, alongside the steps.

Michael slowly opened the shutters. He could look far out to sea. However, as he looked closer at the construction of the windows and various pockets, he discovered something else.

Well I'll be, thought Michael. *I can also pull down a second hinged, stained glass, window panel.*

"I can't believe it; this looks like our Scottish Chambers Family Crest. This is incredible." He exclaimed as he carefully inspected the panel, which held the exquisite Celtic beveled glass and leaded design. He quickly moved to the next window and pulled down the window panel.

Michael exclaimed in total surprise. *This is our Chambers Family Coat of Arms. The colored parts were created from delicate, cut, stained glass pieces. This is beautiful.*

As Michael continued to open window panels in this room, he discovered that every one of them had Scottish themes that connected to the Chambers family.

One of the most beautiful ones featured Scotland's National Emblem, The Thistle. The design was a simple flower made out of lavender and purple, stained glass pieces. It was exquisite.

As Michael opened another glass panel, he smiled as he silently agreed, with pride. *I guess this set of hidden windows, wouldn't be complete without the Chambers' tartan of blue and green plaid.*

Each window admitted natural light to the interior of the lighthouse tower, and even showed beautiful prisms, as the sunlight passed through them. *I've been to many lighthouses, but the timeless beauty of this collection of glass windowpanes is utterly astonishing.*

Chapter 25

Kate was about ready to leave when she had a last-minute thought about retrieving the coffee thermos and cups from the lighthouse. She dumped her handbag, phone, and all the other stuff back in a pile on her bedroom chair and went outside to the lighthouse.

She noticed that she and Connor had forgotten to lock it when they had left earlier. *Oh well, no harm,* she thought, as she opened the door.

When she stepped inside, however, she thought she heard someone talking. She quietly pulled the door shut and listened again. She could not make out what he was saying, but the voice made her stop.

She was not sure why, but she started to tingle with excitement. *What is that?* thought Kate. For a moment, she did not even recognize the voice. (Which was probably because he was not yelling.) Nevertheless, she sure responded to it.

Oh No. She thought, *what on earth is 'He' up to?*

Well, Kate decided. *I know every nook and cranny of this lighthouse, and after a lifetime of playing Hide and Seek, I know how to be quiet and sneak up.*

She crept silently up the spiral staircase. When she stepped into an area by one of the shuttered windows, she was pleasantly surprised by the faint scent of men's cologne. She would never admit it out loud, but it smelled wonderful. The familiar fragrance seemed to trigger a similar reaction as when she walked up the beach to meet him. The anticipation of finding Michael here and the sensual aroma combined, as the pleasant flushed feeling and tingling sensation swept over her again. Kate was surprised by this pleasurable, but unwelcomed, phenomenon.

 She was frustrated by the fact that, *it reminds me of how handsome he looked as I walked towards him at the beach. As I got closer and closer, I was taken completely off guard by him.*

She started to wonder, *how much of my memory is real and how much is part of my dreams I've had ALL NIGHT LONG?*

Kate tried to console herself. *Maybe this is what happens when you engage with someone who is so maddening and obstinate. I need to be careful. Michael is extremely dangerous. He wants to take the storage unit contents, and he is the enemy.*

Remember, she thought with great satisfaction. *I certainly pulled a fast one on him, at the beach. I knew exactly who he was and I truly got to him.*

To be perfectly fair, she also remembered that, *in the ensuing argument, he held his own.* Typically, Kate had been used to most guys handling her with kid gloves. They always seemed to agree or defer to her.

Only Connor, she thought, *shares his true feeling with me. I enjoy arguing and debating with him. Afterward, we agree to disagree and go on our merry way, still loving each other.*

Now, this guy was something completely different. He looked and smelled incredible. The fact that she had spent two whole days thinking about him was very unnerving.

Kate was not sure, but she thought she had seen and felt him looking down at her last night on the helicopter site pad. *Of course, if he were staying at the inn, he would have looked out when the Search and Rescue Helicopter landed.*

She tried to remember. *Anyone would have done that. But did Michael notice me? If he did…, was he feeling anything? I mean, was he feeling anything except anger about the storage units?*

Thinking back even further; *I could have sworn he'd felt something personal and extraordinary for me at the beach. I just had that feeling. Of course, I was an idiot for showing off like that.*

To be entirely fair, if I'd had any idea that I'd be this attracted to him, I wouldn't have acted like a spoiled brat. I was the one that was fooled and it is too late now. I've already performed extremely unladylike and ill-mannered in front of him.

These were among the dozens of things she'd been running through her mind last night.

Now she came back to reality and wondered what Michael was up too. *Why is he talking again? Is he talking to himself? Is somebody up there with him?*

She felt a sudden, fierce jolt of jealousy. Kate was now at the very, top step and she almost tripped. She caught herself just in time and stepped silently onto the mahogany floor.

Kate nervously wondered, *Well, now that I'm up here, what am I going to do?*

She had had several legitimate questions to ask him which she had been compiling as she climbed each step.

What are you doing up here?

You're not allowed up here. That had seemed much more appropriate for this situation.

How did you get up here? (Of course, he climbed) That would make it too easy to sidestep the severity of his actions.

Why don't I get right to the point? Just what do you think you're doing in my lighthouse? I want answers, and I want them now.

Michael was aware of some vague, far away motion which he thought it was a seagull. He had his back to her as he stood gazing out the open window at the beautiful sea.

Michael quietly tried to comprehend the significance of this collection to the Chambers family. What does this all mean? Is our family, somehow related to the Sea Crest Lighthouse? Why didn't I know anything about it?

Again, that odd sense of deja vu, swept over him that he had often experienced, over the past two days. He felt an immediate connection, but it was so much more this time. He could feel a strong emotional pull. This time it was, not alarming, but loving.

Michael thought he could almost feel the voices in his soul saying; You're home now. This is where you belong.

He had completely lost track of time. He thought he heard a seagull fly by outside, but he was at total peace, looking out to sea.

Surveying the spectacular scene, he did not know when anything had so touched him. A memory from long ago washed over him. It was his mother, holding him up at this very window, to see the ocean. He had almost no real memory of his mother because he had been so young when she died, but he could recognize her from all the pictures. This, however, felt real. An experience of heart-warming tenderness and intense love swept over him.

Kate was surprised at how calm and sad, almost melancholy, he looked. In that long, silent moment, she knew she wanted him.

She didn't understand why this ridiculous thought had come to her mind. She had never felt this before. She was suddenly scared, which was also new to her. She was usually sure of herself in all situations. She liked to be in control of her feelings.

Kate was standing very, very still. She was in new territory, and she was unsure of what was happening to her.

Kate quietly watched him with amazement.

What was Michael doing here? she wondered.

Michael slowly turned around and just looked at Kate, with tears in his eyes.

Oh no. Why were there tears in his eyes?

All of the questions, which she should ask, had disappeared when she saw his face.

"Kate..., you're here," Michael whispered tenderly.

Kate nodded slowly. She was so choked up she couldn't speak.

"I'm sorry, but there's something I need to do," whispered Michael. He looked so desperate and so torn-up inside that it broke her heart. He sounded like he would die if he didn't do it.

Kate stood quietly, trying to figure out what had happened to him and how she could help him.

"OK" She whispered back. "It's all right." She meant *everything* would be okay. Whatever brought those tears to his eyes was breaking her heart.

All the thoughts of storage units, his arrogant attitude, his rude remarks about her spoiled surfing students, all of it, had been erased from her mind.

The honest, raw emotion she saw in this man, combined with his desperate appeal, changed everything.

He needed to do something. She had never felt so touched by anyone in her life.

I'm not sure what he needs to do, but I'm not going to miss this for the world.

As for Michael, the good little *angel* on his shoulder, that sounded the alarms for danger, was screaming in his brain. *This is probably a terrible idea. Stop. Whoa. I should probably stop and think about this.*

At the same time, the little *devil* that was on his other shoulder was taking his turn, yelling. *That's all I've done is think about this. She is driving me crazy. I just can't take it anymore.*

Michael looked seriously into her soft blue eyes, took her face in his hands as he whispered helplessly, "This makes no sense at all, but...,"

His lips touched Kate's as he kissed her.

The sheer magnetism, they felt for each other took them both by storm. The growing feelings they had been struggling to understand and suppress, literally exploded.

Well, if they thought this was going to take their mind off each other, they could think again.

Their kiss was the very last possible thing they had expected to happen today or any other day, for that matter. It was forbidden, desperate, the act of consorting with the enemy.

Kate's Mah Jongg Club would never believe it. Michael's brother would have an absolute fit if he found out.

Speaking of James, if Michael had even the vaguest memory of a brother, or anything else except, Kate, right now, he might have realized that he had not heard from James in two days.

What Michael was hoping was; *Maybe now I can clear my head, settle down and function for another few hours.*

They looked into each other's eyes again as they tried to catch their breath and get their bearings.

Michael murmured hotly, "No, that's not enough" and they hungrily kissed each other again, with an urgent need. The raw passion they felt for each other was shocking, as they held on to each other for dear life.

Yes, this was incredible!

Chapter 26

At around this same time, Kate's brother, Connor was working on some unfinished chores around the keeper's cottage. He had enjoyed going with Kate to see the Traveling Lighthouse Library Box, but he needed to catch up on a few things before he left to hang the festival banner. He finished the chores and prepared to leave when he heard the phone ring. He ran back inside to answer it.

"Hey Connor," said his friend, and co-hanger of the Main Street Festival Banner. "I'm glad I caught you in time. I've been looking at the banner, and I think we're going to need to repair a few of the grommets that attach to the fixed cable that runs across Main Street."

"Okay, did you check for anything else we might need?" asked Connor.

"Yes, our street banner seems fine, but some of the fasteners are loose or pulled out," explained Patrick.

"How does Kate's banner that trails behind the airplane look?"

"That looks great," he laughed. "You know your sister. She always repairs everything before she packs it away. Could you drop by the hardware store and pick up three, ¾ inch grommet kits?"

"Will do," replied Connor. "I'll see you in a few minutes."

As he was leaving, he noticed that the door to the lighthouse was unlocked. Since they were not letting visitors enter until it was safe, he thought he'd better secure it.

Then, thinking that they would all be away for several hours, he double locked it using his prize possession, the medieval Viking padlock from behind the flowerpot. He hooked the massive padlock through the shackles and clicked it shut. *Just for good measure,* thought Connor.

Chapter 27

Later that afternoon, Aunt Mary was wondering what had happened to her favorite niece. She had already made the first couple of blueberry pies, and she had expected Kate to arrive hours ago. They were using their family's recipe, and they hoped to win the 1st prize again.

The real secret was in the pie crust. Mary's Grandmother had made it with lard, but Kate and her Aunt Mary had changed it over to shortening, and it tasted delicious. The pie crust just fell apart when your fork went through it. It won the Blue Ribbon for, *The Best Pie at the Sea Crest Festival*, five years running.

Aunt Mary was instructing a few of the Girl Scouts that were working on their Baking Badge.

"First, we need to measure 2 cups of flour into our bowl." Each of the girls took turns sifting the flour into their bowl.

"Now we need to add and mix ½ teaspoon of salt through it."

"We also need to sift and set aside an additional cup of flour in a separate bowl to be used when we roll out the pie dough." She walked around complimenting them on each step of the process.

"Next we'll measure out ½ cup of shortening. I'll also show you a neat trick to measure it that will make it easy. Each of you, please bring your measuring cup over here to the sink."

As they lined up, she continued, "We will fill each one with a ½ cup of water. Carry these carefully back to your workstation. That's right. Now can you guess what we're going to do?"

The girls offered their opinions, and a couple had the correct answer. "That's right. Very good. We will scoop the shortening into the top of the cup and hold it underwater with the spatula until the water is level with the 1 cup line." They played with their ingredients until they got the desired results.

"Very good." she encouraged.

"Next you come back to the sink and carefully empty the water out. Bring your spatulas. I always do this part over a bowl in case the shortening tries to slide out. We don't want it to fall into the sink."

The girls giggled over that, so Aunt Mary chuckled as she explained, "Hey don't think that hasn't happened. I'm just trying to let you avoid my mistakes."

"This shortening goes into a separate mixing bowl. Everyone got it?"

"Now," Aunt Mary smiled. "We come to the secret step which makes this recipe easy to roll out and press into the pie pan. This part is seldom used, in modern times, but it has never failed me, and it's resulted in numerous Blue Ribbons."

The Girl Scouts eagerly watched while she took a boiling hot kettle from the stove. She took a measuring cup and said, "I'll do this part, but each of you needs to whisk it until it looks like fluffy whipped cream."

She poured ½ cup of hot boiling water into each of the shortening bowls.

"Be careful not to let it splash on you. There you go. It's looking great."

"I think they all look ready for the flour. Use your pastry blender utensil, to cut the flour into the shortening mix, until all the flour is moistened."

"Now with clean hands, gather the dough together with your fingers, so it cleans the bowl. Press the whole batch firmly together until you can make a ball."

"That's right. You girls are great bakers. I'll share a hint that will work for the rest of your lives. That extra flour you measured out can be used for this step if your kitchen has a different humidity. You will find that as you bake in different kitchens, your dough might need either more or less flour to work well. The measurements that we used today is the standard that my grandmother used and adjusted from there as needed. It's never failed me."

"Since this dough makes two pie crusts, we'll divide the dough in two. We'll use one for the bottom and the top of our pies. Roll each half into a ball, and we'll prepare the rollout area."

"Today we'll use a sheet of waxed paper and wet down the counter to suction the bottom down. We'll use some of our extra flour to cover the top lightly. I find that if you use the sifter and shake it softly as you pass above the waxed paper, it comes out great."

"Now comes the really fun part. Place one of the halves on the floured area. Take your rolling pin and roll out an even layer of dough, stroking first one way and then diagonally across, the other way, to form a circle. That's right, work it lightly until it makes a circle and we'll need to make it about one inch bigger than your inverted pie pan."

"That's fine. Now fold the pastry in half and carefully transfer it to the pie pan. Wow, you all got it the first time. If it does fall apart, no problem. Just pinch the broken edges together."

Every one of the Girl Scouts soon finished.

"I can't tell you how proud I am of your baking skills," Aunt Mary emphasized with a smile. "We'll take a short break and then finish the blueberry filling and baking."

While they were eating a snack, they started discussing the satisfaction of making their first pies from scratch. Aunt Mary recalled, *Yes, it's great to learn how easy it is to bake our favorite desserts. This simple pie crust can be part of their special collection of recipes that can be passed down to their children and bless their families for their entire life.*

Aunt Mary happily shared these thoughts with the girls over the next few minutes.

"Wow," said one of the Scouts. "I've never thought of that. I do know that no one in my family has ever made a home-made pie from scratch."

"Well then, you are making history today. One of the nicest things about the blueberry pies we are making is that we have an abundance of blueberries here at Sea Crest. We have various well-advertised festivals and contests, to spotlight products from our area. It's easy to find plenty, and our tourists expect us to have plenty of baked blueberry goods, as well as jellies, jams, and other goodies."

"All right, let's get back to our workstations, finish the pies and put them in the ovens to bake."

They all eagerly listened to the directions as Aunt Mary walked them through the simple steps of mixing, pouring, covering and baking the pies.

"1 ½ cups sugar
1/3 cup flour
4 cups fresh blue

½ teaspoon of cinnamon
1 ½ Tablespoons butter

Pre-Heat the oven to 425°. Sift sugar, flour, and cinnamon into berries and mix lightly.

Pour into pastry-lined pie pan. Dot with butter. Cover with top crust. Cut slits in it.

Seal and flute edges. Cover edge with 1½" strip of aluminum foil to prevent excessive browning.

Now we'll bake it 35-45 minutes or until the crust is nicely browned and juice begins to bubble through slits in crust."

While the pies were baking, Aunt Mary gave them something very special. "Gather around," she smiled. "I've got index cards with the recipe for the Blueberry Pies printed on them. I suggest you have these laminated so you can wipe them clean if you spill something. These are to be used many times. However, blueberry stains are permanent, so save yourself the trouble of reprinting them."

"Keep in mind; this recipe can be used for several different kinds of pies. For example, raspberry, blackberry, strawberry, or something called boysenberry, will all use the same measurements. If they are at the height of their season, you might try a little less sugar."

"These skills that you learn to get special Girl Scout badges are useful abilities that will serve you for a lifetime."

The aroma of the girl's pies filled the air as they held the oven door open and set up the cooling racks for Aunt Mary as she carefully slid the pies into place. The Scout's eyes were shining with pride.

"One final thought. These pies are special. If you are in need of a Christmas gift for someone, or perhaps you hear about a family with a difficult circumstance, a pie can bring comfort. They are a blessing, and you can make a generous gesture with them."

"Now you may each take your pies with you in the boxes that you were asked to bring today. You all did a great job."

Later that afternoon, Connor and his buddy, Pat, took a well-planned break from hanging the Main Street Festival Banner, to see how the pies were coming. As they went flying up the driveway and into the kitchen, the aroma of sweet blueberries filled the air.

"Boy, those pies sure smell good," called Connor as they came through the door.

"Yeah, they sure do," replied his aunt. "But you have to wait till tomorrow, and you both know it."

"The Girl Scouts made their pies, this morning in their class and they all earned their baking badge. I'm so proud of them."

"This troop is earning badges and pins, as well as, working on a Journey Project. They told me that one of the Scouting Troops they had heard of, baked over 200 pies for a Thanksgiving Community Project. It's simply amazing isn't it?"

"That's wonderful, but we came here for a piece of the pie," pleaded Connor.

"No way."

"Oh, come on," he begged. "Please, just give us one pie, we'll split it."

Aunt Mary saw the disappointment on their faces, so she conceded, "Okay, I'll be saving a big piece of pie for each of you."

"By the way, I see Kate didn't make it over today. Did she have a Search and Rescue emergency?"

"I didn't think so. I know she was planning to come over earlier. Something must have come up," answered Connor. "Hey, Aunt Mary, that reminds me, can I ask you a question?"

"Sure."

"Grace called us this morning and had Kate, and I come over for a surprise. Do you think you can guess what it was? I'll give you clues."

"Great. Is it bigger than a breadbox?"

"Hey. That's not fair. I was going to give you clues," explained Connor.

"Okay, but is it bigger than a breadbox?"

"Yes, and it has things inside it."

"Is it a bicycle," asked Pat?

"No," said Connor. "And what things are inside a bicycle?"

"Well, the spokes are inside the wheels," answered his friend.

Connor finally said in a very exasperated voice, "It's a Portable Traveling Lighthouse Library Box. Do you remember any such thing, Aunt Mary?"

"My lands, I think I vaguely remember what you're talking about."

"How did Grace find that?"

"It was in an unpaid storage unit, at an auction up in Rosemont," answered Connor.

"Was there anything in it?"

"Yes, it was complete, with a list of contents attached to the inside top of the wooden trunk. It included a Dominoes game, 'The Adventures of Huckleberry Finn', a couple of toys and about 50 other books. Kate and I had never even known they existed, before today."

"Boy, that brings back memories. As I recall, the lighthouse service would leave them for a few months, send it to another lighthouse in exchange for a new portable library for us. Your dad and I thought it felt like another Christmas every time it arrived," exclaimed his aunt.

"Why didn't you ever tell us about this? With all the stories including, what we suspect are tall tales, we've never heard anyone even mention these library boxes."

Aunt Mary could not explain why, except that by the time they had grown up, everyone had just forgotten all about them.

Soon Connor and Patrick decided their break time was over and they needed to finish hanging the sign across Main Street. As they were leaving, (without any pie), Aunt Mary said that if they saw Kate, please tell her she'd be baking more blueberry recipes tomorrow at the church kitchen. She was giving a free baking demonstration to anyone who wanted to learn. Numerous baked goods would be made for the Sea Crest Festival over the next couple of days.

Chapter 28

Michael was the first to speak. "I'm not sure what's happening to me. I have no credible explanation for what I feel for you, Kate. I don't seem to be able to control my emotions where you are concerned, and I don't know why."

"I know," Kate whispered.

"This is totally out of character for me to behave like this," he tried to explain. "I could, of course, apologize for myself, but for the life of me, I honestly feel you are the best thing that's ever happened to me."

"I feel it too."

"Yes," Michael tried to justify how wrong this was. "You've driven me insane. I have not been able to think straight since I met you. I don't believe I'll be able to survive if I have to leave you. I'm dead serious, and it terrifies me."

Kate had tears in her own eyes, as she agreed, "I don't know what's happening either. I am equally baffled, by your effect on me and my feelings for you. Part of me is on top of the world, and part of me feels scared to death that you are going to disappear and that I will never get over it. I would never be the same again, Michael. 'This' scares me and 'Nothing' scares me."

Kate continued to describe her bewilderment, "I usually get along with everyone. I'm utterly confused by my attraction to you, even though I detested the very thought of you."

"Well that's not very nice," laughed Michael. "Now, my feelings are really hurt."

"You know what I mean. Neither of us seemed able even to tolerate the other," she explained. "When did that all start to change?"

"Kate, you know exactly when it started," he murmured with a sarcastic moan.

As he bent his head down and kissed her again, he shuttered to think how he had longed to take the mermaid, with the red swimsuit, in his arms like this.

'Said Mermaid,' was thinking the same thing, *"I've wanted you for days."* What she actually said was, "If you're referring to that afternoon on the beach after the surfing lessons, I'm sure I don't know what you mean."

"Ha. Like you didn't know exactly what you were doing to me" Michael laughed. "I should have RUN. But, did I? No! All the while you were reeling me in hook, line, and sinker."

"But in my defense," Michael continued. "You were like an accident on the highway. You know you should move on, with your eyes straight ahead. However, you cannot resist. You have to look anyway. You have no willpower. Well, you know what I mean."

"That's not true," cried Kate. "I'm like an accident? Thanks. You know, Michael, you are unbelievable."

He continued, "Oh, I know. It's like someone who stops in the middle of the road and watches a big eighteen-wheel truck, coming right for them. The poor guy is frozen; he can't move." They were both laughing by this time. Michael continued for one last shot. "And You, my dear Kate, mowed right on over me, splattered me all over the road and stole my heart."

"Well, if that's true, it's the best thing I ever did," Kate said with a twinkle in her eye. "You've been driving me positively nuts, and it's just what you deserve."

"I've been driving you nuts?" Michael was not going to let this one go. "Oh really? You have me walking into walls. And I'm an architect for heaven's sake."

"Wow," she said. "I didn't know you were an architect. What on earth, were you trying to buy those abandoned storage units for? Nothing I try to figure out about you makes any sense."

"You can multiply that by one hundred, and you'll see how jumbled up your ever-changing information appears. And Yes, I am an architect, who wanted to see what damage the big storm did to the lighthouse. The room service waiter at the Sea Crest Inn said it was unsafe and I thought maybe I could help."

"Oh Michael, that's wonderful," cried Kate as she hugged him. "You're an answer to my prayers."

Embarrassed, she quickly added, "We're having a festival this weekend to raise money for the assessment and repairs. What do you think?"

"It would take me a lifetime to tell you what I think," Michael said seriously. "Oh, you mean about the repairs?" he said with a smile.

"I'd need to have some equipment brought in to test the stability of the foundation and walls, but other than that, the walkway needs to be completely rebuilt. That's not only cosmetic. At high tide, I'll bet the pathway is underwater?"

"Yes," answered Kate, "especially now that we're in the spring tides. The lighthouse will be surrounded by the ocean during high tide tonight."

"Well, I've created a great design for projects like the jetty and walkway. It consists of a network of interconnected triangles. They form a rigid framework called a truss. They can span long distances which are amazingly strong, and they can be designed with extremely graceful curves and arches," explained Michael.

"That sounds beautiful," replied Kate.

"Yes, it can be exquisite, and it would look perfect leading up to the lighthouse door. Also, you would never have to worry about damage, as a result, of a storm again. The truss system is extremely durable, and it can withstand most weather issues with no problem," said Michael as he kissed her.

"That sounds great. Where can we get the supplies and equipment for you?"

"Oh, that's no problem," he said. "My last few contracts have been in Europe, but I have access to equipment here in the states also. It would only take a day to find out how stable both the foundation and the tower are. I could have the equipment here on Monday."

"Oh Michael, that's great, but we don't have the funds yet."

"That's not a problem. It's my equipment and my company." As he said these last words, he got that strange deja vu feeling again. He looked troubled as he pulled Kate close to him.

"I don't know what keeps happening to me," he said. "Did you ever hear of or have a deja vu phenomenon happen to you? It has happened several times since I arrived here at Sea Crest. I know I was here before, but I was too little to remember it. Something happened, and it must have been very sad. I just felt it again when I talked about this lighthouse."

"My feelings are very strong here," he continued. "I even felt my mother holding me up to look out this very window, right before I saw you." He tried to explain, "I've never even been able to remember what my mother looked like, except for pictures, but when I looked out this window, I remembered being here, in this lighthouse with her."

"I know that remembrance was real. I've been in numerous lighthouses here in the States and around the world, but I've never felt her memory before."

Michael looked at Kate with a sincere expression on his face. "This lighthouse is special, and I'll do everything within my power to preserve it," he vowed.

Kate could not have been more touched or surprised. "I don't know exactly what it must feel like, but I saw your face when you felt your mother holding you at the window. She was blessed to have such a loving son." She put her head on Michael's shoulder and thought her heart would burst with the love she felt for him, as she held him tight.

Chapter 29

Around this very moment, a very agitated and baffled, James Jensen, was rolling into the outskirts of Sea Crest in his grandmother's Bentley automobile. He lives in New York City and rarely drove a car, but he had always had the use of his grandmother's car and driver when needed. Now, this car had been left, in their grandmother's will, to James and his brother, Michael.

James had decided to drive himself down to Sea Crest, but he began to doubt that decision immediately. He found driving by himself very hard. He was not accustomed to dealing with heavy traffic on unknown roads. He also did not like having this much time to himself to think about what he had gotten Michael into and why his grandmother had written her will as she had.

James had made one more attempt to get control of his mental situation. He had dressed for success.

James was dressed in a Brioni, Charcoal Gray, Three Piece, 100% Cashmere Suit and Stefano Ricci, finely striped, gray/white dress shirt. He complimented this with a Brioni, solid silk, red satin tie, and matching pocket handkerchief. He completed the look with a pair of Stefano Ricci Alligator Leather Classic Loafers in Black. We will not go into his socks and undies, but suffice it to say, he was well dressed.

These designer pieces of clothing composed one of his typical, everyday outfits. It was, in James' mind, how a highly successful New York City executive dressed. In spite of the fact, that many of his fellow associates and colleagues did not take this path. They preferred to travel a more casual road to success.

At this point in his life, James did not even think of these items as status symbols, as much as a mere convenience, to get the best things in life. The best tables at restaurants, the best service in dealings, everyone took his business calls, etc.

If he wanted to buy a suit, the best stores would have several delivered to him. He would pick out what he wanted and have the tailor fit them for him. Then he would send the rest back. If he wanted a piece of jewelry, the jeweler would close the store for his appointment. He would have one-on-one help for any questions and service to make the purchases as pleasant and private as possible. If he wanted anything, from a haircut to a dinner for two by his favorite chef, he need only mention it to his assistant, and it would magically happen. This is also how he was successfully able to control his day-to-day life. James believed, if he put on his *Power Suit,* the doors would open.

That, however, was not going to work very well in this situation. The normal person that James had to deal with here in Sea Crest would probably treat him just the same as everyone else.

James was in a location, which he had avoided for many years. He did not want to be at Sea Crest, and he was extremely distressed and worried on many levels. In fact, he was fit to be tied.

This was exactly what I'd vowed that I would never do, James, expounded to himself.

Two days ago, his only brother, Michael, was supposed to be in Rosemont, checking on the individual who had bought their grandmother's storage unit contents, at auction. James had specifically requested, almost demanded, that Michael come back from Europe, to handle this. James felt extremely guilty manipulating him like this.

Now, James was beside himself, as he tried to figure out what had happened to him. He carefully tried to go over every detail again in his mind.

I know, for a fact, Michael had landed in New York City. He called me from JFK airport. I know that his flight, had been delayed and he was not going to make the auction on time. It would take several hours to drive to Rosemont. I ordered him to drive down to that ridiculous hick town and find out what happened to our grandmother's stuff.

Next, Michael called, to complain and blame me for letting this happen in the first place.

"As far as I can tell, someone has bought the two units, and he or she has taken all the stuff to a town called Sea Crest," Michael had explained. "I just checked my GPS and its miles down the coast, south of here. It looks like Sea Crest is at least an hour away."

Next, he had continued adamantly, "And James, seriously, I need you to know, I don't want to deal with the likes of anyone who would even think, of attending an auction featuring someone else's garbage."

James had apologized, for what seemed like an eternity, and Michael agreed to go down to Sea Crest to buy back their grandmother's stuff.

James was very alarmed as he thought, *that was two days ago. I have not heard from him since. Michael is not answering his phone despite numerous calls that I left for him.*

Something terrible has happened to Michael.

As James drove through town, he was alarmed even further by all the preparation for some weekend festival. *These people seem unconcerned that my brother is missing, and great harm has probably come to him.*

James drove directly to the Sea Crest Police Station. He parked his car and practically ran up the steps and through the door. He stopped in front of the first person he met and frantically explained, "I need to report a crime. Something terrible has happened to my brother." James was beside himself, as he rambled on, "Something could have happened to him a couple of days ago. I'm not sure when, but he needs help. Now."

One of the police lieutenants holding a clipboard stepped forward, thinking, *Boy, this sounds big.* "Was your brother here for the festival?"

"Of course, not."

The fact of the matter was, Sea Crest's Annual Festival was the biggest thing that this police department ever handled. They directed traffic, helped park cars, made sure that no one littered and handled any situations involving a couple of known, town drunks that lived here. The town did have one solitary jail cell now, and they would use it if they had to. The Sea Crest Police usually escorted the inebriated offender back home. They just slept it off.

The most dangerous thing the police did all year was a joint activity with the Sea Crest Fire Department to put on a safe; Spectacular Fireworks Display, at the Festival.

That is not to say, there was no crime, but the Coast Guard Search and Rescue and the Federal Bureau of Investigation had a very strong presence in this area. The local police had very few criminal offenses to handle.

"I'll help you fill out a missing person report, and we'll see if we can help," he continued.

"Something happened to him. You need to do something right now." James pleaded loudly, out of desperation. With that, he collapsed into a chair, hung his head in his hands and began to run his fingers through his hair.

James was struggling. He could not help but remember, why he had pledged never to come here. *"There were too many memories here. It was real, and it was bad. How can I face losing what is left of my family? Now Michael is missing. I sent him down here alone."*

The police officer stepped closer and kindly spoke to James. "Sir, if you could come with me to my office. I would like to help find out what happened to your brother. That's what we're here for."

As James got up and started to follow, the officer said, "All right, let's start at the beginning. We'll get it figured out."

When they got to the office, he got them both a cup of coffee and sat down across from James. "OK, take a big breath and tell me what your brother's name is and when was the last time you saw or spoke with him."

"His name is Michael Jensen. I talked on the phone with him two days ago. He was up at Rosemont, and he was coming down here the next morning."

"Okay good. Have you tried to call his phone since then?"

"Yes, I've called several times, and I left several phone messages."

"Was he traveling alone?"

"Yes," said James sadly. *I should have come myself. What did I send him for?*

The police officer picked up the phone and dialed. "Hello, this is Officer Jones. Could you see if you've had anyone come to the hospital in the last 2-3 days, the name of Michael Jensen?"

They both waited while the hospital checked. "No? Good, if you do have anyone by that name come in for any reason, please call the precinct immediately." The officer was ready to hang up, then stopped and said, "Just a moment, I'll check."

He turned towards James as he asked, "Michael Jensen's Information; Age? Height? Any distinguishing marks or ways to ID your brother?"

James gave the information to Officer Jones, who relayed it to the hospital and hung up.

"Next step: Was he going to stay overnight when he got here? We are having a big festival celebration."

"He wasn't planning to stay overnight when I talked to him, but it's possible."

The officer picked up the phone again and dialed. Judging from the man who was sitting across from him, he did not think his brother would be staying at a cheap dive, so he started with the Sea Crest Inn.

"Hello, this is Officer Jones, from the Sea Crest Police, could I have a word with your manager, please? "

"Thank you, Sir."

"Hello, this is Officer Jones, with the Sea Crest Police. I wonder if you could check your guest-list and see if you have anyone listed under the name of Michael Jensen. You do? Great, could you put me through to his room please?"

The officer looked at James and saw the relief, "They're ringing his room. He's at the Sea Crest Inn."

The manager came back on the line, "I'm sorry, Officer. He's not answering."

The officer stood up and said, "Do not let anyone enter or leave that room. Do you have security available? Have them watch that room. Remember, No one In or Out. We're on our way."

"Come on." Officer Jones hurried James out of his office while he was calling to his fellow troops. "All-points bulletin; at Sea Crest Inn, check on safety and status of a person in Room 225."

They were now in the officer's police car, lights and sirens on.

Officer Jones was still calling orders as they drove, "Call 911. Have them wait for police assist before entry. Possible hostage situation in progress."

Kate's phone was buzzing and pulsing, to beat the band, from its place inside her purse. However, no one heard it. The purse had never left her bedroom since she returned from Grace's house this afternoon.

Connor had come home to eat supper but didn't think twice about Kate not being home. He did, however, ask his dad why they had never mentioned the Traveling Lighthouse Library Box to them before. He didn't have any logical answers, but he laughed and agreed with his sister, Mary, that they loved it.

Now the stories came for the next full hour. It was wonderful to remember those happy times. He even called Mary to reminisce some more. That also prompted Mary to ask, "Hey do you remember what else caused us sleepless nights wondering what might arrive around Christmas?"

"I think I know what you're talking about. Did it drop out of the sky?"

"Yes, you've got it. Did you ever tell Kate and Connor about the Flying Santa?

"No, I don't believe I have."

Connor immediately piped up and asked, "What else did you guys conveniently neglect to tell us?"

"Oh, it must have just slipped our minds. However, we used to have a Flying Santa, who generously dropped off a bag of Christmas things, every year."

"Oh boy, a Flying Santa. I'm sure you never mentioned that to us. What kind of things can you drop from an airplane?"

"It would always be a surprise, but it was a welcome gift parcel which included basic items, such as newspapers, magazines, coffee, tea, candy, tobacco, soup, yarn, pens, and pencils. The Flying Santa project changed over the years, but I believe it started ... let's see around the last part of the 1920s, during the Great Depression.

To show his appreciation for the dedication and self-sacrifice, of the lighthouse keepers and their families, a private citizen, aviator William Wincapaw, started the first Flying Santa, Christmas gift drop. He loaded his Christmas packages into a vintage airplane with a single radial engine and wicker seats. On that famous original flight, he airdropped Christmas gifts, to lighthouses along the Maine Coast. I think he was able to reach about a dozen or so. As the tradition changed and expanded, goods were sometimes delivered to the Coast Guard, who would take it from there."

"I can't believe you and Aunt Mary didn't ever talk about that," complained Connor. "Just wait until Kate hears about this."

"We just got busy and times change and we just never remembered to share it with you," explained his dad. "By the way,

I believe that The Flying Santa increased to serve at least 91 lighthouses, using 3 Flying Santa planes, within a couple of years. During World War 1, the program had grown to an impressive 115 lighthouses and Coast Guard stations."

However, these memories were promptly interrupted, by the sound of the Sea Crest's entire Police Department, sirens blaring and lights flashing, as they descended full force towards the Sea Crest Lighthouse, the Lighthouse Keepers Cottage, the Sea Crest Inn and the Sea Crest Restaurant. This group included anyone and everyone, even remotely related to law enforcement in this small coastal town.

Every year they would have practice drills prior to the Sea Crest Festival, that would prepare them for crime sprees that might develop during the festival. Just last weekend, each patrol person took turns training on the imaginary crime squad, drug squad, vice squad, fraud squad, and last but not least, the riot police. Tonight, was the first time they had actually had the chance to use this valuable training. This was big!

Soon, the police force was seen, hunkered down outside, all around the area. They were barricaded everywhere. Some were behind their cars. Others had crouched down using whatever obstacles they could find, including the many big pots of blooming flowers scattered along the beach boardwalk in preparation for the festival.

With this huge show of solidarity, the Sea Crest Police Precinct had the unique opportunity to show that it could handle even the biggest crimes. Of course, they were not sure what the crime was yet, but they were ready.

As the lead officers entered the Sea Crest Inn, the security guard outside Room 225, let the police know that no one had gone in or out of the room since the call came in, to the manager.

Officer Jones stood in the hallway, just outside the door to Room 225 and used the loudspeaker to try to communicate with the people inside the room. "This is the Police. Come out with your hands up." Everyone involved nervously waited. Nothing happened.

With no response from inside the room, the officer demanded again, that the occupants, "Come out with your hands up."

No one responded from inside. Officer Jones motioned his troops to come up by the door but stay out of harm's way, just in case the occupants started firing as they exited the room.

Officer Jones asked for the manager's key. He slowly turned the key in the lock. Nothing happened. Now with guns drawn, the Sea Crest Police entered the empty room. They carefully covered each other as they went from room to room and out to the balcony.

The entire suite came up empty.

Officer Jones informed the team that, "Michael Jensen has been in the area for approximately two days and by the looks of this room, with clothes and things thrown everywhere, a struggle has undoubtedly taken place."

He approached the room service tray on the balcony with the food Michael had ordered. "His cold coffee cup is only half-full. The coffee in the carafe is almost full, and the coffee is again, cold. The blueberry muffins are untouched, except for one. It appears to have one huge bite taken out of it."

"It looks like he was interrupted this morning. Mr. Michael Jensen is now presumed hurt, abducted against his will, kidnapped or quite possibly; he was killed."

"His brother, James Jensen, came down from New York City to try to find out what has happened to him."

There was total silence as the solemn Sea Crest Police Force; all looked respectfully sorry for the man in the three-piece suit and the alligator shoes.

Chapter 30

From inside the lighthouse, they heard sirens and all kinds of commotion outside.

"Hey, look," said Michael, "The police cruisers are all flashing their lights and running their sirens. They seem to be surrounding the Sea Crest Inn for some reason."

Kate excitedly said, "Yeah, there must be an emergency."

Kate checked for her phone, but she realized she had not brought it with her to the lighthouse. She asked, "Can I use your phone for a minute? I need to check in."

"Sure... wait, I don't seem to have my phone. I must have left it in my room," Michael answered.

"Come on, let's go," Kate called, as she grabbed his hand. They hurried down the spiral staircase as fast as possible.

They reached the bottom of the staircase and took two steps toward the doorway. However, when they looked up and saw the door, they both abruptly stopped. They both felt the same apprehension. Their cautionary intuitive feeling seemed to mean that, *if they went through that door, out into the night, they might lose this close fragile feeling that seemed to surround them.*

Kate thought, *I can't bear to see this end.* Tears were threatening again as her voice broke, "I don't even know why I'm crying," She said, "I never do this."

Michael was feeling the very same thing. He pulled her to him and thought, *I can't let this slip through my fingers. There will never be anyone to compare to my Kate.*

"It's Okay," Michael whispered as the staggering truth finally dawned on him. Truthfully, it appeared he had needed to be hit over the head, with the big new flash. He finally realized why she had affected him as she did. He had fallen in love with Kate.

 "Kate," Michael began as he touched her chin and turned her face up to look into his eyes, "I'm going to tell you something that may be hard for you to hear and understand."

"What Michael?" she whispered with mixed apprehension and excitement. She had just been thinking; *He's the one.* She felt more for this man that she ever imagined was possible. It felt utterly sensational to be in his arms. *I'm not willing to give him up for anything.*

"Kate, I Love You. I cannot seem to control it. It's complete, and it's forever." He said it so tenderly, and he seemed so Blessed by the fact that she just automatically replied.

"Well, Michael, I don't want to scare you either, but I feel the same way. I'm in love with you, too and I can't think of anything else."

They proceeded to seal it with a kiss. Michael interrupted, with another declaration, "Kate, you'd make me the happiest man on earth, if you'd do me the honor of marrying me."

Kate smiled and agreed, "I'd love to."

Next, Michael had a very pressing request. "Do you have any hopes for one of those long engagements of more than a few days?"

"Well, I honestly don't want you wandering around Free, for one more minute, than is necessary." Kate laughed. "I've, seriously, waited my whole life thinking, I'd never find you."

"Then let's get married as soon as possible." proclaimed Michael.

"That sounds perfect." agreed Kate. "I've never felt happier."

Now they could go out and face the world together, as they held hands and turned to leave the lighthouse. They pushed the door to go out, but it would not budge.

"What's wrong with this door? Doesn't it release from the inside?" Michael asked Kate.

"Of course, it does. Here let's try again," she said as they pushed against it again.

"It feels like it's locked from the outside," said Michael as he looked at her.

"Oh, No. Connor must have put the Irish padlock on it. We were worried about someone getting up here with all the damage, that it wouldn't be safe."

"He must have done that after you came in. I'll bet nobody saw either of us come in here," said Michael. "And I'll bet water also surrounds us."

Kate agreed with very mixed feelings, "No one will come tonight."

"Well, at least we'll have something interesting to tell our grandchildren someday." Michael had no idea where that had come from. He had rarely even gone so far as to think of children.

They both suddenly laughed with joy, at their new possibilities.

Chapter 31

This was, by far, the biggest case in which the Sea Crest Police Department had ever been involved. The United States Coast Guard and the Federal Bureau of Investigation had been involved with many big-time crimes such as smuggling, drugs, and crimes on the high seas, but the local police were not usually asked to assist in any way. Their year-round townspeople were not usually involved in such high-profile crimes.

This situation was an exciting opportunity for Officer Jones to show his superiors, just what he was capable of handling. He was visibly disappointed when those superior authorities suggested the need to call in the FBI.

It is customary for help to be requested, in situations where the FBI has resources and experience where the local law enforcement facilities do not have access. These might include the ability to research and investigate electronic communications.

Officer Jones reluctantly agreed to defer to the FBI, although in reality, it was not a choice at all.

Maggie O'Hara was home relaxing with the newest addition to her life. She felt blessed to have this wonderful dog prance into her life. "Hey, Misha let's go out to the kitchen and see what we can find, Okay, girl?" Maggie said, with such excitement that Misha immediately got up and went to her.

They combed through the cupboards, and sure enough, they found treats for each of them. Maggie was still heartsick over someone abandoning this sweet dog. *What would ever possess, anyone on the face of the earth, to do that?*

Maggie certainly hadn't detected even a single sign of aggressive behavior in the dog. Well, she was thankful that Misha had wandered into her yard. *Maybe she just dropped from heaven,* speculated Maggie with a laugh.

Well, no matter how she arrived, Maggie pondered, *I'm going to make sure we get to the bottom of it and make the previous owners pay dearly for treating you like that.*

On second thought, what if they try to get you back? What if they develop a guilty conscience and try to say that you were lost and they want to keep you?

Maggie could hardly bear the thought. She sat down and hugged the gigantic Great Dane, as she promised, "Misha, I don't know why you came into my life, but I promise I'll work it out so you can stay with me always. Okay?"

She felt strangely heart-broken at the mere thought of losing Misha, and she decided she ought to talk to Joe about what legal steps she could take to maintain the legal owner of Misha. In the meantime, she could change her outlook, look on the bright side, and hope for the best.

"For now," she said to Misha. "I'm going to plan for the event of buying the Chambers' beach house. There is plenty of room for you there. If I can't buy it, I have already offered to buy or lease it from the previous owner. We'll see how that turns out. All right, Misha?"

They curled up on the sofa and Maggie looked over the new information about the Chambers' beach house that Mary Beth had given her. She understood it probably would not be left to her after all, but she was still planning to purchase it, if possible.

When the phone rang, she picked it up immediately, "Hello, this is Maggie."

"Hello, this is Officer Jones from the Sea Crest precinct. We have a possible abduction or kidnapping of a guest from the Sea Crest Inn. We would like to ask you to work this case with us."

"Of course," said Maggie. "When did this happen?"

"We're not exactly sure. We think it was sometime this afternoon, or possibly this evening. We need your expertise if you could come over and help us; we're at the Sea Crest Inn."

"Sure, I'll be right there," she said.

Boy, was this guy confused or what, she thought.

Her dog looked expectantly at her, as Maggie got ready to leave. "Well Misha, it looks like I have some work to do. You're in charge," she called, as she hurried out the door.

As she drove over, her thoughts were racing through her mind. *The Sea Crest Inn had never had so much as a simple wallet stolen on the premises. The possibility of an abduction of a guest was unbelievable. This was highly unusual, to say the least.*

By the time she arrived at the parking lot, she was shocked to see the whole police force present. *What on earth is happening here?*

She quickly got out of her car and hurried to the entrance. The police chief was waiting for her. He briefed her on the events of this evening. While this had been taking place, Maggie was aware of an extraordinary man who looked very out of place.

Who was he, and what was his connection, to the strange abduction scenario?

Maggie followed the police chief to view Room 225: The scene of the crime. "Wow." She observed, "It certainly has been tossed." Clothes were everywhere. She also saw the remains of breakfast from room service.

"Has anyone talked with the person who delivered the breakfast?" she asked.

"He's returning to the inn, to talk with us. We'd like you to conduct the interview, if possible."

Officer Jones pointed towards James as he said, "The victim's brother is very concerned that we find his brother as soon as possible and money is apparently no object."

"May I ask about how his brother came to be involved in this case?" asked Maggie. "Did he appear out of thin air?"

"Well, sort of," explained Officer Jones, rather nervously. "He came down from up north somewhere." He seemed a little vague on the details.

"You mean like, the North Pole?" asked Maggie sarcastically.

"No," answered the officer. He then reviewed the entire evening from the time James came into the police station, to the present.

"Who took his statement?" asked Maggie, with raised eyebrows and a very critical demeanor, as she suspiciously looked over at the man.

"Well, I guess no one took a statement... exactly." He continued, somewhat uncomfortably, "things moved pretty fast there for a while, we didn't stop to check the details."

"I see," said Maggie. "Do you have anyone available now, to take down the details? Get his ID and verify that he is in fact, the victim's brother?"

They all looked at each other awkwardly. The police had not done any of the standard procedures necessary to work a case. Furthermore, where had this self-proclaimed brother been in the time leading up to the crime? They felt like amateurs and appeared to have made quite a few mistakes, where the well-dressed man was concerned.

Maggie, on the other hand, did not seem that impressed with the man in the three-piece suit, (and alligator shoes). She went about her business and inspected the room.

She told the officer in charge, "After you're through taking the brother's statement, I'd like to talk with him if it's all right."

"Yes, of course" he answered. "By the way, the room service waiter that brought up the breakfast is here. We have him in Room 200 if you'd like to speak to him."

"Thanks, that'd be great," she said. "I'll follow you in."

As Maggie left to see Harry, in Room 200, she stole a look at the guy who claimed to be the brother.

Could his cover stand up to the harsh scrutiny I have planned for him? His clothes have certainly kept the local police from suspecting him, but I have an entirely different take on him. It would be a pleasure to take him down a peg or two, for the way the police had reacted to him. He was not above the law, and he was now going to understand that, in no uncertain terms.

Just before she stepped out the door, she whispered one more word of caution for the officer that was to take, the brother's statement, "Don't let him out of your sight and don't let him step even one foot off the premises."

Maggie could see the shock register on the face of the surprised officer. *There,* she thought, *that ought to put some objectivity back in his backbone.*

Maggie continued to Room 200 where she met with Harry. He seemed to enjoy his job as he very good-naturedly, told of the full interaction between himself and the missing guest.

Maggie noted that the missing guest had asked about the lighthouse tours and wondered if that was just faked interest to make small talk, or if it was real. She picked up the phone and called Kate. She left a message on her cell phone and then proceeded to call the keeper's cottage phone.

Connor answered immediately, "Hi, Connor here."

"Hi yourself," answered Maggie. "I'm trying to reach Kate. Is she around?"

"No. She had lots of stuff to do today. I'm not sure when she'll be home. Try her cell."

"That's okay," answered Maggie. "I left a message. I just wanted to know if the lighthouse was open."

"No, I locked and padlocked it when we got home this afternoon," bragged Connor proudly. "Kate and I were both going to be out for the rest of the day getting ready for the festival. I just wanted to be sure no one goes inside until it's been repaired."

"Thanks, you answered my questions," said Maggie. "See you later, no need to have Kate call me back; I'm going to be busy."

She walked back to Room 225. She wanted one more look around before she interviewed the 'brother.' She picked up the newspaper to see if it held any clues of what he was doing here.

One thing for sure, she thought. *From the clothes she'd seen thrown all over his room, he sure didn't dress like the brother.*

Next, Maggie checked with the manager, back at the front desk. She flashed her FBI badge, just in case he did not know who she was.

He nodded acknowledgment, "What can I do for you?"

"I was wondering," she said. "The missing gentleman from room 225; where is his car?"

"Oh, let me see." He brought the computer record up on the screen. "Here is his sign-in. He might be using a rental car."

He motioned her around to his side of the desk. Maggie stared at the screen. *There, at last, was his name.* She could not believe it. *Michael Jensen.*

Oh No, remembered Maggie. *Kate had asked me to run a check on his guy. She said he sounded like a jerk, a real loser.* Maggie had not seen any problems with the FBI's records on him. No Red Flags appeared in the background check. That was a couple of days ago. So, what had happened to him?

"Do you know which car it is?" asked Maggie.

"Yeah, I think it's the red sports convertible in the parking lot."

"Thanks," said Maggie. "I'll want to have a good look at it after I talk to the brother."

She stepped away from the desk and called Kate. She had to leave another message, "Hi Kate; Please call me as soon as possible. It's crucial."

Next Maggie called the lighthouse keeper cottage again. Before he could say anything, she started, "Hi Connor, this is Maggie. When is the last time you saw or spoke with Kate?"

Connor confirmed that he had not talked to her since late morning. This was not good. Maggie hung up.

All right, where is Michael Jensen? More importantly, where was Kate?

She called the FBI to do the background check on Michael Jensen, but she now added James Jensen, as well. She also wanted to know if the brothers had US Passports and had they used them recently.

The agent confirmed that "Yes, they both had US Passports."

"Has either of the brothers been traveling?" asked Maggie.

"Well, it appears that Michael has traveled all over the world and he had numerous large containers of equipment shipped with him and to him," explained the agent.

Very interesting, replied Maggie thoughtfully.

"In fact," continued the agent, "Michael just returned from London, England, on Monday morning, with a last-minute ticket. It was full First Class, and he had no luggage, just a briefcase."

Maggie was instantly suspicious, "What about the return flight?"

"No return reservation, as yet," the agent explained. "However, one had been made, but canceled the day after he arrived in New York."

"Can you check for any credit card or mobile phone activity?" asked Maggie.

"We show nothing since yesterday when he checked into Sea Crest Inn and paid for dinner at the Sea Crest Restaurant," the agent answered. "No mobile phone activity. Messages were left, but none were picked-up."

"If anything shows please, contact me immediately. Now, what do you show on James Jensen? He's here talking with an officer, right now. Do you show anything in the background check?"

"Well, it looks like we have a *sealed record* on him. It's a little strange. It is for a fight, in college. The charge was assault and battery, plus *lying in wait* for the victim. I'll get this looked into and contact you as soon as we can see the part that was sealed and what the outcome was. I can't tell if he was ever tried, convicted or sentenced. I find no jail time...." (dial tone)

"Special Agent O'Hara...?" "Are you there?"

"Special Agent O'Hara?"

But Special Agent O'Hara was running and was half-way across the building by now.

Chapter 32

Maggie entered the room, flashed her badge and sat down across from James. She was not happy as she deliberated angrily, *whatever this guy thought he was going to pull, stops right here.*

She quietly looked over the notes from the report that the officer had finally filled out.

James could not wait for her to realize just, whose case she was handling. He smugly thought, *she'll either pull out all the stops to find Michael or find someone else that is more qualified to deal with someone of our importance and position.*

"Could you please tell me where you were today from noon until you showed up at the Sea Crest Police Station, around 4 PM?" asked a very solemn Maggie.

"What do you mean?" James was not prepared for anything like that. "I was driving down here from New York," he said. "It's all in the report."

Maggie had handled quite a few smooth operators in her time, and this did not faze her one bit. "Can you verify that?" she asked casually.

James was stunned, by this question. "What do you mean, can I verify that?"

"Oh, it's basically very simple. Did you stop along the way?" She explained as if she was talking to a child. "Did you stop to get gasoline for your car? Did you stop to ask directions? Did you happen to have a meal on the way down? Do you have a toll receipt?"

James was so astonished, by this line of questioning, that he could not think straight. "What are you getting at? Do I need to get an attorney?"

Maggie shrugged as if it didn't matter one way or the other. "Well..., if you don't have an alibi for where you were during this period...," she stopped and pretended to think very hard about it. "then..., Yes, I believe that you certainly should consider it," Maggie said thoughtfully.

James practically exploded, "What are you talking about? Michael needs help. Time is critical here. Why are you wasting it on me?" James was dumbfounded.

She mulled it over as she proceeded to waste as much time as necessary before answering, to get his blood pressure to a boiling point.

There I think he's about ready to blow, she decided.

Maggie looked him right in the eye as she explained, "Because you're our Prime Suspect."

Chapter 33

James was positively stunned. "Well, I do not care if it is after hours; I'm calling my attorney right now."

He pulled out his phone, dialed and waited for Atty. Jeffrey Williams in New York City, to pick up. His answering machine relayed the message: "If you hear this message, it's after business hours. Please leave a message, and we will call you back during the next office hours. If this is an emergency, please push #1, and you'll be connected to my answering service."

James said, "This is an emergency." as he pushed #1.

He waited until a live human voice answered very nonchalantly, "This is Atty. Jeffrey Williams after hour's service. How may I help you?" She had heard it all, and she was excellent at putting off these calls until business hours. She considered herself the gatekeeper and very few of these calls were truly enough reason to put a call through to the attorney, after-hours.

Her voice sounded exactly like Lilly Tomlin, playing the character 'Ernestine,' the telephone operator, from the old, Laugh-In Show. James was not only offended by her annoying attitude, but he thought her gum chewing was especially unprofessional for a law office's after-hours answering service.

"Yes, this is James Jensen. I need to reach Jeff immediately. Could you either connect me or have him call me, right after we hang up?"

He gave the operator his number and explained, "The FBI is detaining me in Sea Crest and my brother, Michael Jensen has been missing for several hours."

"I'm sorry, Mr. Jensen, but Jeffrey Williams is out of town."

"Well, that's fine. Can you contact him anyway and have him call me immediately?"

"I'm sorry, Mr. Jensen. He's on a plane, on his way to represent one of his clients on the West Coast."

"I don't care if he's on his way to the moon. I need him to call me as soon as possible. My brother may have been kidnapped, and the local authorities think he may have been killed. Either way, they think I'm responsible."

"Of course, I can try to communicate with him and forward your request to call you." She tried to reason with him. "He should land within the hour, so you won't have that long to wait."

"No, I'm not leaving this line." James, who had lost patience with this broad, demanded through clenched teeth, "You try to reach him and patch me through, and I mean NOW."

"Well, if you're going to get abusive about it."

"No, No, No, I did not mean to be rude. Could you please try to reach him while I'm on the line? Please?"

"Well..., if you put it that way, I guess I could try. Please hang on."

While James was on hold, Maggie popped in to ask, "Did you have any luck with that lawyer thing? If not, we have a nice holding cell downtown, with your name on it."

"I'm on hold," James said. "They're trying to contact him right now."

"Sure, they are," replied Maggie sarcastically.

Then, as an afterthought, she said, "In the meantime, if you can come up with any answers about where you were earlier this afternoon, they may go easier on you downtown."

James resented her insinuation of his guilt. He was not used to being spoken to in this way. He simply could not come up with anything to defend himself in this situation.

Maggie, it seemed was an expert at thinking quickly on her feet. She didn't skip a beat, but continued, "However, that will not help you one iota, when we get our hands on you. The FBI has a whole different set of interrogation techniques at our disposal."

Maggie observed that James had turned as white as a sheet. She thought he might come clean, so she pushed on. "And, for your information, we're not as gullible as you thought."

"Are you threatening me?" he asked in a small voice.

Maggie just about lost it as she shouted at him, "Yes. We found out about the girl that is missing with him. She is my very best friend. If we see that you guys have harmed one hair on her head, I can guarantee you'll never see the light of day."

James couldn't believe his ears. He wanted to wake up from this nightmare, but he couldn't.

Then, Jeff Williams came on the line. "James, what's going on? Did you really go down to Sea Crest?"

"You need to help me," James almost begged. "Michael is missing, and they think I did something to harm him."

Maggie stepped out before she overheard something that could potentially jeopardize the case in some way. She was not taking any chances with this one.

Jeff Williams continued to direct James on the next steps, "I've got a colleague that will fill in for me. He is in the area, and I believe he can be there quickly. Tell him everything you can."

James insisted, "I've already told them everything. They don't believe me."

"Calm down. I'm going to contact the best attorney in the whole area. He will be there soon. Trust me."

James felt a little better. His world was righting itself again. "Okay, Jeff. What's his name?"

Jeff knew everything would be okay now. "His name is Joe Lawrence."

Chapter 34

Joe picked up his phone on the first ring, "Hello, Joe speaking."

"Hey Joe, this is Jeff Williams. I'm handling an important case out on the West Coast. In fact, the plane is landing in the next ten minutes or so. I was wondering if you could help me out with a small problem."

"Oh, hello Jeff, what's up?"

"I have a client who has gotten involved with a big mix-up with the Town of Sea Crest, and I was wondering if you could check it out for me."

"Sure, what's the problem?"

"I didn't get the whole story because my plane is trying to land, but I guarantee, he didn't do anything illegal. Well, not knowingly, at least."

"Okay, where is he now?"

"I think he's on his way to the police station."

"Fine, I'll go see what the problem is"

"What's his name?" asked Joe.

"It's James Jensen."

"All right, I'm on my way."

A short time later, Joe arrived at the Sea Crest Police Station. He was shocked to see a Bentley automobile parked outside.

Oh well, thought Joe, *it must be someone here to see the festival.* The town was raising money to repair the lighthouse, and they had reached out to several wealthy benefactors from near and far.

He entered the Police Station and asked, "Has James Jensen been brought in?"

"Yes, but what are you doing here?"

"I was asked to come in and see what the problem was and help if I could," answered Joe. He was very confused by this question in the first place. He'd been to this Police Station a hundred times before, and no one had ever asked him, 'what he was doing here.'

"Oh Boy," answered the desk officer. "This I gotta see."

117

"What?" asked Joe.

"Please come with me."

They proceeded through the maze of offices until they got to the jail cell. There was only one. There had only been one since the jail was added. The officer stopped in front of the cell. Joe looked in and saw an extremely well-dressed man in a gray three-piece cashmere suit.

However, Joe thought, *what especially sets him apart from the norm are, his Stefano Ricci Alligator Leather Classic Loafers in Black. They look spectacular.*

Joe told the officer, "We'll be a while," as the officer unlocked the door and Joe stepped inside.

The officer relocked the door and left.

"Hello," said Joe, as he extended his hand. "I'm Joe Lawrence."

The man stood up and shook his hand.

"Thanks for coming," said James. He immediately started to explain what had happened.

Joe noticed at once that James was extremely nervous. He talked very fast, and it was hard to follow what he was saying. He was almost rambling as he said, "I can't believe what's been happening. I came down here to try to find out what happened to my brother. They think I did something to him and I'm part of a big kidnapping and cover-up. Now a woman is missing too. The FBI is planning to torture me."

"Let's start from the beginning," Joe said. "When did your brother come to Sea Crest? Was it related to the festival?"

"No, of course, not. Why does everyone keep asking me that?"

Joe could see James was very upset about this.

"A couple of days ago, we discovered that the payments on our family's storage units in Rosemont had lapsed and it was sold."

"How were the payments usually made," asked Joe?

"They were automatically paid by the year, I suppose," answered James vaguely. "We didn't know anything about the units."

"So, your brother went to Rosemont?"

"Yes, but when he arrived, the auction was over. The contents of these units went to someone from Sea Crest. He planned to negotiate with them to buy the items back. Money was, of course, no object."

"Of course," said Joe agreeably, glancing briefly at this alligator shoes. "So, when did you hear about this?"

"It's been a few days," said James. "I haven't heard from my brother since he said he'd have to come down here to Sea Crest to get our things."

"And you've called him?" asked Joe.

"Yes, I've made numerous calls over the past few days. The phone connects and takes the messages, but Michael has not returned my calls or gotten in touch with me in any way. This is highly unusual. I know something terrible has happened to him."

"I can see why you'd be worried," said Joe. "When did you get here?"

"Late this afternoon. I came right to the police station to tell them my brother was missing and something had happened to him," explained James sadly. He could hardly control his emotions.

What on earth happened to Michael? he wondered.

"Okay James. Tell me what happened when you got here."

"Well, Officer Jones, asked me his name. I said, Michael, and he called the hospital, and they denied having anyone come in by that name or description over the past few days. That was a relief."

"Yes," answered Joe. "Then what happened?"

"Well, Officer Jones called the Sea Crest Inn, and they said he'd been there the last couple of days. They called his room, but no one answered," James said.

"He could have just stepped out, but go on," said Joe.

"Next, Officer Jones asked the hotel security to guard the door, no one in or out. He then led the whole police department down to the Sea Crest Inn with full sirens and lights flashing."

"Wow, that must have been something," said Joe. "They usually don't have any crime at all around here."

"Well, they ended up with guns drawn, and the police were hidden, barricaded behind their cars, potted plants and trees. They used a loudspeaker and instructed whoever was in the room, to come out with their hands up."

"Wow," exclaimed Joe. "What happened next?"

"In the end, no one came out. The room was empty," finished an exhausted James.

"I'll bet Officer Jones felt silly," said Joe. "Now I just need to know what you're doing in jail."

"I'm sure I don't know, but some crazy FBI lady, said, I'm their *Prime Suspect*," answered James.

"How do they figure that?" asked a very surprised Joe.

"I don't know, but a very close friend of hers is missing also, and I can't verify my alibi for the time I drove down here today. She was furious with me, and she holds me responsible. She also said; *the FBI has a whole different set of interrogation techniques at their disposal.*"

Joe could not believe it. *Could this have been dear, sweet, levelheaded Maggie?* "Could you please describe the FBI woman?"

"I'll never forget her. She had auburn red hair and a horrible temper that exploded when she yelled. It was terrible." James shuttered as he finished.

Joe was amazed at Maggie's behavior. *This missing woman must be someone she truly cares about to lose it like this.*

Joe shook his head as he called out for the police officer to release him from the cell.

Next, he promised James, "I'll get to the bottom of a few things and be back to touch bases with you in a little while. Of course, my primary concern is for your brother's safety. I am going to see what the status is on that first. Then we'll unravel the rest of this."

"In the meantime, please try to think of anything else that your brother might have been involved with while he was down here. Did he have any friends or enemies in this area?"

"Not that I know of," said James.

"Fine, I'll be back."

The police officer let Joe out and relocked the door.

They each took one last look at the well-dressed man, with the alligator shoes. He was the one and only incarcerated man in Sea Crest. He was after all *The Prime Suspect.*

Chapter 35

Joe Lawrence asked the police officer who was walking him back out of jail, "Do you have any information on the brother, Michael Jensen?"

The police officer shook his head, "Nothing new. We still haven't received any ransom note or demands from the kidnappers."

"I don't think you have any evidence to arrest James on. Why is he your Prime Suspect?"

"FBI Special Agent Maggie O'Hara has placed him in this situation. It appears her best friend, Kate Walsh, has disappeared also and Maggie thinks they are connected."

Joe was shocked, "You mean Kate is missing too? Boy, she is all about safety, and she teaches self-defense. I can't believe someone could take her against her will."

They turned the corner, and there was Maggie, pacing back and forth in the lobby of the Sea Crest Police Station.

"It's about time you finished talking with the suspect. Did you learn anything? What did they do with Kate?" asked Maggie in a nearly panicked voice.

"I can't talk about it with you, but rest assured, he had nothing to do with what happened to either of them." Joe was very convinced. "What have you found out so far? Who was the last person to see Kate? Well, what was she doing and, what time was it?" asked Joe.

"We don't know yet. We have our best team working on it. In the meantime, I don't intend to let Mr. Alligator Shoes leave."

"Yah know, Maggie," Joe said patiently. "It's not against the law to look nice and wear a pair of shoes that are worth six-seven thousand dollars."

 "Well, Mr. Smarty Pants, I'm waiting for a warrant to have that vehicle out front searched before he goes anywhere."

Joe was stunned, "You mean that Bentley? That is his car? You cannot be serious."

Maggie was very pleased with Joe's reaction. "Of course, I'm serious. I know the FBI mechanics would *Love* to get a look under the hood of that jewel. Why, they might even decide they need to take it entirely apart, screw by screw."

Maggie was on a roll now. "In fact, who knows how long that may take? They may request special help from other FBI units which would, no doubt, jump at the opportunity to work on a Bentley. I hear they sell for over $200,000 and can easily eclipse the $300,000 mark depending on what extras have been ordered. This one looks like it has all the upgrades available."

Joe could not believe her, "Now wait just a minute here."

However, Maggie kept right on expounding on her *search and seizure* theme. "I'll bet it's got lots of places to hide contraband and stuff. I certainly hope they do not have to call in the canine unit. That can be especially messy, you know. But surely, James sprang for the Scotch Guard treatments for those seats…, don't you think? You know what can happen when those dogs get excited," she dejectedly shook her head in fake dismay.

"Who knows?" she continued. "By the time, we find out what happened to Kate; it might be scattered all over the place in six to seven thousand, separate pieces."

Joe was flabbergasted. "Now Maggie, I'm warning you, don't get carried away here."

"I want to know what happened to Kate!"

Joe wanted to know what happened to Kate also, but he was not going to let Maggie and the FBI take apart the Bentley until he had a chance to get a few answers himself.

"Maggie, I'm going over to the keeper's cottage and ask a few questions that may shed some light on her whereabouts."

Joe wanted this whole terrible situation solved as soon as possible. He was also worried about what he would tell Mr. Jeffrey Williams if he called him for an update on James' status.

Chapter 36

Apparently, Kate and Michael were going to be spending the night alone, in the Sea Crest Lighthouse. They barely knew each other. However, over the last few hours, they had decided to marry. EACH OTHER. They suddenly looked timidly at each other.

Michael was smiling as he said, "Well, imagine that; being locked in the Sea Crest Lighthouse, with the Woman of my Dreams. I never saw that coming."

Kate quickly countered with, "Well, even more shocking, imagine this, having You, Michael Jensen, turn out to be the Man of my Dreams. I never saw that coming either."

Kate also shared, "This seems strangely reminiscent of something I've felt before. Like being so exhilarated over the sheer surprise of it all. I'm not sure how to explain it, but it's similar to the feeling I get for example, ... what I experience, regarding the famous Kissing Couple in Times Square. You know; The sailor and the nurse in New York City on VJ day."

Kate continued, "I feel like; Wow. Now That's a Picture Worth Taking."

Michael thought seriously, for a minute. He looked at Kate with new insight as to who she was, as he agreed, "I know exactly what you mean."

They both laughed and proceeded to kiss each other for good measure.

"Now, how do you suppose we're going to get out of here?" asked Michael. "Previously, I've contracted to build or repair a few lighthouses, and you've lived in the keeper's cottage. What do you think?" asked Michael.

Kate laughed, "I got nothing. If it's bolted shut from the outside and the water is surrounding the lighthouse, that's enough, but apparently, nobody even knows we're in here."

"Well then, I've got a splendid idea," said Michael. "If we go back up to the top, we'll be able to share our very first beautiful full moon from the best seats in the whole world. We can eat cheese and crackers and snack on anything and everything we can find."

"I think Connor and I left some blueberry muffins and a thermos of coffee up there this morning. My friend Grace called us to see if we wanted a look at an exciting discovery, she had just made. I can tell you all about it tonight."

"This unexpected window of time is a valuable opportunity to share our lives with each other." Michael laughed as he added, "The only thing I know about you is that you drive me crazy and that I can't live without you. Oh, except for that thing about, I Love You, and I can't wait to marry you, as soon as possible."

"I love you back," said Kate in a serious loving voice. "Now before we go back up, I might as well give you the guided tour of this magnificent lighthouse's lower floor."

"I'd love to hear it, Ma'am."

"Here, on this first level, there is a full kitchen with a working refrigerator, stove, and oven," said Kate in her best official tour guide voice.

"That sure looks grand, but what if we run out of food?" replied Michael, as he played along.

"I'm confident that we have more food and supplies than you'd find in most older lighthouses," she added defensively.

"We have a full working bathroom down here with a shower and an antique claw foot bathtub. We also have a half-bath upstairs on the level with the mahogany floor," she continued softly, "where you first kissed me and where I fell in love with you."

Michael took that as a mutual desire to try it again. He touched her face with his lips and gently kissed her eyes. By the time he got down to her sweet lips, he had taken Kate in his arms and kissed her soundly.

A short time later, they decided to check out the kitchen to see what was available. Michael inquired, "I don't understand why you have so much food in this kitchen."

"It's all very simple. Did you notice the extraordinary number of boxes of Girl Scout cookies? How about the number of cans of peanuts and bags of popcorn that the Cub Scouts and Boy Scouts sell?"

"Well, now I do," replied Michael.

"We have the whole community involved. That's part of the joy of living in the shadow of this marvelous lighthouse," explained Kate.

"We schedule and support many things related in some way to the beach and lighthouse," she continued with pride.

"That's very commendable," Michael nodded his approval.

"For example, my aunt Mary is making blueberry pies for the Sea Crest Festival. I was supposed to join her this afternoon to help the local Girl Scouts earn a baking badge. We are going to teach them her grandmother's pie crust recipe, which is a very old-fashioned way to make it. It has earned numerous awards and the crust flakes apart with the touch of a fork. It has been utterly foolproof over all the years."

"Wow, now you're making me hungry."

"Well, let's look in the freezer. The seniors and many retirees use the lighthouse twice a year for Elderhostel programs, which also operate under the new name of Road Scholar. They had a group here last week, and I think they usually have good lunches. I believe I even noticed some Angus Cheeseburgers. They are delicious."

"Yeah, here they are," Michael said, as he found them. He asked, "Do you want one or two?"

Kate answered, "I'll take two since I haven't had a real meal since coffee and the blueberry muffins around noon." They put them in the microwave and pulled out the sodas from the fridge.

"Kate, I think I saw French Fries in the freezer if you want them," Michael offered.

"That sounds perfect," she said as Michael went back and pulled them out.

While he opened them and arranged a bunch on the tray to heat up, Kate added, "the ketchup and mustard packets are leftovers from the last group that was here."

After a minute, and a couple of kisses, she continued, "by the way, the Scouting Clubs are only part of the activities that the lighthouse sponsors. Numerous other projects including the church, schools and several adult resource groups, meet here. But the Boy Scout and Girl Scouts probably have most extensive training sessions."

"What else can the Scouts do here?" Michael was surprised by the whole community spirit aspect of the lighthouse.

"The different merit badges that they earn are associated with learning many things that they can work on here. For example, the Boy & Girl Scouts have badges for learning about many important things such as Astronomy, The Night Sky, Constellations, and the International Space Station. We have sleep-overs for many clubs and organizations that want to use our telescope and have a safe and exciting place to learn. We involve the parents as well as teachers and Scout leaders."

"I've never thought of using the lighthouse for any of those things," said Michael. "I just assumed guiding the ships and boats was enough. It sounds like the Sea Crest Lighthouse helps guide people safely through life."

"We have many of the same types of activities for the church groups, Sunday school classes, and various school field trips. We would like to establish a museum to help fund the care and upkeep of the Sea Crest Lighthouse. It would be a teaching project that would bring education and higher goals to the residents of Sea Crest as well as employment on the off-season."

Michael smiled as he said, "and don't forget your water safety program. That's my favorite by far."

"Very amusing," laughed Kate. "You do know that I saw you at the beach and knew you had to be Michael."

"No, you don't say. I had no idea."

"Well did you know that I was shamelessly showing off for you?"

"No. The only thing I knew was that I had never, and I mean NEVER, seen anything like you looked in that red swimsuit. I have not watched much surfing, but I never imagined anyone on earth could be as graceful and do the tricks you could do on that surfboard. You are amazing."

"Thanks, but don't get too carried away. I knew I could do that routine with my eyes closed. I have won a couple of championships with that triple combination of aerial maneuvers, with a couple of cutbacks. It's kind of my signature trick that I like to do. I was just showing off for you."

"Well, you can show off anytime you want for me. I loved it. I can't help but get carried away. You're marvelous."

"I felt embarrassed and quite foolish when I got close enough to see you. Then you took my hand and held it, my heart just melted. My reaction to you was unexpected. Can you ever forgive me?" asked Kate.

"Well, I'll try, but it will take a lot of remembering about you in that red swimsuit," Michael said with a grin. "Oh well, I guess I can suffer through, for the sake of our future happiness."

Kate laughed. "Little did you know that red swimsuit is part of my water safety project."

"Well, you almost gave me a heart attack, young lady," Michael laughed. "That's something that you need to feel sorry about."

"No way. I'm only interested in all the other lives that I can save," Kate explained with a laugh. "The greater good, you know?" She shrugged playfully as though he meant nothing to her.

Kate continued, "Seriously, right now our safety objective is to make sure all our residents know how to swim, and each person is licensed and certified to perform cardiopulmonary resuscitation (CPR), which consists of mouth-to-mouth respiration and chest compression. They also need to know how to use Automated External Defibrillators (AED). The American Red Cross has given us a grant to help teach, and an anonymous donor has given the Town of Sea Crest, five, brand new Automated External Defibrillators (AED). These will be spread out to the community in five locations where most people congregate."

Michael could hardly believe it, "Do you mean places like the school and church?" he asked.

"Yes." She continued, "also the town library, which has several activities, open and free to the public. They have an extensive computer program and several volunteers on hand to help. My friend Maggie was able to get ten new computers donated with a grant from the FBI. They agreed, it's better to help people be successful than to have them turn to crime because they feel they have no options, for a better life."

"I had no idea, the FBI or the Red Cross, gave grants to anyone," replied Michael. "That's fantastic."

"Well, a couple of us work together to apply for grants that don't need to be paid back but benefit everyone that lives here. We are truly blessed to live and work here, beside the Sea Crest Lighthouse, which we love."

Michael replied with a solemn and heartfelt, "Kate; I'm the luckiest man alive. I get to share my first moon-lit dinner, at the top of the Sea Crest Lighthouse, with you."

Kate replied with a smile and a long hungry kiss. "Who would have ever guessed I could feel so much love for a man that a few days ago, I didn't even know existed?"

"Did you ever imagine you'd be eating with me, by the light of a Fresnel Lens, of the first order, and the full moon?"

As they started up the spiral staircase with their arms laden down with food, Kate stopped. "Here, let's put our hamburgers and drinks and stuff in the dumbwaiter," she said.

They had several delayed stops on the way to the top. It seems they could not stop kissing each other. Michael had never come close to feeling this desperate magnetic attraction to anyone before. They had barely left the bottom steps when Michael reached out for her. "Oh, Kate." Michael felt like; he was drugged with the want of her, as his thoughts were drowned in warm kisses. "...I'm literally and helplessly blown away by this powerful pull you have on me. Even when I was furious with you, Kate, I was incapable of breaking off from both thinking about you constantly and urgently wanting you, as the mermaid in the red swimsuit. I'm telling you kiddo; you're something I can't resist."

They slowly climbed higher in the tower almost to the top. On one of the highest steps, Michael stopped, turned to her and looked into Kate's eyes. Then, he held her tightly as he reflected and softly whispered in her ear, "Kate, you have many natural gifts, each one a bright promise of ecstasy. It's who you are, one layer after another. You're the real deal, you're genuine, and you're the most precious thing in the world to me. I love you."

Kate felt utterly broken with love and feeling for Michael as the tears rolled down her cheeks and she murmured, "Oh Michael, I love you too."

I'm afraid I'll never get enough of you, Michael thought to himself.

Chapter 37

After they finished their moonlit meal, Kate looked loving over at Michael and asked, "Why did you become an architect?"

"From a young age, I was interested in how buildings were put together and constructed. I didn't know that it was called architecture, but I was fascinated. Based on this interest, my grandfather showed me things which I'd study for hours."

"I spent a lot of time staying with my grandparents. Especially after my mother died. It made me feel close to her, knowing that she had grown up in this home. You know, touched the same things, slept in the same bedroom, and when I pulled the same soft quilts around me at night, I felt a great sense of well-being from familiar things like that — surrounded by a family who had loved her too. It was the most comforting feeling in the world.

"I remember my grandparents had a beautiful library in their home in New York City. I'd always gravitate to one corner which had a comfortable chair and a large table with a lamp. I could spread out the largest books and pour over them for hours. It was an ideal place to spend an afternoon. But what made that nook particularly inviting, was the wonderful collection of pictures hanging on the wall. Each one was more amazing than the next.

"In fact, there was one oil painting, in particular, that held my attention from my very earliest memories. It was a large picture of a giant Ferris Wheel. I studied the steel spokes of the colossal wheel, reasoning in my young mind, how it must have been put together. It looked like several people were seated in each of the compartments. They resembled railroad cars. I was fascinated with the structure of the moving wonder, and it was right at the top of my own personal seven wonders of the world list.

"When I was a little older, my grandfather and I shared the best afternoon of my whole childhood. I was inspecting my favorite piece of art, contemplating the Ferris Wheel when my grandfather walked in to join me. He was sipping a cup of piping hot coffee for himself

and brought a cup of cocoa with marshmallows for me."

Kate agreed, "I'd have to say that's a great start to any afternoon."

"My grandfather was the best. He smiled when he saw what I was looking at and asked, 'Do you think you've figured it all out? How it's constructed?'

"I pointed to various parts of the picture and explained how I thought it all worked.

"He rubbed his chin, like he was debating with himself, then said very seriously, 'Michael, you've done well. I would ordinarily wait until you were much older, but you are ready now.'

"I couldn't imagine why he seemed so proud, but I wasn't going to disagree.

"He motioned me to follow as he strolled over to his desk on the other side of the room. The wall, behind his desk and chair, had a built-in bookcase filled with various shelves of books, photos, and figurines."

"Next, he asked, 'Michael, can you keep a secret?'

"I replied, 'usually; unless it was an emergency situation.'

"He laughed and instructed me to find the book titled 1893 Chicago Colombian World's Fair. It took me a minute to find the book because I never spent much time near the desk. I started to pull it out and noticed it was stuck.

"My grandfather offered, 'Here, I'll help you with that. If you slide the book up an inch higher and turn it to the right, look what happens.'

"The entire bookcase moved aside and opened like a doorway, to display a secret room. I'm sure my eyes were as big as saucers.

"Wow," I exclaimed in amazement. "I never knew this was here."

"Well, your mother dreamed this up, and she constructed the whole thing," he said with a hoarse, emotional voice.

"I had a lump in my throat, as he told me, 'She would be so proud of you Michael.'

'Now I'll show you a couple of things she was working on in here,' he continued with a brighter smile.

"I looked around in surprise. There was a full-sized drafting table, lots of pens, pencils, slide rules, Staedtler templates, compasses and all kinds of various drafting tools.

"You mean she made this secret room, and she came in here to work on stuff?" I was stunned.'

"Yes. That's exactly what she did. Your mother was one of the finest architects in the country," he boasted proudly.

"Now over here in this cubby-hole, let's see what we have."

"With his eyes now twinkling, he pulled out a large tube and placed it on the table between us.

"We managed to pry the metal top off the cardboard cylinder.

"I helped him unroll the large sheets of navy-blue paper, onto the table.

"Kate..., what do you think it was?"

"I don't know, but the anticipation is killing me. What was it?"

"Oh, I think I'll wait awhile," teased Michael. "Do we have any cocoa around? I think I'd like a cup."

"What?"

"Well, I think we should make some cocoa, with lots of marshmallows. Then we can make a proper toast for the big reveal."

"Honestly, Michael, you tell me right now," Kate demanded with a straight face..., that collapsed into laughter as she fell into his arms.

Michael grinned with delight as he teased, "Or what? What are you going to do, Kate?"

"Something terrible. You won't even know, what or when I'm going to do it."

"Oh, the suspense is killing me. And by the way, your threats are meaningless. You're all about saving lives. You wouldn't hurt a fly."

"That's true, but PLEASE tell me. Then we can make cocoa. I promise."

"Oh, all right. We unrolled the sheets from the tube, and they were the blueprints for the construction of the Ferris Wheel."

"What do you mean? Oh no, you can't mean the real one? The original one built for the World's Fair in Chicago?"

"That would be the one. The first Ferris Wheel was built for the Chicago Colombian World's Fair in 1893."

"That's incredible. Do you think those blueprints could be real?"

"Yes, I do. They are signed by George Washington Gale Ferris Jr., himself. Dated 1893."

"I can hardly believe it."

"There was an old document included in the cubby-hole which explained that George Ferris was a structural engineer from Pittsburgh, Pennsylvania, who inspected steel for the Exposition. There were numerous proposals for Chicago's spectacle attraction to outshine the Paris 1889 Exposition Universelle's, iconic structure, the Eiffel Tower. However, the fair's lead architect, Daniel Burnham chose to allow the Ferris Wheel to be built, hoping the reduced steel framework structure would be safe."

He had a smile on this face as he confessed, "Those funny rail cars I saw on the painting, were actually 36 gondolas capable of holding up to 60 people each—for a total capacity of 2,160 people."

Chapter 38

Joe Lawrence, headed over to the keeper's cottage to confirm what Connor had said about Kate's last few hours, before going missing. The entire family was in a state of shock and wanted to know what they had found out. They also wanted to know what Joe thought and if he had any ideas on what had happened to Kate.

Joe said, "I need to talk with Connor, and I'm also at a loss for an explanation for today's events."

When he spoke with Connor, the story was the same as he'd said earlier. He verified everything: Grace called; they met with her to see the Traveling Library and returned to the keeper's cottage. Then they both left to prepare for the Sea Crest Festival: Kate left to help Aunt Mary bake pies and Connor went to help hang the Festival banner over Main Street.

Later in the afternoon, Connor went to Aunt Mary's to see how the pies were coming. Kate had not come or called, but no one was worried. Something must have come up.

There was no mention of locking the Sea Crest Lighthouse.

No one had asked anything about the lighthouse and Connor did not think to say anything because it seemed so routine.

Joe headed back to the police headquarters to see James. He talked with the duty officer that was in charge for the night shift. "Hi, how's it going this evening?"

The officer responded, "Well, apart from the two, missing people, nothing is going on. Did you find out anything new from Connor?"

"No, he doesn't remember anything that he hasn't already given in his statement. He's pretty shaken up."

"That's to be expected. How's the rest of the family holding up?"

Joe let him know, "they were all very surprised that anyone could take Kate, without a fight. They're all hoping for the best, but they're incredibly worried."

Joe continued, "Actually, I came back in to see about my client, James Jensen. I do not believe he is guilty and I know you don't have any evidence to charge him with a crime, at this time. I'm his attorney, and I will take full custody of him for the next day or two. I will be one hundred percent responsible for him until this case is solved."

The officer-in-charge asked suspiciously, "What if we do get some evidence that he's guilty of something?"

Joe was quick to answer, "I will guarantee that neither one of us will leave town. If anything comes up that points to James breaking the law in any way, I will agree to bring him right back to the jail. If that happens, he will, of course, be charged and prosecuted for a crime."

"All right, Officer O'Brien will take you down to the cell and give you a few minutes to explain the ground rules to Mr. Jensen. When you and Mr. Jensen are checking out, stop at this desk, and I'll have the papers ready for you to sign."

"Thank you," Joe said, and then shared another thought with him. "This may save both our necks and keep him from filing a lawsuit against the Sea Crest Police Department."

"Do you really think so?"

"James Jensen came in here to report that his brother is missing. Now he is in jail, and there is no evidence of any wrongdoing on his part. The FBI is trying to intimidate him with this crazy Prime Suspect label. Both brothers have loads of money. What do you think they'll do?"

That gave him something to reflect on as Joe and Officer O'Brien left to go down to the jail cell. Joe had the police officer open the cell door, let him in and asked him to return in five minutes.

"Hello James," Joe started as James immediately stood up.

James asked, "Did you find out what happened to my brother?"

Joe tried to sound more hopeful than he felt. "No, I'm sorry. Not yet. I hoped to get some additional information from the witness who last saw the other person that's missing. He had nothing new at all."

James was a little confused, "Well, why isn't he sitting in jail with me? If he was the last person to see her, maybe he is at least a person of interest. I think he may be the Prime Suspect."

"I see what you mean. I guess the credibility of Connor's information, goes much further because he is known to us. We have some reference as to his character, etc. which leads most of us to believe his statement."

"Well, what about me? It's not my fault that no one knows me."

"You're right, of course. There is something I can do that will prove to everyone that I know you are above reproach."

"What do you mean?"

"I intend to sign you out and take you home to stay in my guest room. You'll be my responsibility, and you will be legally in my care while we sort this out."

"Thanks, that sounds good to me," said James. "I appreciate it."

"Good, let's go," Joe said as Officer O'Brien returned. They proceeded to leave the jail area and signed out at the front desk.

When they got to Joe's home, they decided to order Chinese food. While they were waiting for their order to arrive, James seemed to settle down.

He asked Joe, "What can I do to help with the investigation and find out what happened to my brother?"

"We can go over everything about what, why, and how, Michael spent the last few days leading up to his disappearance. Something might seem odd, unusual or out of the character for him to do. That might be a clue to help us solve this, even if it seems unimportant. If we follow up all possibilities, we hope to have answers that will lead us to what happened to him. With any luck, we'll find a connection, if there is one, to solve what happened to Kate Walsh also. We don't have any proof that they are linked. It may be a coincidence that both individuals disappeared on the same afternoon, from nearby areas."

The Chinese order came, and they both ate as if they were half-starved. James was impressed at how good the food was. After all, he was used to the special luxury Chinese of New York City. After they had finished, Joe showed James where his guest room was. He was giving him the low-down on where the extra towels and toiletries were when the doorbell rang. This ringing was very persistent, like a child, fooling around. They were just laying on the doorbell with a constant ring, ring, ring. Both Joe and James looked at each other with a feeling that something bad was about to happen.

They were right. Joe opened the door and in charged Maggie. She was furious, "I can't believe it. I just heard that you signed out our Prime Suspect. That is unconscionable. Where is he?"

Joe started with, "Now Maggie...."

She cut him off immediately, "How could you just leave without clearing it with me?" She was beside herself with anger. "He's my prisoner, and I demand to see him now."

Joe tried again, "Maggie, calm down."

James peeked out from the bedroom and said, "Oh, hello. You again?" He was feeling much braver, now that Joe was on his side. He continued, "Are you following me? Joe, I think you had better contact her superiors and file a complaint. They're paying her good money to find Michael and that other woman, but she insists on following me around. It's obvious; she's got a crush on me. She just can't stay away, almost like a stalker, I'd say."

"All right James," said Joe, "I'm sure the FBI just wanted to confirm that we got here safe and sound. Maggie's just following up, as she should. She's an excellent agent."

"If you say so, but personally, I think she's got a thing for me," said James.

Maggie was ready to explode, "I want to know what you did with my friend."

Joe tried to remain level-headed in the middle of all this. "OK, James go ahead to bed. It's way after midnight, and we have a lot to do tomorrow to find your brother. Maggie and I are going to have a little talk before she leaves. She has a big day ahead of her tomorrow too."

"Okay," said James as he walked back toward the guest bedroom.

As an afterthought, Joe added, "just make yourself at home. If you need anything you can't find, knock on my door, and I'll help."

"Thanks again," said James seriously, as he went into the bedroom and closed the door.

Now Joe turned to Maggie. "Maggie," Joe started, "Why are you here?"

"You know exactly why I'm here," she demanded. "You took my suspect and let him go."

"No, I've got full custody. That is not letting him go. He is not going anywhere. He's worried about his brother. Why can't you understand that?"

"Kate's missing. She's my family, my cousin and my very best friend for my entire life." Maggie was full of guilt as she whispered, with tears starting to roll down her cheeks, "Kate's missing and it's my fault."

Joe expected many things to come out of Maggie's anger, but what just happened was a complete surprise.

Joe was at a total loss as he said, "What are you talking about?"

Maggie was afraid she couldn't disclose that Kate had asked her to run a check on Michael and that he seemed like a real low life. Maggie had failed to do that, and now Kate was missing, and heaven only knew what else. Joe was James' attorney. She could not cross that line.

All Maggie could offer for an explanation was that "I can't tell you, I'm not allowed."

Joe was perplexed by this but didn't press her any further. "Listen, whatever is going on, we'll try to solve it again tomorrow. For now, why don't you try to relax and get some sleep?"

Maggie said, "All right." as she sat down on the sofa and took off her coat.

"Wait just a minute." Joe was flabbergasted. "I didn't mean here. You can't sleep here, Maggie." Joe put his hand on his hip and ran the other hand nervously through his hair.

Maggie, on the other hand, seemed quite satisfied, for the first time all day. She had removed her light coat, thrown it over herself and pulled it up around her chin. She nestled down in the sofa pillows as if she was all comfortable and sleepy. "I'll be perfectly fine right here. Please turn out the light on your way to your room."

Joe was at his wit's end, "So help me, if you set one foot inside his room, I'm going to citizen's arrest you."

"I'm extremely shocked that you would think me capable of anything of the sort. But I Promise; I Will Not Set One Foot Inside The Prime Suspect's Room."

Joe said in a very firm voice, "I'm going to hold you to that, seriously." He slowly turned and shook his head as he wondered, *what am I going to do? Maggie and Kate are two of my closest friends. I can't understand what could have happened to Kate, but my gut is honestly telling me that James didn't have anything to do with it.*

He went on past the guest room and when he heard James' soft breathing, that confirmed, *he must be innocent if he could fall asleep that fast.*

Joe walked on down to his bedroom, and his last thoughts as he fell asleep were, *one of my best friends is missing, another one is asleep on my couch, and the Prime Suspect is asleep in my guest room. Wow. What a mixed-up mess.*

Later, in the still, quiet, middle of the night, Maggie thought she heard the guest room door open. She laid perfectly still and tried to stop breathing, while she strained to hear. She watched as the shadow of a man's body came out into the living room. She was planning her next move as she thought, *Yes, the Prime Suspect is going to make his escape. Well, not on my watch, Buster.*

As James walked by the couch to get a drink of water, he was hit with the first karate kick. The roundhouse kick was executed to James' side as Maggie hit him with the ball of her foot sideways.

James immediately blocked it and followed up with a significant counter-attack. James gave Maggie a double leg reverse, which turned her legs off the couch and catapulted both of them onto the floor, in one swift move. The lamp and a plant of some kind crashed loudly onto the floor beside them.

Maggie is shocked to realize that James was underneath her and he was holding her so she could not move her arms. Next, he yelled at her, "Is that your gun?"

"You are lucky that you're holding my arms so I can't reach it, or I'd be asking you, 'Is that your bullet hole?'"

"I don't know who you think you are, but you are the first woman who has ever tried to tackle me, in the middle of the night," James said very sarcastically. "In fact, all a normal woman has to do is ask, but I know you're more desperate than normal."

"Let go of me," Maggie whispered. "What if Joe hears you?" Maggie continued to struggle, but this was getting her nowhere.

James, on the other hand, loved every minute of it. "Maggie? May I call you Maggie, as opposed to FBI Special Agent Maggie O'Hara? I mean, now that you have me in this very compromising position, I think we should be on a first name basis. Don't You?"

"James, I'm warning you, if you don't let me up immediately, you will be very sorry."

"Oh Maggie, you started this and besides; I kind of like to see the helpless female side of you. I like it much better than your FBI, blazing pistol; if I may quote you, 'You're our Prime Suspect,' persona."

Maggie was furious as she thought, *how dare he speak to me this way.* She whispered with clenched teeth, again as firmly as possible, "Let-me-go-right-now."

James was enjoying this way too much, so he continued, "Back in your day, didn't you ever have anything similar to a Charm School, you know, where you could learn how ladies are supposed to act? (all dainty and pretty... and quiet?)" He heard her gasp, ready to erupt.

But before that happened, James thought of one more point he would like to make. "You know when you were threatening me with FBI torture techniques? Is this what you had in mind?"

Maggie could not believe this idiot had the nerve to talk to her this way. "You'll pay for that remark."

Just then they heard Joe, who was standing in the doorway, say, in a very parent-like voice, "I'm not even going to ask what's going on in here, but if you two are done fooling around, would you please hold it down? Some of us are trying to sleep."

He wearily turned to leave, and then called out, "By the way, if you guys broke anything, you're paying for it."

Chapter 39

Michael and Kate had a wonderful dinner at the top of the Sea Crest Lighthouse. They decided to take turns answering questions or sharing things that they wondered about each other.

Michael asked, "All right young lady, I'm dying to know how you can do the things you do? You couldn't have learned it all in Coast Guard Training. You seem to have a natural talent for flying a helicopter, surfing and you're a born leader. How did you learn it all and how can you be an expert in everything?"

Kate laughed as she finished the last of her cheeseburger. "Well, I grew up here. That will explain a lot about what seems natural to me. My family has been the lighthouse keeper here, at the Sea Crest Lighthouse for at least three generations.

"However, it certainly isn't unusual for women to be lighthouse keepers."

"Well I've heard of some in Europe who helped out, but I guess I never connected them with the abilities that you have, Kate," said Michael slowly. *He hadn't thought about this at all.*

"That's where you are way off base," Kate softly explained. "At least 80 females have been American Lighthouse Keepers. Most of them were wives or daughters of a lighthouse keeper who either died or became unable to continue due to failing health."

"Hannah Thomas was one of the first. She took over the care and keeping of the Gurnet Point Light, in Massachusetts, when her husband left to fight in the War of Independence in 1776. We have no record if her husband survived or not, but she continued until 1786."

"Her selfless undertaking is an early glimpse of what became a lighthouse family tradition, of passing the torch, to the brave and courageous women to keep the lights lit."

"I guess I just wasn't aware of that," marveled Michael. "I just went about my work without being aware of the history that accompanied any particular lighthouse."

"Of course, during the 1800s, life as the daughter of a lighthouse keeper was much different from our present-day customs," explained Kate. "It was not unusual for the children to help with many of the chores and even take over for their father, in time of need. This assistance was sometimes continued until a replacement arrived or they just plain took over the job in place of their loved one."

"Ida Lewis-Wilson was one of my personal favorites. She lived from the mid-1800s until the first few years of 1900s, as the female Lighthouse Keeper at Lime Rock, Rhode Island. She received the Gold Lifesaving Medal and was awarded the American Cross of Honor for her heroism in rescuing numerous people from the seas. She was something special."

"Another one of my hero's is Abbie Burgess. She lived in the 1800s. Michael do you know any young girls approximately 14 years old," asked Kate.

"I'm sure I have some associates and one neighborhood girl about that age. She babysits for a couple I know," said Michael with a smile. "Why? I know I'm going to be sorry."

"Well, Abbie started her heroic and often dangerous life at age 14 when her family moved to the Matinicus Rock Lighthouse in Maine.

"During one horrific storm, she continued to keep the lights lit in this remote location for weeks during a raging storm in which her father was unable to return to help, due to the extreme hazards along the rocky coast. Abbie moved her mother and siblings to safety in the tower, while they watched the rough waves wash away their home," stated Kate proudly.

"Wow, it's hard to believe how capable that young girl was. How was she able to do that?" Michael exclaimed.

"We don't even compare to those super lighthouse keepers," she finished.

She thought for a minute and then continued. "We don't know the original history for us here in Sea Crest because our community lost most of our town's records in a major hurricane a few years ago. Our courthouse was literally, destroyed. We have been trying to reconstruct Sea Crest's history, piece by piece. One of my friends, Grace, has studied both American History and Ancestry. She has an educational grant to help with expenses she incurs in this endeavor." Kate looked thoughtfully at Michael, and she was wondering if she should tell him that was why she had bought the storage units.

Michael was wondering that exact same thing. In fact, he thought he knew she had bought them to see what background information on Sea Crest, they might hold. He felt ashamed that he had thought she was looking through other people's garbage. He now understood that Kate was working on an incredibly important project. As he continued to ponder over this new information, he made some decisions. Ultimately, in his mind, he felt she was welcome to anything of value that she and Grace could uncover from his grandmother's storage units. Granted, his new enlightened feelings were clouded with so much overwhelming love that his previous judgments went right out the window.

Neither of them wanted to rock the boat by bringing up the Chambers' storage units. They looked at each other and could not help but kiss again. This was the peace treaty they constructed from the love they felt for each other. Each was unwilling to hurt the other.

After a minute, Kate continued, "As for my flying skills with the Coast Guard, my grandfather was one of the first Coast Guard trainers for the Air/Sea Plane Division that conducted search and rescue missions along this coast. My dad also followed his father by joining the Coast Guard, flying the Air/Sea Plane and transitioning over to the rescue helicopters, when they came into use. My dad received the Distinguished Flying Cross, for Heroic Achievement in Flight, which is one of the Coast Guard's most esteemed awards."

She chuckled as she continued, "I have very fond memories of my dad and grandfather's dream of owning a Grumman HU-16 Albatross, air/sea rescue plane like the one they had used as Coast Guard Pilot Trainers. Of course, there was only a slim chance of ever having the opportunity. These were amphibious flying boats developed to land in open ocean situations to accomplish rescues, which embodied the very core of who they were."

"The search was on, and I joined them on a trip to visit the National Museum of Naval Aviation at NAS, (Naval Air Station) Pensacola, Florida, which had one on display there. As they looked at this important symbol of both of their careers, they each wondered, "How many lives had been saved, by using this extraordinary plane?"

"What did you think when you saw the air/seaplane, Kate?"

"When we crossed the floor where it was displayed, I got goosebumps," she laughed. "I remembered when they had both used this in their daily Search and Rescue Missions. So many lives were saved, it was hard not to respect and love it."

"So, what happened? Were you able to purchase one?"

"This was their first choice, and they were successful in purchasing one from a Military Surplus a year later. There have only been 466 built by Grumman, and we feel privileged to have the honor of taking care of ours."

"That plane has been a part of my life, ever since. I have access to many aircraft, but this is my favorite. It's in my blood," she said happily. "To put it simply, my dad and my grandfather, are both Career Coast Guard Search and Rescue Pilots, and now, I am too."

"Yeah," said Michael, "I guess it seemed natural for you to follow in their footsteps."

"Well, I learned to fly before I could even drive. They took me flying every opportunity they had. I loved it, and I used to fly even when they had to put blocks on the pedals, so my feet would reach. I don't remember not knowing how to fly planes.

"When I experienced the rescue part of the job first hand, I knew I could really make a difference. Meanwhile, I found that I was very good at all kinds of water sports. I went to college on a swimming and surfing scholarship."

"I believe it," said Michael.

"I was the first woman rescue swimmer to be certified in the Sea Crest Area. If you roll that all together, you end up going into the Coast Guard, at the top of your game and doing well." Kate laughed. "When the Coast Guard upgraded to the Search and Rescue Helicopters, I took advantage of that opportunity."

"I'm so impressed with you," said Michael earnestly. "You know that don't you?"

Kate thought for a moment and said, "I'm just happy that you're okay with who I am. I don't feel like you are trying to change me. I doubt I fit into the cookie-cutter image of the runway models you normally date."

"Well, you're certainly right about that." chuckled Michael. "As a matter of fact, I didn't even know they made women like you, and I certainly never met one."

"Now, what about you?" asked Kate. "I know you're an architect, and some of your last contracts were in Europe? Tell me about them."

"Yes," Michael began quietly. "I have had quite a few exciting design opportunities in various places, around the world. In fact, you might be interested to know, that over the weekend I was in London, England, delivering the keynote speech at The International Summit for Disaster Preparedness and Recovery."

"What?" Kate asked. "Are you serious?"

"Yes," answered Michael. "I've been working for six months on a project for shelters to be used after a disaster occurs anywhere in the world. The other attendees at the summit have been working with me as a sort of think-tank, you know, a meeting of the best and brightest minds, to help areas recover from natural disasters."

"Wow," Kate marveled at the news that Michael was sharing with her. "That's incredible."

"And now; excerpts from my speech, without the slideshow," stated Michael with a flourish. "These are some of my main points, that are important to me, and what I wanted to stress," Michael explained as he laughed. He could not believe that he was lucky enough to have even met someone who seemed as interested in safety as he was.

"Now this quote is from my speech," Michael clarified as he started to explain again. "Our primary focus for prevention is a plan for coastal preparedness in the event of a tsunami reaching the shore."

He went forward with his insight into damage he had seen in Japan recently and how areas could prepare ahead of time to result in much less damage.

As Michael talked, Kate could truly understand his need to protect these complete strangers in countries where he could not even speak their language. His goal was to save their lives and make their survival a priority. Kate understood how important this work was. Talk about being on the same page. Meeting Michael seemed like a miracle to her.

Next, Michael told how "Our think-tank met to come up with answers as well as admit that we have problems. My opening talk included a plan for the mangrove trees and shrubs, which not only have very strong root systems, but they also thrive in saltwater areas. This truly makes them a very logical answer for a very effective buffer."

Finally, Michael concluded, "My specialty project for the summit this year, was to design a unique, modular, snap together shelter made out of special walls that are lightweight, but five times stronger than concrete. The shelters are durable for up to five years. These panels can each be taken apart and then reassembled as needed. It's a very simple concept."

Kate was truly amazed by this project, in particular, because this was the second time, today, that she'd heard about a click together scenario with the goal of safety and survival.

Michael continued with what the other teams had developed to add to the shelters, such as solar panels, generators, and clean water.

Kate was grateful that this wonderful man had walked into her life, as she said, "Oh Michael, I'm so proud of you. What a valuable project you've developed."

"I'm glad you approve. It means a lot to me," he replied.

"You'll have a wonderful surprise when you see the journal we came across. The captain describes a click together swimming pool designed to use on the ship deck for teaching the sailors to swim."

"Oh, come on now?"

"No, really. You'll see," said Kate teasingly, as she kissed Michael.

Chapter 40

Michael thought this was an ideal time to show his love of the sliding pocket panels in the windows he had discovered, and asked her what she knew about them.

He smiled at her as he started, "I discovered the beautiful stained-glass hidden windows in the shutter pocket on this floor. They were pretty, surprising. Kate, what can you tell me about them?"

Kate just stared at him. "I'm not sure I even know what you're referring to."

Michael got up and held out his hand for her. Kate smiled and graciously accepted his hand, as she stood up. He led her over to one of the windows. "This is what I'm talking about," Michael said. "I expected to see another hidden shutter in this pocket, but when I saw this, I was stunned. What does it all mean?"

Kate was also stunned as she looked carefully at the glass. She vaguely remembered something about it. "We tried to look at it when we were young and our parents told us, they were very special and not play with them. We never pulled them out again. I guess we just eventually forgot about them."

"Well, I was astonished to see them. I can't for the life of me explain why they would be in this lighthouse," said Michael.

"Wow, these are very beautiful, but I don't know why they are here," exclaimed Kate.

Michael was slow to continue because he wasn't sure either, but he gave it a shot anyway. "Kate, are you Scottish?" He asked.

"No, we're Irish through and through," she proclaimed proudly. "My last name is Walsh, by the way."

"What is your mother's maiden name?"

"O'Hara" explained Kate. "My best friend is Maggie O'Hara. We're cousins. Maggie's dad and my mom, are brother and sister." Kate saw no connection to his questions. "These glass window pieces don't look familiar to me at all."

Michael looked at her very seriously as he slowly said, "Well... Kate, every single one of these ten glass windows on this floor, is very familiar and very meaningful to me. I understand all of them, and I have no idea what they are doing in the Sea Crest Lighthouse."

"Well, that's strange."

"I know," Michael answered very solemnly. "And I'm puzzled as to why they are in this particular place." He took a big breath and explained, "Kate, I'm Scottish. These are all Scottish. How did they get here?"

"Michael, I haven't seen them in years, but I'm sure they don't go with my family. The Walsh's are at least three generations of Irish Lighthouse Keepers. I wonder if my dad knows what they mean," Kate stated, more confused than ever.

"Come, look at this glass." Michael opened the window and slid out the beveled glass with the delicate, purple and lavender flower, buried in the prickly-leaved stem, etched in the design. "It's Scotland's Thistle... the floral emblem of Scotland."

"How beautiful," marveled Kate.

"The Scottish history behind choosing this special flower spans centuries, all the way back to James IV in 1470. He was the first to use the Thistle as a royal symbol of Scotland when he issued silver coins with the imprint."

"Now, look at this next glass," said Michael. "It's heather. Wearing a sprig of heather is believed to bring good luck."

"That's amazing." Kate's eyes were shining with excitement.

"It goes on and on, around the room, each window has one. They're all Scottish." Michael was still humbled, by the wonder of all these connections to him.

"Then we come to these last couple of glass pieces." Michael opened the window and cautiously pulled out the glass. "This is a Scottish green and blue tartan for the clan of my family."

Slowly he walked to the last window; he carefully slid open the last glass. He took Kate's hand and kissed it.

Kate felt actual goosebumps as realization was dawning on her.

She looked at Michael. Everything felt surreal.

Michael tenderly said, "My dear Kate, this represents my family's bloodline and will be passed down to my children. This last window holds the Family Crest for my mother's family..., The Chambers."

Chapter 41

It was starting to make sense now. Kate was piecing all the fragments of what they had found in the Chambers' storage units with what she had just heard. Add in the fact that Michael had been trying to buy them from her.

Kate was trying to understand; she started with, "Michael, it's all connected somehow."

Michael agreed, "You mean about the storage units? I think so too. Neither of us knew the why, we each wanted those exact storage units. I still don't know why, but I know they're important to my family."

Kate exclaimed, "Yes. The Chambers are YOU! I had No Idea."

"From what little we have seen of the contents, we knew that ethically and morally, it should be given back to the Chambers, if there were any remaining family members. We were going to protect the contents from you because we knew the Chambers should rightfully have it."

"You mean that your friend Grace, you and the others were going to keep it from me, to make sure the Chambers could have it?" Michael was floored.

"Hey, we didn't know who you were. Chambers is not spelled: J- E- N- S (as in Sam) E- N." laughed Kate.

"Hey, be mighty careful there, with that name. It's going to be your name very soon," said Michael.

"Michael, the first thing Grace shared with us was a handwritten journal from the late 1860s. Guess who wrote the journal?"

Michael said, "Well I have no idea. Why don't you just tell me?"

"No, just guess. You won't believe it." cried Kate.

Michael agreed, "Okay, the late 1860s? OK I guess…, President Lincoln."

"No, of course not. It's in your family's belongings. It is Sir Michael Chambers. He was Captain of the Scottish ship that shipwrecked off the coast here. The name of the Scottish ship was *Sea Crest*. He and an Irish lighthouse architect, named Joseph Walsh, were aboard when the ship was dashed against these rocks and sunk along our shore. They built the Sea Crest Lighthouse here and settled the Town of Sea Crest here, in memory of their ship."

"That's why all the little windows are Scottish and Chambers. Why, I must be named after Captain Michael Chambers," marveled Michael. "This is unbelievable."

Kate was so pleased, "Michael, all this is exactly why we all felt these belongings were meant for your family. We have no idea how they ended up getting auctioned off, but we knew it was a mistake."

Michael could hardly convey his gratitude. "I'm so glad you're the ones that bid and won these things."

Kate explained, "Michael, I took Grace's place at the auction because she was sick that day. We always bid on any auctions or sale items, up and down the coast that may help us piece back together our history. Even though we won't be keeping any items, we were able to get an enormous amount of historical information about our town and the people who live or have lived here."

"We never dreamed we'd find that journal."

Michael was struggling to come up with the words, "I never dreamed, I'd find the love of my life, because Grace got sick." They fell into each other's arms laughing.

Chapter 42

"I'm interested in the various projects that you and your friends take on. How are you able to accomplish everything," asked Michael?

Kate smiled and said, "It's a secret."

"Come on," laughed Michael. "Out with it."

"Honestly, I'm not at liberty to discuss most of it. However, I can tell you something that everyone close to us already knows."

"You are full of surprises, aren't you," he joked as he took her hand.

"Well, the part I'm allowed to tell you is that we are die-hard Mah Jongg players."

"Wait a minute," Michael said thoughtfully. "I've heard that name somewhere. Ah yes," he laughed with great sarcasm.

"What?"

"That's the game my grandmother used to play, with her friends," he shook his head from side to side. "You know I spent summers with them, and I tried to follow how they played. You know, it's not like checkers or chess, where each piece always has a standard move, they can make. I'd watch some of the basic combinations, and the next summer that was all out the window and the tiles had a whole new set of hands that were played."

Kate was laughing as she agreed, "Yes, that must have been confusing for you if you didn't know that The Mah Jongg League comes out with a new card every year."

"So what's that have to do with it?"

"Each year they come up with a new set of winning tile combinations. A few of the hands on the cards might stay the same, but a majority will change slightly. Some change just enough to trip you up at first, if you're not careful."

"You're pulling my leg, right?"

"No, I'm not," she answered with a gleam in her eyes. "I'm sure it was very confusing for anyone who didn't know about the modifications that took place every year."

"Thanks, I feel so much better now," he turned his lower lip out as he pouted.

"I'll give you a consolation kiss to make it all better," she agreed with pleasure.

Michael felt surprised as he thought, *It's wonderful to feel her calm, soothing, natural cheer as opposed to the menacing evil attitude that I had first envisioned, Kate, having. I've never enjoyed the pleasant banter that we seem to possess, with any other woman.*

Kate broke into his comparison with a question, "Did your grandmother ever tell you anything about where Mah Jongg originated?"

"No, I've never heard much about the game. I guess it's strange that you and your friends even know about it."

"Well, here's the scoop, or at least what we've been able to learn, so far. We don't know for sure how much is true. However, it's pretty much agreed that it started in China."

"Really," reflected Michael. "I guess that fits. From what I remember, the tiles certainly looked Chinese."

"Well, that's where my friend Maggie first encountered them."

"Wait, is Maggie, the same Maggie that met you at the helicopter the night of the rescue?"

"Why yes, how did you know?"

"She was the Maggie seated at the table next to me, at the Sea Crest Restaurant earlier that night. She and the man with her were not only discussing the rescue but singing your praises, throughout the entire meal. I didn't know *Their Kate* was *My Kate* until you removed your helmet and I saw your braided hair drop down your back. Believe me; I was in Shock."

"How do you feel now?" laughed Kate with delight.

"I'm still flabbergasted," he defended himself. "I'll never get used to you. But I feel like the luckiest man alive."

"Well, then we're even. I thought I saw you looking down at the helipad, but I didn't want you to see me looking for you. I was so scared of what I felt." She looked deeply into his eyes as her voice broke into a whisper, "I think we better get back to the history of Mah Jongg."

"That sounds like a safer topic," he tenderly replied.

"All right, I'm going to see if there is any coffee left in the pot we made," she said as she got up. *Boy, that was intense,* she thought as she got them each a cup of coffee.

As they settled back again, she said, "Well, Maggie was traveling in China on FBI business, and she was so fascinated with the game, that when she returned to the states, she bought an American version of the game."

"Well, is there a difference?"

"Yes, but I'll get to that in a minute," she continued. "Legend has it that the famous philosopher, Confucius invented the game. However, it was not called "mahjong" by the Chinese who played it. That name was used in the early 1900s. Do you remember that dragon tiles on your grandmother's set?"

"Oh yes, I was most interested in those."

"Great. Historians think that those three dragons perfectly represent the three noble virtues that Confucius mentions. These are sincerity, loving family, and benevolence. The additional piece that supports their opinion is based on the fact that he loved birds and the name Mah Jong has the word sparrow in it. If this myth is true, that means the age of the game dates back as far as 500 B.C."

"Wow," marveled Michael. "That's amazing. I wonder if my grandma knew where and when it originated."

"We know about it because of Maggie's contacts in China. By the way, there are other theories that claim someone else invented the game."

"I wouldn't be surprised. A game this old probably disappeared for a while and surfaced somewhere else at a different time. Are the tiles the same?" asked Michael.

"That's a great question because another group of researchers believes it started as a card game in the Ming Dynasty, which ruled China from 1368 to 1644. It's similar to the tiles, but this version has additional flowers with the game. We heard it's even resurfaced as paper or cards. One theory explains that some of the poor peasants could not afford the expensive tiles and used cheap paper to play."

"Our American version of the game is a little different. Our sets include 8 Jokers. Most of us are members of the National Mah Jongg League, Inc. and we follow their rules and standards. It is based in New York City and they produce a new set of winning "hands" for each year.

Well, I'm impressed with your knowledge. I wish my grandmother could have met you," said Michael.

"Do you remember anything about her game?"

"Not very much, but I'd probably recognize it if I saw it again," said Michael cautiously. He was wondering, *what if my grandma's Mah Jongg set is in the storage units Kate bought? I don't want to mention anything about that right now.*

To steer the conversation away from where his mind had wandered, he asked, "are there any other theories about who invented the game?"

"The only other ones Maggie told us about were a nobleman in Shanghai, sometime in the 1870s. Our favorite was from the mid-1800s when a set of brothers claimed to have started the game. One was supposedly famous for his ivory carvings. We'd love to see a Mah Jongg set like that," she stated wistfully.

Chapter 43

Later that night they retired to the pillow filled hammocks to sleep. They were surprisingly comfortable and a relief after a full day.

Michael woke up in the middle of the night and glanced over at Kate, peacefully sleeping in the hammock across the room.

He smiled as he thought, *she looks so sweet in the reflected light of the Fresnel lens. But, looks can be deceiving. When I saw her surfing the other day, I was looking through the eyes of someone so taken with her physical appearance, that the outward beauty of Kate was all I saw. I certainly appreciated her graceful surfing ability and that red swimsuit, but that was all that mattered to me. I have never been that attracted to anyone in my life.*

Michael was embarrassed to realize how shallow that was. *Now, I have to rationalize those feelings by recognizing how very human that makes me. Also, in full disclosure, I will admit that it would take a whole lot of negatives to cancel out how good she looked to me.*

He had to smile again as he recalled, *Okay, she did leave me standing alone on the beach. I was furious and frustrated beyond belief. No one had ever treated me like that in all my dating experiences. I know, I know, we weren't exactly dating.*

Michael was also perplexed to realize that, *I still wanted her, even when she hurt me by tricking me on the beach and even though she had stolen my grandma's belongings. These major digressions didn't turn out to be valid, but I know in my heart, it wasn't enough. I can't help myself; I still wanted her.*

He continued to wonder about the surprising events that continued to occur.

Boy, this trip to Sea Crest sure isn't what I'd expected. Although could anyone anticipate meeting a woman like Kate? I honestly didn't know they even existed. Someone this smart and talented, on so many levels, is unheard of.

Michael was wide awake now. *All right. Can I think of one other woman, past or present, that can fly any of the Coast Guard Aircraft, including the Coast Guard Search and Rescue Helicopter? No.*

Can I think of one other woman who is a rescue swimmer and has saved even one life? How about many lives? No.

What he had learned about the women who keep the lights, was astounding to him. He remembered what Kate had shared with him this evening.

I can't seem to get it out of my mind. The heroic lives of the lighthouse keepers had always been something that I've respected and admired. After all, a good portion of my architectural career has involved lighthouses from all over the world. I don't think I've ever thought about the brave women who were in the picture.

My assumption regarding the lightkeeper's job has been that it involved the men. I guess, if I ever thought about it, I would have believed the women, have a life similar to other homemakers. That scenario is nothing like Kate described.

Michael's train of thought was interrupted when Kate turned over in her hammock. "Oh no," she yelled, with arms flailing out of control as she almost rolled out onto the mahogany floor.

Michael laughed, "Nice. You're not so graceful when you're sleeping are you?"

Kate looked up in surprise as she tried to acclimate herself to the fact that she and Michael were in the Sea Crest Lighthouse together. She blinked, and as she tried to regain her balance in the hammock; she almost flipped onto the floor again.

"Hey, you try to suddenly wake up and find yourself in a tumbling freefall and see how great you look," she laughed.

Michael cheerfully explained, "I never said you didn't look great. In fact, you've looked downright ravishing, since I've met you. It's nothing like I imagined in our conversations over the phone."

"Thanks. I'm going to take that as a compliment," she replied happily.

"Now I'm wide awake, Michael."

"Good, I can't sleep. I keep thinking about everything we've learned about each other. I'm down to the things you shared about all the women lighthouse keepers. I feel terrible that I've never known about their heroic lives. I've worked on many lighthouses all over the globe, but I missed a very important fact about the people who took care of them."

"The lack of credit for the women's contributions to lighthouses, in general, seems strange to me also. But I'm most disappointed that women's successful rescues appear to be practically invisible, in spite of a large number of lives they have saved."

"That's certainly not fair," agreed Michael sadly. "And I'm guilty of the same offense. I feel awful."

They remained quietly reflecting on the situation until Michael asked, "Kate can you tell me how you handle all the rescues? I watched you from the Sea Crest Inn the other night and the fact that it affected two children broke my heart. How do you deal with it?"

"Well, I can tell you something important that I overheard my mom say when I was a child,"

"Okay."

"After I tell you, I can share about the rescue that goes along with it, if you'd like. But I never forgot what my mom said, and I feel the same way."

"That would be great," he replied with love.

"The rescue wasn't sad at all, but it involved a family that ran out of gas or something. They weren't capsized or anything bad. I don't remember what the trouble was, but we were digging clams on the beach for a clambake, and we saw them. It was around Christmas time, and that was always exciting for my brother and me."

"Wow, as a child I never thought about Christmas near the beach. It was usually snowing in New York City," Michael laughed.

"This family was nice, and they had two kids, so we had a wonderful time for the next few days. They ended up staying over through Christmas, and that's when I heard the other mom, gratefully thanking my mom for such a wonderful Christmas. Best they'd had in years.

"My mom thoughtfully explained; 'My children have seen way too much tragedy, in their young lives. I am concerned that they will see life through that prism of grief and mourning. My husband and I chose this life, on purpose, because we love it and it reflects our values for saving lives. I don't want our kids to feel the death and sadness, we see, but instead feel the spirit that we can save lives by choosing to be lighthouse keepers.'"

"Wow," said Michael quietly. "That's one of the most selfless things I've ever heard."

Chapter 44

"How would you feel about some more of that delicious cocoa," asked Kate?

"I'm always ready for a midnight snack. Do we have any more blueberry muffins left?"

"I think so," said Kate. "I'll be happy to tell you that bedtime story about our special Christmas Rescue if you'd like. I promise it will be from a kid's perspective and we had a blast."

"That sounds great. Did you ever imagine it could be this much fun being trapped in a lighthouse?"

"Well, since I hadn't met you, I wouldn't have dreamed it would be this entertaining. You are a joy to be around, and I love you."

Soon they were all set with their tasty goodies, and Kate began.

"It happened quite a few years ago, but this is the way I remember it.

"Also, keep in mind, kids don't usually know all the details of adult problems, but it seems that someone had the bright idea of giving this family the 'gift' of, a 3-hour boat rental. The fine print, on the gift certificate, explained, in little tiny letters, that it needed to be used on the 23 of December, or as we like to call it, Christmas Eve, Eve. I'm quite sure the benefactor in question had only their best interest at heart. I mean, nobody 're-gifts' a 3-hour boat rental.... Do they?"

Michael interjected, "Are you just making that up?"

"No, honest. We are very good friends with this family to this day. We get together often, and it has come up in conversation about a million times."

"Now back to my story. The mom in the story insists, there was *no way,* that she had any time to spare, leading up to Christmas. She still had Christmas baking, shopping, wrapping and  decorating to do. The preparation for her annual Christmas Eve Gathering, before the candlelight service at the church, was daunting, to say the least. She always liked to have things just right; even if it nearly killed her."

"We all tease her saying stuff like *La De Da* and *Well, Excuse Me;* when she talks about it."

"So naturally, she never intended to go on this *boat thing.* However, the rest of the family, (who didn't have anything better to do,) insisted that it would be *Fun.*"

"They pulled that, *let's take a vote, stunt,* on her. Of course, in the end, she relented, and they packed up the SUV, and embarked on a *3-hour boat ride,* two days before Christmas."

"At the beginning of the ride, their mom and dad started to relax and look forward to this special time with the family. That lasted until their mom peeked back at her marvelous children, with the expectation of seeing them happily excited about this fun escapade that they had campaigned so extensively for."

"Now Michael, this is her side of it, but to hear her tell it when she turned around, she saw Lucas, their twelve-year-old, with his head down, his eyes glued to the screen of the game he was playing, and his thumbs were working a mile a minute."

"Their daughter, Sofia, who had recently turned eleven, was equally engrossed, with her headphones over her ears, watching a movie. Her attention didn't deviate one iota from her engrossing monitor. According to their mom, their daughter had checked out from all human interaction by activating her cone of silence and engaging her do not disturb shield. She was now in a fully inaccessible mode."

Michael nodded his head, "You know, that's so common nowadays. However, some of the adults are worse than children. Some parents totally ignore their kids. I've seen it both ways."

"I know. In this case, neither of the kids seemed aware of anything except their gadgets. The way their mom described it was that she felt sad and melancholy and she missed them, even though they were right in front of her."

"Does that even seem possible, Michael?"

"Yes, I think it's more common than we know. It's like feeling lonely when you're in a whole crowd of people."

"I think it's sad," she said. "I hope we will always feel connected to each other even when we're not talking. Like if we were at a meeting or someplace where we couldn't make a lot of conversation, we'd still be aware of each other."

With that, Michael kissed her and told her how much she meant to him.

When they finally got back to the story, Kate said, "When the family arrived at the rental pier, the only boat that was not already in dry dock, was pretty rundown, to say the least. It had a wheelhouse on a platform, and the equipment looked dilapidated also. Truth be told, the boat appeared, just plain worn out.

"Now get this; They tried to justify being out in this terrible excuse for a boat, by blaming Rick, the rental agent. He had informed them, that it was positively seaworthy. However, no one could take any electronic gadgets onboard, because it might cause the boating equipment to malfunction."

"What on earth was that about, Kate?"

"I have no idea. However, the kids were very attached to their electronic devices. You'd think Rick had just taken away things, as necessary to them as, air to breathe.

"Now it was the kid's turn to feel shook up, as they sadly walked back to the vehicle to deposit all their paraphernalia. The separation process from all their offending devices was definitely painful. According to their mom, the kids actually looked traumatized as they gathered back by the boat.

"While this was going on, their dad, Joe, had been working with Rick to get the boat started. When nothing seemed successful, Rick went to get some additional gas, to see if it might be low on fuel.

"Joe asked the kids to look down below to make sure there were life jackets in good condition. When they found them, the family got a kick out of Lucas reporting back, that they seemed to be in better condition than the boat.

"Soon Rick returned with some gas. He and Joe continued to try to start the old vessel, until, at last, the sputtering motor took hold."

Michael advised, "That should have been their first clue that they should turn around and go home."

"Yes, you're right. We have discussed that at length, however, we always conclude that we would never have met each other. So, we eventually concede that it turned out great."

"They always try to save face, by insisting that the mom and dad hesitated, and exchanged looks that indicated that this might not be a good idea after all. They proceeded to blame Rick who decided to sweeten the deal. He explained that they were going to close in about half an hour. He was going to lock up and he wouldn't re-open until the week after New Year's. So..., they were welcome to use the boat for as long as they wanted. He only asked that they tie and lock it up at the dock when they returned.

"With that terrific deal, they climbed aboard the forlorn boat, and cast off.

"Now, with no schedule to keep, they decided to go all the way out to a couple of the barrier islands along the coast. As they approached one of the beaches, our lighthouse came into view. When they drew closer to get a better look, we were digging clams and waving at them. That's about the time their sad little boat started losing power.

"They soon discovered that their seaworthy boat had officially given up the ghost and abruptly stopped running.

"My dad saw their trouble, and came to their aid immediately, as he quickly threw a rope and proceeded to pull them safely to shore. I'll never forget their relieved smiles as he helped them.

"'Wow, I appreciate what you did for us,' said Joe with relief. The men shook hands as Joe continued, 'Thanks, I'm not sure what we would have done, without you. This is my wife, Beth and my kids, Lucas and Sofia.'

"My dad smiled as he replied, 'Oh, glad I could be of help. That's what I'm trained for. These two ragamuffins are my children, Kate and Connor. I smiled and shyly hung onto my dad's arm as I objected, 'We're not ragamuffins.'

"Connor had been chewing on a piece of straw and assessing the situation. 'What happened to your boat? Did you run out of gas?'

"'I'm not sure, but we had quite a bit of trouble starting it today. It did look questionable, but the rental man assured us that it was definitely seaworthy. I guess he was wrong.'

"Dad frowned at the boat as he explained, 'Everything back in town is closed until after Christmas. In the meantime, I'll introduce you to my wife, Katherine. We have ample room and food to put you up.'

Kate laughed as she retold the amusing memory that, "Joe always reminds us that, Dad sounded as if they'd just dropped in for a cup of tea."

"Boy, you have to admit your dad was unusually good-natured about everything. I hope he's that kind when I ask him for your hand in marriage."

"When he sees how much I love you, I'm sure he'll be happy to wish us well, although I am his only daughter and I'm extremely spoiled."

"My only hope is to convince him that I can't live without you and I'll love and cherish you forever."

"Thanks," she whispered as she looked into his eyes.

After a few minutes, she continued, "Well, back to my story. Next, Dad invited them to the keeper's cottage to meet our mom. Joe always insists that she turned out to be very attractive and as good-natured as our dad."

"You must take after her," Michael quickly added with a smile.

"Oh, of course!" she laughed.

"Well, mom was just her normal self, immediately asking if anyone had been hurt. Then she showed them around the keeper's cottage, with the extra sleeping areas for them. Her calm, sincere, attitude led them to believe that this was somehow, normal for us.

"To their utter amazement, Mom continued, 'I hope you folks are hungry because we are going to have a clambake down on the beach. By the way, kids, how is the clam digging project coming?'

"Well, Connor who was always starving, answered, 'So..., I guess we need a few more.' He turned to Lucas and said, 'You want to help?'

"Lucas smiled and answered, 'Sure.'

"Hey, wait for me," I cried, as I signaled to Sofia to join me, as I started running after the boys.

"Later, we all pitched in and helped dig out the fire pit. Michael, we had so much fun as we gathered seaweed, driftwood and smooth rocks for the fire. We are friends to this day."

"Our family had designed some permanent seating, surrounding the fire pit area, by using logs and a couple of huge boulders. Although we seemed authentically suited for this life, it seemed like this surprising new family, did too."

"Kate, I think it's because your family is kind and warm and you all made them feel safe and welcome."

"Of course, I'm sure that's it," laughed Kate. "Michael, you're making it impossible for me not to love you."

"I love you more," replied Michael as he kissed her.

Later, Kate explained, "I'm going to fast forward through our tasty Clam Bake and the campfire on the beach, where we saw a spectacular orange and pink sunset, drop into the ocean, as it set."

"By the way, Michael, have you ever sat around a fire and made Smores?"

"I'm not sure, but I'm sure if you twist my arm, I could be convinced."

"Very funny. I was just remembering; I don't think those kids had ever done it before. They were so happy and excited to share it with us, although, they seemed surprised to get to share it with their parents. I don't think they used to spend a lot of time with them.

"Afterward, the stars appeared in the night sky and I heard their mom look at the stars and remark, that she could hardly believe it. She sat there trying to remember when she had ever had even 10 minutes to sit down, to say nothing of hanging-out, on Christmas Eve, Eve.

"Beth sadly confided the fact that she keeps their home on the Christmas Home Tour each year and this was a huge inconvenience for the whole family.

"As a child, I wondered what made her say that. She had remarked that she had that big Christmas Gathering every year. It didn't sound nearly as fun as I thought it would be.

"Sofia told me later, that her mom always tried to be the best Christmas Hostess in the area. This extravaganza was the highlight of Christmas Eve. Yes, the dessert table alone was staged to display an array of crowd-pleasing treats which included all the classic favorites, as well as an ice cream bar.

"Now that sounded great," said Kate. "By the way, Michael, I love ice cream."

"Me too. I also love all those desserts at the decorated table you were describing."

"Well, that was only part of the food. The long buffet table was strategically arranged to show off its stunning ice sculpture centerpiece with flowing ribbons, soft candles, and beautiful flowers. This was, of course, surrounded by an extensive spread of delicious food."

"The house decorations both inside and out were both warm and inviting. Everything right down to the beautiful ribbons and bows on the presents under the tree resembled an elegant work of art. However, what did all of that have to do with the real meaning of Christmas?

"Soon the stars grew brighter and we heard Lucas pointing out the North Star and the Big Dipper. He also wondered aloud, if that was the star that the shepherds saw in the sky, on Christmas. My dad shared the fact that the sea captains of old, used the stars to guide their ships. Dad and his brother-in-law, both know a vast amount of knowledge about the stars.

"What happened next, really reinforced, his knowledge of the night sky as Lucas wistfully shared his hope; 'I always wanted to see Saturn and its rings.' He turned to my dad and continued, 'I think we can only see it in the early morning, this time of year. Right?'

"My dad smiled in agreement, 'Yes, towards the end of December, in this hemisphere, you can view it about 45 minutes before sunrise, just above the horizon.'

"Right before bedtime, Mom and Dad announced, 'Don't forget, tomorrow is the Christmas Eve Treasure Hunt.'

"Connor and I joined in an exuberant yell of glee. 'Great,' 'Super,' as we practically jumped around for joy.

'That will give them something to think about,' laughed Mom. She went on to explain that we each plan a surprise. It starts with the Christmas Eve Treasure Hunt which is actually more like a scavenger hunt. We have to follow the clues to find something to either share with that person or something special that will show that we care for or love that person. Sometimes the clues are puzzles or games. Often it includes finding a clue in a book. Our family's, most often picked book, is our 'Tom Sawyer,' 1st Edition. They need to locate a particular passage on a specific page, which will indicate the next step in the journey.

"Dad smiled as he added, 'Yes, the journey is just as important as the gift or prize at the end. Eventually, our games became more complicated. But believe me, they've come up with some challenging ones for us too.'

"Connor piped up with, 'Yeah, like our chess games.'

"Dad immediately said, 'Oh, come on, now. No fair bringing that up.'

"Lucas joined in with delight, 'Tell us, please. This sounds good. I love chess.'

"Of course, Connor agreed with excitement, 'Okay, I'll tell you.'

"At that, Dad quickly defended himself, 'Hey, he's only going to tell his version. He out and out, tricked me.'

"Connor was not deterred, as he eagerly started, 'Well, a couple of years ago, the clues went from checkers to chess. Now we had to play a game of chess before we can proceed to the next step. But the year Dad was trying to teach me how to play, of course, I wasn't very good. However, I liked the game, and I wanted to surprise him the following year, at Christmas.'

"Connor smiled as he continued, 'I didn't tell Mom or Dad, that I joined the Chess Club at school and played as often as possible. The teacher would give us pointers and strategy coaching. By the time our Christmas break came around, everyone in our club was fairly skilled at competing.'

"Our dad proudly joked, 'Hey that was no fair, keeping that from me. I wasn't prepared.'

"Connor cheerfully resumed his story, 'Christmas Eve came and sure enough, one of the clues was: *'Play a game of chess, and you will get your next clue.'* Well, I beat my dad in 4 moves. He just couldn't believe it. He looked at the chessboard, and then he just looked at me. He finally shook his head in confusion.'

"We were all laughing and joking with Dad, and it was just plain fun."

Michael thought, with an odd sense of regret, *I'm trying to remember when I've shared such a warm, delightful evening with my dad and brother, James. But nothing similar comes to mind.*

"Well, we kids were all up early the next morning, secretly plotting and trying to figure out what was in store for us. Our part was to do extraordinary deeds to make Christmas special.

"At breakfast, Mom explained, 'I know you kids have been busy planning for our Christmas Eve Treasure Hunt. We each share something special and give clues to find it. We can help each other with the clues and set up the surprises throughout the day tomorrow.'

"Connor told Lucas, 'I've always dreamed of actually decorating and lighting the outside of the lighthouse with a great design. It would normally be way too hard for me to do by myself. But if you're game, we can do a spectacular job this year. We can take decorating to a whole new level, with lights all around the railings at the top, and everywhere we can reach.'

"Lucas immediately agreed, 'Sure, you can count on me. Where are you going to get all the lights? We'll need a bunch if we plan to do a super, great job.'

"That wasn't a problem. Connor explained, 'We always buy strings of Christmas lights on clearance after Christmas. You won't believe how many we have.'

"Meanwhile we girls had discovered our own Christmas gift to the family. Sofia had been in a Christmas Play on the last day of classes at school, which ended with them all singing, '*I Heard the Bells on Christmas Day.*' The words are a poem by Henry W. Longfellow, which was put to music. Sofia was absently humming the melody of that song, as she climbed the steps of the spiral staircase in the lighthouse.

"I knew the song also and as we began to sing together, the echo of our sweet music filled the tower.

"That's when we came up with the idea to sing some Christmas carols for our Christmas gift to our two families. I remembered that we had an old Christmas songbook in the cellar with the other Christmas stuff and that's where we met up with the boys.

"Upon seeing them, I demanded, 'Hey, what are you doing down here?'

"Connor suspiciously wanted to know the same thing from us. 'We're looking for Christmas lights. What are you girls doing?'

"I explained, 'Sofia and I want to surprise our parents, with singing Christmas carols and I thought I remembered a songbook down here.'

"Lucas suddenly relaxed as he said, 'We just heard you singing in the lighthouse. That was amazing.'

"That's when we decided to join forces, as Connor said, 'Hey, I've got an idea. We wanted to decorate the lighthouse with all the lights we can find. I know Mom wants to have the lobster bake on the beach tonight for Christmas Eve. Why don't we surprise them with our own Christmas Eve surprise?'

"This project was what we spent most of our day working on, which was ironic because this essentially put our Christmas Eve Treasure Hunt on the back burner. However, after lunch, Dad announced, 'If you're done eating, look under your chairs, and you will find your first two clues are taped under two of the seats. Good luck and we'll see you at the finish line.'

"I felt under my chair and yelled, 'Look, I have one! It says, *'Let's hope it didn't sink.'*

"Sofia called, 'Mine says, *'It might be docked.'*

"Connor called out, 'I'll bet it means your boat. Let's go,' he shouted as he took off toward the water, where their sad boat was tied up.

"This was the exciting start of the annual Christmas Eve Treasure Hunt. The next few hours were filled with guesses, clues, cookies, hot chocolate, and along the way, games of chess.

"One of the last clues was: *'Go to the shed and check the rack.'*

"I remember yelling with delight, 'Come on, let's go to the tool shed.'

"We all took off running. When we got to the shed, the note on the door said:

'Don't dig and labor in the sand,
Till a metal detector is in your hand.'

"As Connor threw open the doors, he yelled, 'Wow, this is great!'

"Hanging on the rack were two brand new metal detectors, with giant red bows.

"We couldn't believe it. Connor shouted, 'Hey, look at this. A metal detector is the only thing we asked for.'

"Now we had two. I agreed, 'This is the best.'

"Connor and I put our heads together and agreed to let Lucas and Sofia use the new metal detectors while they were visiting. We took the two older ones from the shed, and the four of us happily took off to see what we could discover in the sand.

"After hours of chasing the clues and some great detective work, another successful Christmas Eve Treasure Hunt came to an end.

"Lucas and Sofia's parents walked up to the top of a hill to watch the sunset. It was gorgeous. The ocean waves, the sea breeze, the sky: it was wonderful. We overheard them talking about how many years it's been since they've been this happy on Christmas Eve and they'd enjoyed the last couple of days with the kids more than they ever remembered.

"Joe chuckled as he added, 'Do you realize those kids haven't complained about their gadgets or mentioned how bored they were, even one time?'

"Mom and Dad had set some lobster traps, and the next activity was a delicious Christmas Eve cookout. We all helped build a fire and gather and spread the seaweed over the lobsters and corn on the cob. The food was delicious.

"Just as the sun was sliding out of sight, we kids were doing a lot of whispering and giggling. Our parents knew something was up. A couple of minutes later, Connor stood and nodded as a signal to us kids. With his eyes beaming, he announced, 'To the best parents in the whole wide world; this is our Christmas Surprise for you.'

"We four children each kissed our Mom and Dad and waved to them as we headed to the lighthouse. I turned backward for a few steps as I called to them, 'Please give us five minutes.' However, I noticed that they weren't planning on going anywhere.

"Well, they knew we were up to something special this morning. Moments later, the whole lighthouse burst out with a magnificent display of Christmas lights. At the very top of the lighthouse, along the outside edges of the Cupola Roof, as well as both the railings along the Widows Walk and the Gallery Walk of the lighthouse, was strung with endless, bright, glowing lights.

"The large tree outside the keeper's cottage was also decorated with so many lights, that it could be seen for miles. Mom explained, 'We don't have a Christmas tree inside the house because the huge tree outside makes a perfect Christmas tree that we can share with anyone that might be sailing in these waters around Christmas.'

"The next thing they heard was totally unexpected. The sweet melodic sound of Sofia and me, singing, 'I Heard the Bells on Christmas Day,' drifted down to them. The echo and the acoustics from inside the lighthouse tower were astonishing. Our voices blended into pure, innocent, clear notes, reminiscent of a children's choir. (At least that was how we heard ourselves, anyway.)

"Our angelic voices sang all four verses, which told the poignant story of what Christmas meant. That simple, yet powerful song was the sweetest carol I'd ever sung.

"Between the beautiful Christmas lights and the equally amazing Christmas carols; tears rolled down my mom's cheeks, as I wondered if I would ever have another Christmas, this great again.

"Christmas morning, right before dawn, Joe and Dad had a surprise, as they woke up Lucas and Connor. They asked them to come up to the top of the lighthouse to help them finish setting up the telescope, on the Widows Walk, outside the Lantern Room.

"Lucas scrambled to find his shoes, as he asked, 'Can you believe it? Do you think we can see Saturn, with its rings?'

"Well, that was the plan. We were having a Christmas breakfast up in the lighthouse Watch Room, on the floor below the Lantern Room.

"As the boys raced up the spiral steps of the lighthouse stairway, Lucas cried, 'Wow, this is the best Christmas ever.'

"My mom and Sofia's mom were setting up the breakfast table, when we overheard all the commotion about Saturn, and they heard Lucas's comment.

"Mom turned to her mom and said, with tears in her eyes, 'Yes, it is the best Christmas ever. Thank you for coming. Your family is the best.'

"Sofia's mom was dumbfounded. 'What are you talking about? We didn't, *come here*. Our boat rental sputtered out, and your husband was able to get us ashore safely.'

"Mom just shook her head. 'The only thing I prayed for this Christmas was for our children to be around happiness and to feel-goodness touch their lives, this year.'

"Well, Christmas that year was life-changing for Joe and Beth. They took a very long walk along the shore and tried to figure out how they could duplicate the time they had just spent together, the last couple of days.

"Next, they asked Mom and Dad to join them as they shared their new plans. Together, they created a handwritten contract, for Joe and Beth to buy a scenic 3-acre plot of land, just a short walk from the lighthouse. They were able to build a delightful get-away cottage, which was finished by summer vacation that year.

"To this day, this couple and their kids are the best friends we could ever ask for. They now have a wonderful place to visit several times a year."

Chapter 45

The next morning Kate and Michael were hoping someone, namely Connor, would come back to the lighthouse and unlock the Irish padlock when the tide receded, and the walkway dried off. They wanted to get married as soon as possible.

However, that did not seem to be a big priority for anyone else. It appeared that the police presence was keeping people away from the beach and the lighthouse.

Kate remembered a secret way she and Connor had communicated while growing up. She had no idea if it would even work, but she asked Michael if he knew anything about DSC VHF radios. Well, they work just like normal VHF radios but with some added extras. Only the person at the number you are calling, responds. When they recognize your number, they accept, and the two parties can start a conversation.

Kate explained, "Connor and I used to call each other and talk all the time. We have not done it in years, and I am not sure both of our radios even work. But it's worth a try."

Michael asked, "Where is the lighthouse's radio?"

Kate responded, "If it's still here, it's in one of the hidden cubbyholes on the staircase."

"Let's see if we can find it, then we'll see if it works," said Michael.

"Yes, it was set up just for fun between the keeper's house and the lighthouse. Connor and I thought it was a big deal. We pretended like we were engaged in matters of life and death."

"Like the red phone in the president's office," laughed Michael as he added, "Well, truth be told, I feel like it is a life and death matter. If we don't get married soon, I'm going to go out of my mind."

"I'm in as much of a hurry as you are," Kate confided as they stopped for a few lifesaving kisses.

"Wait, I think the cubbyhole was about one-third of the way down," said Kate, as they were stepping down the spiral staircase.

"Look right along here, on one of these steps."

"Here's an opening in the wall," said Michael as he gently swung the cover open.

Kate stepped over to join him, "Yes, that's it. Now let's see if we can set up a call. I'll start the call exactly the way we used to do it," she said. "But I must admit I'm glad we didn't think of this sooner. I loved our uninterrupted time together."

Michael agreed, "Boy you can say that again. Now, all we can do is send a message and see if it goes through."

"Well, here goes," she said as she spoke loudly into the receiver.

"Connor, this is Kate, of course. I am in the lighthouse with Michael, and it appears that you put the Irish padlock on the outside. We cannot get out. By the way, we have some thrilling news for our families. Michael and I have fallen in love and we are going to get married. I can't wait for you to meet him."

"Now please unlock the Irish padlock as soon as possible. If that tide comes back and we are in here for another night; we will go to plan B. Love you. Bye, Kate."

Michael laughed, "I can't wait to hear what Plan B is."

"Well, I was wondering. How can we get their attention?" said Kate.

Michael came up with a couple of ideas. "Maybe lower a basket down from one of the lower windows that can be seen from the beach?"

Next, Kate spouted off, "Lower a note in a bottle from a rope?"

Then they were each calling out ideas: "Wave a flag from the catwalk on either or both of the levels?" "Put a flag out the window at the top?" "Fly a kite?"

Michael had one more very important question. "Kate, I have something very important to ask you."

This seemed to take Kate off guard, but she answered, "Okay, I'm ready. What do you want to know?"

"Did Grace find a wedding gown in the storage unit contents? If she did, it would be my mother's dress, and I'd love you to wear it."

Kate was so shocked all she could do was look at Michael with love and tears of sheer joy. "I don't know if she found one or not, but I'll be honored to wear it if she did."

"There is a family history connected with that dress. My grandfather was a paratrooper in World War II. He was stationed in Europe and the plan was to marry my grandmother as soon as he returned home."

"He was set to come home in about one month, and our family was trying to buy a wedding gown. During the war, many items had to be rationed. Silk and nylon were among the materials that were saved, for the war effort, and unavailable to the public."

"On his last parachute jump, my grandfather had an accident. Although he was injured, his parachute had saved his life. He went to a hospital in Europe to recuperate. Since that was his last mission, he mailed his parachute home."

"My grandmother opened the package and saw the white parachute silk. She had several friends help her make a wedding gown out of it. My grandmother Chambers married my grandfather in a wedding dress made from the parachute that had saved his life. During the remainder of the war, my grandmother let many other brides wear her Parachute Wedding Gown to get married."

"When my mom married my dad, she was the last bride to wear that sacred parachute wedding gown that my grandparents were married in," Michael said proudly. "I'm pretty sure my grandmother would have saved it for my brother and me. It just might have been in that storage unit."

Chapter 46

"OK," said Michael. "We have one idea in the works. Now, which project should we try?"

Kate answered, "Your choice, Michael. What do you think would be the most visible or get the most attention?"

Michael thought about it for a minute. "I say we go for some kind of kite. It needs to be huge, a bright color, something unusual and eye-catching. Plus, we need something that will bring someone near, so we can at least yell at them."

"That sounds good to me, too," said Kate. "Earlier this year the Scouts had a Kite Fair. They used many beautiful materials. I wonder what we can find. Let's go to their stock room and see what's available."

Soon they were looking through yards of different material.

"Look. This awesome red silk print is perfect," exclaimed Kate.

"That's spectacular. That will get lots of attention," agreed Michael as he watched the fabric wave gracefully in the breeze. "I'll bet it will fly beautifully. Should we make a box kite or the diamond-shaped kite with the crossbar and a long tail?"

"I think the diamond-shaped type would be simpler to make and take less time. The sooner we can get it in the air, the better."

"Yes, we need to convey the idea that we are locked in the lighthouse," said Michael.

A short time later, they had a spectacular red kite in the air, flying from the top of the Sea Crest Lighthouse. It looked magnificent.

"Well, we're getting lots of attention but no help," observed Kate.

Michael noticed the tide was coming in even faster than it did yesterday. He said, "If someone doesn't come close enough to realize we're locked inside here, the window for getting out tonight will be gone."

They promptly used some of the kite string to tie to the tops of bottles with notes in them, which said; 'We're locked in the Lighthouse,' and 'Please HELP.'

Next, Michael made a homemade megaphone to call for help.

Some people waved, but they did not seem to notice that they needed help. Michael made a big sign with 'HELP' on it, but no one could get close enough to read it.

"It's getting pretty late in the afternoon. In another few minutes, I think the tide will be too high," grumbled Michael.

"Well, Connor hasn't gone back to the keeper's cottage, so I guess checking any messages on his radio, is out," said Kate.

Just then, a Coast Guard Cutter came into view. As it got closer and they could see the couple waving frantically from the top of the lighthouse, they called through a bullhorn, "What seems to be the problem?"

Michael used his homemade megaphone, to reply, "We're locked inside. We think there is a padlock on the lower door. We were stranded inside by mistake."

The reply came back, "Could you please identify yourselves?"

"Our names are Michael Jensen and Kate Walsh," called Michael, as they waved frantically from the lighthouse catwalk.

"Great! A massive search has been underway for you. We are part of a widespread search to rescue both of you. The local police and the FBI have been looking for you on both land and air, while the coast guard was searching the water."

"Are you both well? Do you need medical assistance?"

"We're both fine," both Michael and Kate called out, smiled and waved.

The Coast Guard Cutter called, "We need to put the news out that you're safe." Within a short time, the Captain returned to tell them, "The Search and Rescue Team wants me to ask if that's really Kate up there."

Kate stepped out and waved while someone took a picture to ID Kate for the Search and Rescue Team. She held up her hand and called for them to take another one. Kate stepped up to Michael, with her eyes twinkling.

Kate whispered, "Let's give them a Kiss."

"For a Picture Worth Taking." Michael finished as he smiled.

As their eyes met, he gently tilted back her head, and just like the iconic couple in the Times Square photo, on VJ Day... They Kissed.

They held the elegant kiss and embraced for a full minute, as numerous pictures were taken. When Michael tipped her back up, she smiled as she turned back to the cheering guys on the Coast Guard Cutter.

Someone new stepped up on deck. They watched as Chaplain O'Reilly took the microphone and shouted, "Hey, Kate. We are very relieved to see you."

She happily waved back as she held the home-made megaphone in one hand and hugged Michael close with the other, "Hey Brian. Let me introduce you to Michael Jensen. Michael that is Chaplain Brian O'Reilly. My family has known him for years."

Michael smiled and waved, never raising his other arm from Kate's shoulder.

The Chaplain strained to see what almost looked like an embrace.

"We're sorry for all the worry we have caused you," Kate apologized. "We are both fine, and I might add, we're both grateful that your Coast Guard Cutter finally spotted our signal."

"Yes, so are we. I've kept in touch with your family, and of course, they've been extremely anxious. I'll let them know we found you and you're safe."

Wow, he thought. *I've never seen Kate looking better.* He removed his glasses and wiped them quickly. As he replaced them, he tried to focus more clearly as he whispered, "Why, she has just been through a harrowing ordeal and yet, she looks radiant."

"By the way," he stated, "a hurricane is headed for the Caribbean Islands. The rest of my unit has already deployed to the Grand Bahamas. I stayed behind because you were missing. The Bahamas and the Turks and Caicos Islands are currently in the direct path and are projected to sustain the most damage. You know our motto, *Semper Paratus. Always ready for any emergency.*"

The Chaplain's thoughts were echoing, *Semper Fi, always Faithful (to your God, to your family, to your country, and to your fellow Marines). Leave no one behind.*

Kate gratefully responded with a heartfelt, "Thank you. I know you need to rejoin your unit but I want you to be the first to know, we're getting married. We're going to have the ceremony up here at the top of the Sea Crest Lighthouse, and we'd like you to marry us as soon as you get back."

Chaplain Brian O'Reilly was speechless.

Kate didn't miss a beat as she breathlessly asked, "When will you be returning?"

The stunned chaplain cleared his throat as he slowly regained his composure, "Let's see, I'll have to leave with a shipment of supplies at 2400 tonight. I don't know how long I'll be deployed, but I'd expect at least two or three months, but probably more like six months."

"No, no, no. We want to get married and start our life together as soon as possible," Kate pleaded in disappointment.

Michael stepped in and took the megaphone, "Chaplain, please, wait just a minute. We need to talk ..."

The chaplain wasn't going anywhere.

Michael then turned to Kate with love in his eyes, "All right Kate. I know we're not a couple of complete strangers who are in Las Vegas for the weekend, but how would you feel about getting marrying tonight before midnight?"

Kate took a breath and tearfully said, "I'd be thrilled. And we're already at the top of the lighthouse. Yes, Michael. A thousand times, Yes."

With that agreement, they asked, "Chaplain, is it possible for you to marry us tonight before you leave."

"Wait," replied the Captain. "We think the tide is already too high to rescue you. Will you be all right through tonight?"

Michael responded with an emphatic, "No, we plan to be married as soon as possible." He turned to Kate and tenderly whispered, "Kate, I'm not waiting another day for you to be my wife."

Michael didn't take his eyes off Kate as he lifted the megaphone once again, "Can you airlift the Chaplain to us by Coast Guard Helicopter, please?"

"What?" The answer came back from the very confused Coast Guard Cutter Captain, "I don't think we got that last part."

"As you probably know, Kate Walsh is a decorated Coast Guard Search and Rescue Helicopter Pilot-in-Command. She is responsible for saving many lives. After all, she's done; is it too much to ask to have the Chaplain airlifted down to the catwalk of this lighthouse so she can marry me?"

"We'll check on that. Wait right there." The poor guy was trying to salute and immediately called back, "Sorry about that last part."

Within the next few minutes, they had their answer. "The Chaplin said he'd be honored to marry you. He will bring the license. Do you have anyone for the two witnesses?"

"Kate wants Maggie O'Hara from the FBI. I want my brother James Jensen from New York City, but I am sure he cannot get down here tonight to join me."

"As a matter of fact, your brother is here."

"What? You mean he is here in Sea Crest? Well in that case, sure, I'd love to have him as my Best Man." Michael was shocked as he turned to Kate and said, "My brother is here!"

Then Michael had one more request as he lifted the megaphone and said, "Maggie is Kate's Maid of Honor. Please ask her to see if Grace found my mother's wedding gown in the storage unit stuff. We'd like Kate to wear it. And Yes, of course, we're talking about the Chambers' storage units."

Now Kate had a few instructions to her team, "Please air-lift those three people in a Heli-Basket, from the Search and Rescue Helicopter."

Kate then explained to Michael, "It's able to fit five people or more, without needing to load them into the helicopter itself. The helicopter hovers over the site and rests the basket on the ground or another surface. Evacuees board, where they are transported to the desired area. The basket hangs on a 125-foot cable below the helicopter, without landing."

She continued with her instructions to the USCG Cutter, "We'd like them to use the catwalk below the Lantern Room to load and unload from the basket."

The Coast Guard agreed that this would work and it should come off very smoothly. As an afterthought, Kate added, "If an emergency should come up and the basket is being used at a different rescue, please use the Sproule Net."

She turned and explained to Michael, "This was like a rope net, which looks like a macramé plant hanger suspended from the helicopter. The helicopter drags it through the sea, scoops up the evacuee and lifts the person into the aircraft."

The thought of the Coast Guard fishing his brother, James, out of the sea was positively too much, as Michael laughed out loud. "Personally, I'd vote for that macramé scooper thing."

The Coast Guard agreed that this would be used if need be. Kate also had another critical request for this evening.

"Please be sure to come back and pick Chaplin O'Reilly, Maggie and James Jensen, back up. About an hour later would be fine."

"On your return trip to the lighthouse to take the Chaplin and witnesses home, please, bring us a Large Pepperoni Pizza with Extra Cheese."

The Coast Guard confirmed that would work out fine.

Michael also had one final wish, "We'd like all those fireworks you've been saving for the Sea Crest Festival this weekend. Yes, all those fireworks and any more you can get a hold of. We'd like Sea Crest to see a massive Fireworks Display tonight to celebrate our wedding."

The Coast Guard was not sure about that. "Well, those fireworks are for the festival. It's to raise funds for the lighthouse repair."

"Let them know, Sea Crest now has an architect and his company, to restore the damage that's been done to the lighthouse. We also have a backer for the funds and equipment to get it repaired."

As cheers went up, Michael answered, "No Problem. Thanks."

While this was taking place, the FBI finally reached Maggie concerning James' sealed case from the background check.

It happened when James was in his first year of college, and he returned home for spring break. Several of his friends were home at the same time and they would often get together to play a pickup game of football.

One day a new boy and a few of his friends showed up to play. He had a pretty smart mouth, and during a heated moment, he spouted off with some very mean-spirited remarks about James' Mother. Of course, the kid had no idea that she had died. Since James' friends did know about it and how terrible this had been for him, they defended him. Push came to shove, and a fight started. Within a few minutes, the ugly skirmish turned into an intense street brawl.

Someone called the police. They all ended up having to go downtown to the station, for assault and battery.

In the end, it turned out that the boy and all his friends apologized and eventually all the charges were dropped on both sides.

The case was sealed because no one was ever actually indicted.

Chapter 47

A few minutes prior to this, Kate's family heard all the excitement over the loudspeakers with the Coast Guard Cutter and ran outside of the keeper's cottage, to see what all the commotion was.

"What's going on," called Kate's mother?

"How on earth did anyone get in the lighthouse," asked Connor? "I put the Irish padlock on it because it was too dangerous to have the public go inside until it's been repaired?"

"That's our Coast Guard Cutter," said Kate's dad. "I hope it's not a couple of foolish teens. With the tide so high, the walk won't be safe to walk on until tomorrow."

"Dad, I locked the door with the padlock yesterday morning. I don't know how anyone could possibly get it open," explained Connor.

A few other people had gathered on the beach to see what was happening. One lady said, "We saw a man and a woman up there earlier, flying a beautiful red kite." Her husband added, "They were waving to us and looked so happy."

"And so much in love," added his wife.

"Well, it looks like the Coast Guard is going to put an end to it," said Kate's dad, gruffly. "They've got some real emergencies to handle, and they don't have time for all this foolishness."

"Come on Ma," said Kate's dad, as he put a protective arm around his teary-eyed wife.

They started to make their way back to the keeper's cottage when the next megaphone called out, "Can you airlift the Chaplain to us by Coast Guard Helicopter, please?"

Kate's dad stopped dead in his tracks at that and yelled, "Just who do those people think they are?" He was fired up now. His daughter was missing. He added, "This jerk wants to use Coast Guard resources on this foolishness?"

"Connor, I need to talk to those guys," yelled Kate's dad, but Connor was already running towards the keeper's cottage to get his dad's Coast Guard radio.

The Coast Guard Cutter megaphone responded, "What... I don't think we got that last part."

The lighthouse's megaphone response changed everything, as a man's voice came on from the lighthouse and said, "As you probably know, Kate Walsh is a decorated Coast Guard Search and Rescue Helicopter Pilot-in-command. She is responsible for saving many lives. After all, she's accomplished, is it too much to ask to have the Chaplin airlifted up to the catwalk of this lighthouse so she can marry me?"

Kate's mother and father felt the first surge of hope that Kate was all right, since they were told that she was missing. They hugged each other and wept for joy as they jumped up and down, half-laughing and half-crying.

That's what Connor saw as he came running back from the cottage. "What's going on?"

"We think Kate's up there," they shouted. Connor joined in the celebration.

They ran over to the edge of the beach to see if they could see Kate. They could just see the edge of the catwalk where Kate and Michael were communicating with the cutter.

They had missed a couple of the interchanges, but they heard the Coast Guard Cutter calling back, "The Search and Rescue Team wants me to ask if that's honestly Kate up there."

Kate's mom prayed, "Dear Lord, Please. Let it be our Kate."

When Kate stepped out and waved, her whole family "Cheered and thanked The Good Lord."

They looked up in time to see Kate step into an embrace with the young man. He gently tilted back her head and just like the iconic couple in the Times Square photo, on VJ Day; they kissed.

Kate's mom was ecstatic as she proclaimed, "It's Real. Our Kate's in love."

As the couple held the elegant kiss and embraced, her mom began telling anyone and everyone, who would pay attention to her, "That's my daughter!"

She proceeded to point to the couple, just in case any newcomers had missed them, "Yes, up there, that is our daughter, Kate. They're going to get married."

At the same time, Kate's dad was mumbling, "Doesn't anyone have to ask the father's permission anymore? Who is this guy? Does this Lighthouse Romeo even have a job?"

Kate's brother, Connor, told him confidently, "Oh yeah, Dad. She definitely knows what she wants in a husband. She was just telling me all about it the other day. I just knew she was talking about this guy."

Kate's dad looked at Connor as if he had just lost his mind. "Let me get this straight; Kate was talking to you about this guy? Kate told you she wants *This Guy* for her husband?"

"Well, yes. In a way," replied Connor. "She had a whole list."

"Her husband needs to Laugh Easy and Love Deeply. He doesn't want to change her, and he'll be a great Dad, like you." With great satisfaction, he added, "That must be who this guy is. What did you say his name is again?"

Chapter 48

Across town, a jubilant Maggie was asking, "What do you mean?"

The Coast Guard Cutter Captain repeated his information. "We just discovered that Kate Walsh has been located and is unharmed."

"That's great. Where is she?"

"It seems that she was trapped in the Sea Crest Lighthouse when the tide came in. The door had a padlock on the outside so she could not get out. That's where she's been the entire time."

"That's amazing."

"That's not all." said the Captain. "She intends to get married this evening, and she'd like you to be her Maid of Honor."

"You've got to be kidding."

"No, I'm not. Kate wants you to have Grace find a wedding dress from the storage unit stuff."

"What?"

"That's right, and she needs you to pick it up and bring it to her. She has arranged to have you airlifted along with Chaplin O'Reilly, to the top of the lighthouse. They'll meet you at the beach in about one hour."

"That's insane," cried Maggie. "What does she mean, get married? She doesn't even have a boyfriend."

"I'm signing off now; I have to contact the Best Man."

"I don't believe it." Maggie was in shock. "Kate wants to get married? Tonight? Why? What wedding dress from the storage unit? Who is the best Man? Well, more important: Who's the groom?"

Misha danced around, sharing Maggie's excitement but was very confused. Was Maggie happy or upset? She looked relieved  and delighted when she talked about Kate. Misha had met Kate a couple of days ago and liked her a lot. She received dog treats and food from her, however, she hadn't seen her since. She watched Maggie dial her phone again as she gave Misha a reassuring pat on the head.

"Hi Grace, Kate's alive. They just found her trapped in the lighthouse."

"What on earth do you mean? She lives right next to it."

Maggie replied, "I guess she was inside it when someone put a padlock on the outside door. The high, spring tides came up, and she couldn't get out."

"Who on earth would lock Kate inside?"

"I don't know any details, but something even worse is going on. Kate wants to get married *Tonight*, at the top of the lighthouse and she wants me to be her Maid of Honor. I'm supposed to bring a wedding dress from the storage unit stuff. The tide is high again and she wants me to be airlifted up with Chaplin O'Reilly in about an hour."

Grace said, "Oh my, how romantic. Come on over; I'll start looking for the gown right now."

She hung up before she heard Maggie yell, "What? Romantic? You're going to go look for the gown?"

Maggie was beside herself, as she pleaded, "What's going on? Doesn't anyone else think this is crazy?"

Misha was getting some mixed signals again as she watched Maggie dash out the front door.

She drove on over to Grace's who had, amazingly enough, found an old vintage wedding gown. Grace also knew the history of the beautiful dress. "This is what's called a parachute wedding gown. They were made out of the silk parachutes during World War II, because of the rationing of material, including silks and nylons."

"I've never even hoped to see one in my lifetime. Oh, this one is truly exquisite," Grace sighed.

"What do you think it's doing in with this stuff?" asked Maggie suspiciously.

"Well, I know precisely what it's doing here. It's the dress that Mrs. Chambers was married in."

They looked at each other with surprise, and both said together, "Why did Kate ask for this dress?"

Maggie was the first to form an answer, "How did she know it was here? Does it have something to do with who she's going to marry?"

Grace was nodding her head, "It must mean she knows about it, but how could that happen? Good heavens, I wonder who is she going to marry."

"Let's get going. I wonder if her family knows anything about this." Maggie was on her way out the door with the dress and Grace in tow.

James' notification was not any clearer. The Coast Guard Captain had gotten in touch with Joe, who put James on the line after verifying that Michael was found safe and sound."

"Hello James, I was asked to notify you that your brother is going to be married tonight at the top of the Sea Crest Lighthouse and he's requesting that you be present as his Best Man."

"What?" exclaimed James? "That's impossible. Michael doesn't even have a girlfriend."

"Well, girlfriend or not, he's asking for our Coast Guard Chaplin to be air-lifted to the top of the Sea Crest Lighthouse in about an hour and he'd like for you to be there."

"You're talking about my brother?"

Joe asked James what happened and then offered, "Listen, I can take you over to the lighthouse right now, and we'll see what's going on."

James replied, "Great. This is crazy. My brother has NEVER even thought of getting married. What is going on?"

They headed over to the lighthouse. The whole time James was going off about how this whole thing didn't make any sense.

Joe and James arrived right when Maggie and Grace were getting out of their car with the beautiful parachute gown.

James yelled, "Hey. What is she doing here?"

Maggie looked at him warily, hoping against hope, that James was not connected in any way with her arrival at the lighthouse, as she said, "What are you doing here?"

Joe stepped between them as he said, "Maggie, James has just found out that his brother, Michael is safe and sound and we are here to find out a few details."

"What are you talking about?" Maggie asked, near hysteria in her voice. "Those details better not have anything to do with our Kate. We just heard that she'd been locked inside the lighthouse for the past couple of days."

"I'm warning you, if this is connected, I'll sue this town for every penny it's got." James was approaching outright panic as he saw what they were holding in their arms. "What is that?"

"It's nothing to do with you, believe me." Maggie was filled with dread as she and Grace looked at the gown and then at James and finally at Kate's approaching family.

"Oh, Maggie, Grace, isn't it wonderful?" came the emotional declaration of Kate's mother as she tearfully hugged the other women. "My Kate's going to get married tonight."

"What happened?" asked Grace. "We didn't know she was even seeing anyone. Who is he?"

They all leaned in to hear who Kate was going to marry. "Well, we don't know his name, but we saw them kiss at the top of the lighthouse and Kate used the megaphone to ask the Coast Guard Cutter Captain, 'Now, could you Please get us a Chaplain?'"

"Now wait just a minute, that better not be my brother you're talking about," stated James, who was now positive that it was indeed, exactly who they were talking about. "He's way too level-headed to be mixed up with something like this."

"What? You think your brother's too good for my Kate?" asked her Mom.

"I don't know anything about your Kate, but I can tell you that my Michael is the best husband that anyone could get," James said with pride.

Maggie had heard just about enough. "We don't know who she's going to marry, but I'm sure he's not a deadbeat character named Michael that she was supposed to meet a couple of days ago. She described him as a real loser."

Just then, the exceptionally jovial Chaplain O'Reilly arrived on the beach. He appeared to be, on top of the world, as he explained about the helicopter airlift arrangements. It was dusk, and it would be dark within fifteen minutes. Since the helicopter was due any minute, they should be in the lighthouse before nightfall.

He was so pleased that the Best Man and the Maid of Honor would be able to join him. "Kate and Michael are so happy to have you stand up with them. Michael was surprised and especially pleased that James was here from New York City."

"Are you saying that their Kate and my brother Michael are going to be married?" James struggled to get it out.

"Yes, and I've never seen Kate so happy," said the Chaplain as the helicopter came down the coast with the heli-basket.

As they moved toward the basket, Maggie was close enough to James that he whispered, "You and your friend Kate have probably put some sort of voodoo on Michael."

Maggie turned and said, "You are unbelievable."

James finished his accusations, "But rest assured, this marriage hoax will be annulled, as soon as Michael recovers from whatever drugs you've got him on."

"Oh Yes. You can count on it. I'm going to make sure your brother pays for it if he conned Kate into this," added Maggie.

The Chaplain was joyously helping them into the basket, and as he closed the latch on the door, he smilingly said to them, "This is the most delightful wedding I've ever performed."

James and Maggie just looked at him in stunned disbelief.

They tried to get settled, and keep their balance, as the five-person cage started to ascend higher and higher. When the basket got even with the catwalk, it carefully edged closer to the railing of the lighthouse.

It was during this careful maneuvering, James' anxiety over this crazy wedding was overwhelming. *I've got to stop this whole thing before they actually get married.*

James glanced over at Maggie, and he especially hated her. He wanted to strike out at her and just couldn't help throwing a zinger at her. He said sarcastically, "Are you planning a Karate Demonstration at the wedding, for entertainment? It's a long way down the spiral staircase if you goof up again."

Maggie couldn't believe he had the nerve to say that. "You better be careful yourself. It's a long, way down over the outside of the lighthouse, too."

In one smooth stroke, she reached down and grabbed one of his famous alligator shoes, right off his foot. Before James knew what happened, Maggie flung it right over the side of the basket.

As they both watched it plunge into the crashing waves below. Maggie said casually, "Wow, that certainly is a long way down."

James could not believe what she had just done. He was more than stunned. *That was unthinkable. I mean what kind of person does something like that? Are there No Limits to how far this woman will go?*

While he was reacting to this, the basket stopped, and his brother was standing there on the other side of the railing, just beaming. James thought he had never seen Michael look like this before.

James stepped out of the basket and climbed onto the lighthouse. It had gone very smoothly, with the exception of the loss of one alligator shoe. The gathering crowd of well-wishers below cheered.

Chapter 49

Kate hugged Maggie with all the excitement of a *real* bride. *How could this be?* wondered Maggie. *Her eyes are shining with happiness.*

"Is that the wedding gown?" Kate asked, as she carefully took the dress from Maggie. Kate reverently hugged it to her tightly, with love.

"Can you believe how blessed we are to have it? This was made for Michael's Grandmother during the second world war," marveled Kate.

"Whoa, how did it end up in the Chambers' storage unit?" asked Maggie. "I'll bet that's a story on its own."

"I'll tell you later, but during the war, many things were rationed. The silk and nylon material were only used for the troops."

Maggie thought about that and agreed, "Yes, I remember hearing about ladies drawing a seam on the back of their legs to look like nylons."

Kate continued, with such excitement, that she could hardly contain herself. "This dress was made from her husband's silk parachute that saved his life. He sent it home while he was recovering in a hospital, in Europe."

"Really?" Maggie said calmly, as she wracked her brains for some idea to put a stop to this nonsense. She just kept repeating various things to prompt herself to act, *I've got to stop this stupid wedding. Think of something, Maggie, Come On. I'm running out of time.* But she couldn't think of anything.

Kate was happily continuing with this charming story. "When he got back to the states, she got married in this dress," exclaimed Kate. "Many brides used this very same dress to get married. The very last bride to use it was Michael's mother."

At that very same moment, James promised himself that he would stop this whole wedding *thing* for Michael before it actually happened. *Of course, this will be 'for his own good' and 'he will thank me later' for stopping him from making the worst mistake of his life. I mean, what was he thinking?*

If there were any vows taken tonight, it would be James desperately pledging, "Michael is not getting married to anyone tonight."

He took Michael aside, "Hey, what's the hurry? You just met this girl. Don't you think you're rushing things here?"

Michael was just beaming. "James, I don't think I can pass up this opportunity to marry the Love of my Life," Michael explained as best as he could, but he didn't understand his feelings either.

"I've never felt anything like this. My attraction for her is so strong that I do not think I can live without Kate. I truly need her. I want her so badly I don't want to spend one hour without her."

James was flabbergasted that his brother had gone so far off the deep end over this girl. He tried again, "Please tell me you've known Kate before you drove down to Sea Crest. And please tell me this isn't the lady that bought our storage units."

"No, I didn't know Kate before; I only spoke to her on the phone regarding the storage units. Granted, I didn't think much of her at that time, but the afternoon I met with her at the beach, everything changed."

James thought he had an opening, "Well, what happened to you?" He would try a logical chain of events, "Think very carefully, Michael. Did she give you anything to eat or drink that could have drugs in it?"

"No. For heaven's sake, I was eating a hot dog with French fries and a coke. She did not give me anything to eat or drink. I just watched her giving the girls a surfing lesson, and I was completely and utterly taken with her."

All right, thought James. *That indeed was not working. Michael was almost drooling just thinking about it.* He simply had to get through to him somehow, "Okay, forget about that."

His frustration and bad temper surfaced as he practically yelled, "Did she practice voodoo on you or something? I don't understand."

Michael said in a solemn voice, "I don't understand everything yet, but I know I want to spend the rest of my life with Kate. I truly love her. There are many things that I will share with you tomorrow, that will help you understand. Right now, I need to get married. I'm at my breaking point, and I need to be with her more than I need the air to breathe. I can only hope that someday you'll meet someone and feel even half of what I feel for Kate."

As James thought about it, he conceded at last. *There was much truth in what Michael had said. Of course, I couldn't understand. I have never had anyone who had drawn such deep emotions and feelings from me. I seem to always stay above it all.*

"Okay Michael," he said. "I trust you, and I'll always be on your side. If she returns even half of what you're feeling for her, you are a very lucky guy. I'll be honored to stand up to be your Best Man."

A sudden realization dawned on him that maybe his protective layer of material things was part of it. As James looked down at his feet, with his one shoeless foot, he remembered, *there is one person who did not care one iota about my feelings or my fashion.*

He usually didn't have to deal with people like FBI Special Agent Maggie O'Hara. He was careful not to let anyone get close enough to hurt him.

Well, this broad got plenty close last night. And while I'm on the subject;the nerve of her actually grabbing off my shoe and flinging it over the side of the basket and into the sea. Really, what kind of a person does that? It just showed what a wild, uncouth person she is. I just can't tolerate her."

James finished off his mental tirade with, *let me tell you, No one on the face of the earth would ever marry her.*

At that moment, Chaplin O'Reilly came to the front of the room and set up a table with the license and papers. They needed to be signed by the witnesses after the ceremony.

He had Michael stand in front of him, with James at his side. The chaplain waved his hand to come forward, and Maggie stepped forward looking absolutely, serene. Michael had never even met her before, but he was glad Kate had her best friend there to stand up with her.

James was surprised that she could look so nice. *It must have taken an army of disaster workers to salvage that wreckage.*

It made him smile just to think about it.

Maggie, trying her failed karate moves on the poor victims that were sent to make her presentable. They have to manage all that flying red hair, all over the place, to say nothing of that mouth. How would they ever get her to stop talking long enough to ...what? He'd better stop thinking about this and pay attention to the bride.

Kate followed Maggie in a billowing white silk gown. It was extremely elegant in its simplicity and classic style. It looked like the dress had been made especially for her. She was beautiful as she smiled at Michael.

Both Maggie and James wondered if anyone would ever look at them that same way. The love was so apparent that it was hard to deny it was real.

The Chaplain read a Biblical passage from I Corinthians 13, which explained Love and ended with, *'And now Abide faith, hope, love, these three; but the greatest of these is love.'*

He did not ask if there were any objections. No doubt, the Chaplain could not imagine anyone objecting to this couple. They recited their vows, which they'd had lots of time to write. They could not have been more tender or loving. There were tears all around.

The Chaplain pronounced them, Man and Wife. He followed with a heartfelt: "You may now kiss your bride."

They smiled at each other and performed their now famous, 'Kissing Couple.'

They all clapped and congratulated them with Best Wishes. It seemed like everyone was hugging and kissing them both.

When things settled down for a minute, Michael asked, "James and Maggie, could you both to come back tomorrow morning after the tide goes out and the walkway opens up?"

"Sure," answered Maggie, "I'll make sure Connor opens the Irish padlock on the lighthouse door and lets us in."

Michael said, "Thanks, it's crucial that we share some information with you. Please ask Grace to come also, since she's a historical expert. She might have some additional information that would help us all."

"Yes, we'll be back. In fact," offered James, who seemed in a much better mood, "Maggie and I could just stay over."

"Why that's a splendid idea," Maggie joined in with delight. "I also think this is the very best place to view the fireworks this evening. I also understand they have ordered pizza. The helicopter will bring it when it returns for the Chaplain. Oh, James, that's a terrific plan."

Michael and Kate were objecting to anything along those lines. "Sorry, but you two will NOT be staying up here," declared Michael in a thunderous voice.

Kate threatened, "If I have to order the Helicopter Team to make sure you re-board the Heli-basket when it arrives, I will."

"Well, I guess we know, when we're not welcome." the Chaplain added with a laugh.

A short time later, the helicopter with the Heli-basket returned. Before they got into the basket, the crew onboard handed them the large pizza with a blanket wrapped around it to keep it warm. They also brought a hamper filled with a few other goodies that Kate's mom had thrown together. It included a homemade blueberry pie, baked that day for the Sea Crest Festival.

The bride and groom said their goodbyes, with hugs all around.

Maggie, James and the Chaplain boarded the Heli-Basket and returned to the beach.

Chapter 50

When they got on land again, it was dark, and the fireworks were ready to start. James looked very subdued as he said, "Well, I haven't seen a fireworks display in years. I think I'll stick around for the show."

"I know you are probably used to extravagant fireworks displays in New York City. I watch them on television sometimes if I'm not working."

"Yes, but I rarely get to see a nice display like this."

"Oh, I wouldn't miss this for the world. I understand James asked for the entire 50,000 fireworks to be displayed tonight. They were intended to be spread out over the weekend."

"I wonder if Sea Crest was able to get any of the pattern shaped fireworks for the Festival. It would be so nice to have some of those red stars arranged in the form of hearts. I mean especially for Kate and Michael," added Maggie.

The fireworks started, and they were spectacular.

"We could sit here on this pizza blanket if you want to," said Maggie. "The best seats will be along the hill, but we don't have time to get up there," she meant at the Chambers' beach house, but for some reason, she did not want to say it. There had been many hints, and mysterious coincidences lately and she could not trust what anything meant.

As they sat down and got settled, she looked over at James. "You know James; I don't have the slightest idea why I threw your shoe over the side. I'm usually very calm and great under fire. I can handle anything."

James agreed sarcastically, "Oh yeah, I can see that." He laughed as he said, "I saw that right away, while you were yelling, *'You're our Prime Suspect.'* and again when you threatened me with, *'We have special torture that the regular police don't use.'"*

Maggie began to laugh as she said, "Well, you just made me mad. I thought everyone was giving you special treatment because of how you looked. That's not fair."

"What's that supposed to mean?" asked James. Now he was sure Maggie meant that he was incredibly handsome. He wanted to actually, hear her admit it.

"You looked like a rich snob. I don't like people who think they're better than what they consider, *the common man.*"

Since that wasn't a battle, he felt like fighting right now, he just added, "Oh, sorry, I didn't mean to come across like that."

They continued to watch the fireworks, saying the occasional "Ah," and "Look at that."

"That's my favorite," Maggie declared as she unconsciously touched his arm lightly. She felt an instant magnetism drift through her hand, and she quickly pulled it back.

What on earth was that, she wondered.

It was enjoyable to the end.

"Well," said James, "now that these fireworks are over, I guess I'll go back to the station and pick up my car."

"I hope you're not referring to the Bentley that was outside the Sea Crest Police Station," said Maggie quietly.

"What if I was? Is that a problem?" said James nervously.

"Not if you know a good mechanic."

James bolted up and stammered, "Maggie, What Do You Mean?"

"Well, I thought you were an arrogant jerk, who needed to be taught a lesson."

"All right, that's enough. What did you do?"

"Well, I asked the FBI guys to check it out for drugs, etc. you know, anything suspicious."

"Well, did they find anything?"

"No, but it's in a thousand pieces. They're calling in outside help for anyone who knows how to put a Bentley back together."

"You better be kidding me. Just who do you think you are?"

"Boy, you certainly need to lighten up," laughed Maggie. "Do you truly think I'd let them take your car apart?"

"What?" said a semi-relieved James.

"I mean if they didn't know how to put it back together?" explained Maggie. "It may take a couple of weeks, but I'm sure it will run okay when they're done. You can carry the big box of leftover parts back to the dealership. I hear they're worth plenty."

"Are you crazy?"

"Come on James; I'm just kidding."

"Well, you're coming with me to see if my Bentley is at the Police Station or not."

"I have lots to do tonight. If you're afraid to be out after dark, you have a problem."

"I'm going to call Joe right now and get some answers."

"Okay, I'll see you tomorrow morning at the lighthouse. By the way, James, if you need a place to stay tonight, the Sea Crest Inn is pleasant. Oh, that's right, you already know all about it." Maggie laughed as she got into her car.

James quickly darted around to the passenger side and yanked the door open. He quickly jumped into the front seat of her car. "Take me to the Police Station, right now," he demanded as the door slammed shut.

"Hey, what do you think this is, a Taxi Service? Oh, all right, I'll take you, just because I feel sorry for you," Maggie said, as she triumphantly turned the ignition switch.

James could not believe this treatment. "What is it with you people?" he fumed as she sped off.

A few minutes later, they arrived at the Sea Crest Police Station. There was the lone Bentley, sticking out like a sore thumb.

James was ready to wring her neck as she casually said, "Oh, I guess they didn't start on it yet."

James replied, "That's a good thing for you, lady. You're something else."

Maggie answered as if it was a compliment, "Yeah, I know. By the way, out of the goodness of my heart, I will have a couple of pairs of shoes for you to try on tomorrow morning. It'd be hard climbing all those stairs in only one shoe."

James just shook his head, as he got in his grandmother's Bentley and drove towards the Sea Crest Inn. James knew he had never seen the likes of her before.

"Man, that totally, untamed red hair is flying, every-which-way, all around her face and swishing freely, about her shoulders. Doesn't she know she's supposed to use some kind of clips or something? Grown women just do not look Wild, like that. She's an FBI Special Agent, for heaven's sake. Don't they have rules for the likes of her?"

James drove on toward the Sea Crest Inn. His mind wandered once more as he remembered how Maggie looked at the wedding.

Those innocent looking eyes are the worst. Beware of those huge green eyes that peek out of her face, as if she could see right into your soul if you ever looked directly into them. That's right; make sure you never actually look into Maggie's eyes.

James turned into the Sea Crest Inn's parking lot. As he turned off the car, he thought, *Well, it's almost impossible not to look at her, that's ridiculous.*

He stepped out of the car and his shoeless foot hit the pavement.

Now, why did she have to go and fling my shoe over the side of the basket? She obviously has a screw loose.

James continued his mental assessment of her outrageous conduct: *However, the worst part was that mouth. You could not even think up the stuff that comes out of that mouth. She seems to have no limit of smart, irritating digs to throw at me.*

As James walked into the inn, he tried to remember even one other person on the face of the whole earth, who treated him like this. She not only didn't want anything from him, but she was also so unimpressed with his *dress for success* shoe, that she threw it 117 feet down into the ocean. He was shocked to realize that he was smiling as he strolled into the inn.

Chapter 51

The next morning as James was walking over the sand towards the lighthouse, Maggie called out to him, "James, my dad has something for you."

Her father, Sean O'Hara, walked out to meet him. He was getting ready to go fishing, and he had brought an extra pair of shoes for James. As he approached James, he smiled, held out his shoes, looked him straight in the eye as he said, "Here take mine." James felt something so strangely familiar that it jolted him. James had no intentions, of accepting the shoes, but he took them and said, "Thanks." as he shook his hand. Maggie's dad made him feel safe and protected. James couldn't help but sense, *He must be a very kind man. Does he affect everyone this way?*

"Thanks, I appreciate this," said James.

However, he was thinking, *Boy, he's nothing like his daughter.*

Grace showed up and was very excited to be included. "I've also brought something of interest to share with all of you when you're done."

Maggie had brought donuts and a tray of fruit to share at the top of the lighthouse. Kate's mom brought out a thermos plus a carafe of coffee for them to take up. The three of them entered the door as Connor took off the Irish padlock. They all cheered.

They put the food and coffee in the dumbwaiter and sent it up to the top. They all yelled, "Here we come, ready or not," as they headed up the spiral staircase.

Everyone congratulated the newlywed couple with hugs and kisses. Michael and Kate never looked happier. It was refreshing to experience such joy.

"Kate, your mom sent up loads of coffee, and we have lots to eat, so everyone, please help yourself," said Maggie.

 After a few minutes, when they were all settled and happily indulging on brunch, Michael said, "I suppose you're all wondering why we asked each of you to join us this morning. I mean, after all, what could be so important, that it could not even wait twenty-

four hours after our wedding to share it with you? Well, Kate and I had quite a bit of time to talk and what we discovered will blow your minds."

Kate started, "As you may or may not know Michael and I couldn't stand each other a few days ago."

That brought a big laugh from everyone. Maggie added, "That's an understatement. If I remember, you asked me to run a check on this guy."

James said, "Michael called you a nightmare of a lady, Kate."

Michael stepped in, "All right, we admit we brought out the worst in each other. Our feelings grew from each of us protecting some precious things purchased at the storage auction. We each misjudged the motives of the other, and consequently, we didn't trust or like each other."

Kate added, "Now please try not to interrupt, and we'll try to explain. I think Grace might have recognized some things earlier, that we were all missing."

"Thank you," Michael said as he kissed Kate. "First of all, James, would you please come to stand by this little, shuttered window?"

"Why, does it have a trap door on the floor?" he asked as he joined his brother.

"Of course not, but you're going to see something just as shocking."

Michael slid the little shutter into the pocket on the side, to reveal the beautiful, stained glass panel. The beveled glass had the etching of the purple and lavender flower. "James, if you know what that flower is the emblem of, please don't say it."

James nodded, yes, as he wondered, *why did Michael ask me that? Of course, I know, it is the Scottish Thistle.*

"Maggie, you're next."

"Wow, that's truly beautiful. Kate did you know that was here?" asked Maggie.

"Do you know anything particular about it, Maggie?" asked Michael.

"Well, I've seen it before, and I like it, but I don't know what the name of it is. I'm surprised that it's in this little window and we never saw it."

"Grace, please don't say it yet," smiled Michael.

"All right, James, come to this window," Michael directed, as he opened the shutter pocket to reveal the etched with inlaid cut glass. It was Scottish Heather in shades of pinks and violet. "Do you know what it is and what it means? If so, don't say it."

James again nodded, yes, and wondered, *what is the 'good luck, sprig of heather' doing in this window?*

"Okay Maggie, step on over and look." Her face lit up as she saw the beautiful window. "Do you know what this stands for?"

She shook her head 'No.'

"These are all connected. The windows mean something."

"Maggie, are you Scottish?" Michael asked softly.

"Of course not, I'm Irish, what do you think? Did you ever hear about anyone name O'Hara that was not Irish and proud of it? While we're at it, Kate is Irish too. Her last name was Walsh until last night. We are cousins, you know. We've been here for at least three generations and maybe more."

"Well, I understand from Kate, that Grace is the town historian. I also know that she's trying to research your Sea Crest historical roots," explained Michael.

"Now Grace, can you tell us what these two windows mean?"

"Of course, they are both emblems of Scotland," she answered. "The Thistle is the Floral Emblem; the Sprig of Heather is for Good Luck."

"Wonderful. Now James, do you agree with Grace's answer and how would you know this?" asked Michael.

"You are well aware, they're Scottish, and we recognize Scottish things from when we were babies because we're Scottish through and through."

"Thank you for that excellent answer. Now could you please step over to the final two windows, I'd like to show you?" asked Michael. "Now, please tell me what you think."

"Well, this one is ... Wow, that looks like our plaid, Scottish Tartan. Michael, what on earth is that doing here?" James was at a complete loss.

Michael motioned him over to the last window and pushed the shutter into the pocket. The beveled cut glass revealed the Chambers', family crest. "Does that look familiar?" asked Michael.

"It's our family crest. I can't believe it. How did it get here? What does this mean?" asked James.

"What family crest is it?" asked Michael, with a smile.

"It's our mother's, family crest. It's the Chambers. Wait! You mean our grandparents, that have the beach house here, had something to do with this lighthouse. This is unbelievable," James almost shouted. "If Sea Crest meant so much to them. Why weren't we ever told about this?"

Michael continued, "I know it's a shock. I slipped into this lighthouse after I saw Kate and Connor leave. I've worked on so many lighthouses, throughout the world, that I couldn't pass it up."

Michael added, "James, the strangest thing happened when I looked out this window. I swear I could remember our mother holding me up to this window to look out. I thought I was about the age of a toddler. James, I could feel her love, at that moment. I swear it was like I've been up here before."

Maggie's quietness was uncharacteristic. She was near tears as she felt the pieces fall together. *These two men are 'The Chambers.'*

Wow, now everything was starting to make sense. *No wonder they wanted the Chambers' storage unit. No wonder they were trying to buy the contents back, and money was no object.*

This explained the Parachute Wedding Gown. It was their grandmother's dress. The last bride to wear it was their mother. Now Kate had worn it at her son's wedding. Wow.

Maggie struggled to speak, "We just didn't know."

"If Michael and I hadn't been locked in this lighthouse and had a chance to talk, we never would have figured it out," said Kate. "And I told Michael about Sir Michael Chambers' Journal; he'd like to know if that might be his great, great grandfather."

"Yes," said Grace, "I believe it is. I also have some further information that is specifically meant for both of you gentlemen." She took out a letter that she had brought with her and handed it to them. "This was in the storage units. I think it explains a whole lot about what your grandmother did and why she did it."

"I think it's okay to let the girls hear it also," said Michael. "What do you think James?"

"Of course, it's perfectly all right. We owe so much to you all. We had no idea about any of this."

"Well, that's good because most of it's about you, James," said Grace.

Chapter 52

James opened the envelope up, which held their grandmother's letter and read aloud:

"Dear Grandsons: James and Michael,"

"I'm going to tell you both about something that happened over two decades ago. It involves both of you. However, I don't think Michael will remember much about it, (You were much too young at the time), but it regards the last time you came to visit your grandfather and me here at the Sea Crest."

James got a very uneasy feeling as he tried to hold the papers still. Maybe he should not continue reading this. He looked at Michael who was alarmed at James reaction to the story that happened on this visit.

"James, do you remember this visit? I don't remember ever being here before, at all," said Michael.

Grace spoke up softly and told James, "It's OK. You need to read it, and you will feel much better about everything. I promise."

Michael said, "Would you like me to read it?"

James nodded, "Yes," and braced himself for the worst.

Michael picked up the pages and continued with his grandmother's letter.

"This is what I was able to piece together from your grandfather, both of you boys, your father and a wonderful man who we didn't even know. I believe you're both old enough now to understand how important his 'act of kindness,' was to our family.

Your grandfather and I were heartbroken after the death of your mother. We could not get over the loss we both felt. We were devastated at losing our only daughter. Your grandfather was not in good health himself. We thought that maybe, we would all recover better if your dad could bring you both to Sea Crest, for a two-week visit, that summer. All of us might be able to heal if we helped each other.

Your father was agreeable and thought it might work. He also wanted to be able to share some quality time with you boys away from all the memories of your mother's death.

One of your dad's suggestions was to assist with James' first open water scuba dive. Both of you boys were excellent in the water. James was taking scuba diving lessons, and he had completed the certification & turned old enough to do open water dives with your dad to accompany you since he was also certified. We were all looking forward to relaxing with a change of scenery for a couple of weeks.

The day you arrived was beautiful, and you seemed happy to settle in. After lunch, you decided to take the boat out and dive just off the reef, not far from the lighthouse.

Your dad and James decided to check out the site of the shipwrecked Sea Crest Schooner. Michael and your grandfather remained in the boat. Your father and James had planned to stay down below for 15 minutes and then resurface.

While they were diving at the wreck, a violent storm suddenly approached. Your dad and James had not resurfaced as planned and had been down for half an hour. Michael and your grandfather were very alarmed by this, especially because of the impending storm.

They decided to radio an urgent SOS from the boat. The coast guard was already in the process of rescuing another party in the opposite direction, south of the Sea Crest Lighthouse. However, that same afternoon, an off-duty Coast Guard Rescuer, was spending the afternoon fishing offshore. He also saw the weather worsening and was just about ready to head back to shore, when he heard the distress call come over his radio. The troubled vessel had luckily used their radio to call for help, which enabled everyone to hear the distress signal. That is what saved their lives that day.

The boat in trouble was in the vicinity, of the fishing boat. The off-duty man turned his boat around immediately and headed for my husband's boat.

He soon saw their boat, with Michael, who was approximately seven years old at the time and his granddad. They appeared to be the only ones aboard. Michael was waving his arms and yelling that his dad and brother were diving near the shipwreck down below.

He was scared and wanted them to come up so they could get away from the storm, but they did not know what to do. Your grandfather said that they had been down there approximately 30 minutes and they had planned to resurface after 15 minutes. He was also very shaken.

The Coast Guard man asked them, "do you have any additional tanks?"

Michael told him, "yes, we have two, and both are filled with air." His dad and James were also using two of them below the surface.

The man quickly put on a wetsuit and tank. He also grabbed the other full tank as he fell backward over the side. The man was no stranger to this particular wreck site. This was one of the Coast Guard's favorite spots for scuba training exercises.

He descended as fast as he safely could. As the sunken ship came into view, he saw, what he described, as a heart-breaking sight. The young boy, James, (about twelve years old), had gotten his line cut on the sharp metal in and around the wreckage. His dad was sharing his oxygen from his tank with him. The boy, James, appeared frozen with fear and was too scared to move. This had gone on for at least 15 minutes. It was evident that the dad was not going to leave him.

The Coast Guard Rescuer quickly approached the pair and gave the frightened boy a long fresh breath from one of the new tanks. He then helped him pull on the oxygen mask. Next, he secured the new tank on the boys' back. He made sure the boy was breathing OK before he turned to the dad and gave him his full tank. He took the dad's tank and signaled them to ascend slowly to the boat above. The rescuer then took their near empty tank and ascended slowly, controlling his air as he had learned in the Coast Guard training and practiced many times over the years.

When the man surfaced, they learned that his name was Sean O'Hara. He had served and trained Search and Rescue Teams, with the Coast Guard for many years."

"Hey. That's my dad." Maggie called out, in astonishment.

"Your dad? The one that just gave me these shoes?" asked James. "No way. I wonder if that is why I had such a strong feeling, this morning. It was strange, but I suddenly felt so 'safe,' and I remember, I thought he must be such a kind man, not like his daughter."

Everyone chuckled at that and Maggie said, "Well, Thanks a lot."

"I just call them as I see them," said James as he shook his head in confusion and continued, "but really, I had no idea why I even thought that."

Michael kept reading; *"This rescue was what he did, a normal part of his life. He often put his life at risk to save the 'summer people,' who didn't know the Sea Crest shoreline and hazards under the sea.*

Our family returned safely home that day, due to the extraordinary skill and generosity of this complete stranger, who had saved your dad and James' lives.

Sean O'Hara would accept no reward, no compensation and no headlines telling of his heroism. He was embarrassed at the very mention of any attention. He was just a very good man, doing a very courageous act of kindness because that was who he was."

"Wow," James whispered as he tried to control a shudder. He tried to explain, the shaky tremor of doom that had just filled his body. "This whole letter from our grandmother is bringing up a very traumatic time in my life. I still wake up from nightmares to this day. I'm usually stranded, helplessly, under the water. I'm frequently gasping for air," James said sadly.

He looked hopefully at Maggie as he said, "I'm grateful to your father, Maggie, for saving my life and my dad's life. That never happens in my dreams."

Michael put in, "I don't remember about the rescue by your father, Maggie, but I sincerely want to thank him."

"I'm sure he'd like that," said Maggie quietly. It dawned on her that these two brothers had never talked about this. She glanced over at James with concern, and recognized the lonely burden he'd carried.

Michael read on; *"Later that summer, Maggie O'Hara, and Kate Walsh, knocked on the front door of the summer house to sell Girl Scout cookies."*

"Remember when we went to the Chambers' mansion?" Maggie asked Kate.

"I sure do," answered Kate. "That was the highlight of our whole summer."

"Well if you're good," said Michael as he kissed her. "I might take you there again. How would you like that?"

Maggie suddenly remembered that Joe had given her the last will of their grandmother stated, she had left the beach house to her. She also remembered that "The Family" was contesting it. When Kate went missing, she stopped thinking about everything except how to get her safely home.

Michael continued with the letter; *"When I realized who they were, I knew that maybe we couldn't pay back Sean O'Hara, but I'd keep my eyes and ears open for some way to thank his only daughter, Maggie."*

Maggie looked at James teasingly and pointed out that, "At least somebody in your family appreciated me."

Everyone laughed, and Michael continued; *"Maggie's dad served in the Coast Guard along with Kate's dad. I soon learned that I couldn't keep my eyes and ears on one, without noticing what terrific people they 'each' were. I grew very proud of both of these inspiring girls as they continued to grow up. I subscribed to the Sea Crest Newspaper and kept up on all the local news."*

"All right. OK." Kate and Maggie were high-fiving each other and acted as if they were really stuck-up and arrogant. "Can you believe it? She was checking up on us," said Kate.

"I see she knows class when she sees it," said Maggie, "unlike some of her own family." That shot was directed at, Mr. Alligator Shoes. Oh, she forgot, he lost one of them.

Michael continued with the letter; *"I have a few friends that I keep in touch with. They tell me about numerous, anonymous acts of kindness that have been happening to people along the Sea Crest Coast. They are unexplainable, and they seem to materialize from out of nowhere. It is all very mysterious. These acts of kindness always make a huge positive impact on the recipient's lives. No one can figure out who's doing it."*

Kate, Maggie, and Grace almost fell out of their chairs. They looked at each other in amazement. Grace said, very innocently, "Gee, I wonder what that's all about?"

"Good Heavens, why is she bringing it up in this letter?" asked Maggie.

"Go ahead and read on, Michael," said Kate. "This is really something."

Michael continued eagerly; *"Well, it makes me smile because I know who's doing it."*

"What? How on earth would she know," said James? He looked at the women and asked, "Do you even know what she's talking about?"

No one answered his question, as Maggie, Kate, and Grace sat quietly and avoided his eyes. They wished the floor would open up, so they could disappear.

"Come on Maggie; I know that look. What's going on here?" said James. He was enjoying the focus turning to someone else, and Maggie was his first choice.

"I don't know what you're talking about." she defended herself.

Michael laughed and continued reading his grandmother's letter; *"The apple doesn't fall far from the tree. I have helped them whenever I could. I know everything they do is for someone else. Take the water safety lessons for example. Each of those girls knows how to swim like a fish. The water safety is to stop these unnecessary drownings. Put an end to them, finally. They have each experienced the tragedy of watching too much senseless sorrow. Every project Maggie and Kate start is a selfless, worthwhile cause."*

"Ah Ha! I knew it! You guys are guilty as charged." James was ecstatic. He jumped to his feet, as he pointed his finger at Maggie, and said, "Thought you could keep a secret from our grandma. Well, think again, Sweetie."

Now it was James' turn to wish the floor would open up and he could disappear. He had just reacted on such an emotionally charged level, specifically to Maggie, that it was astonishing to everyone. This was totally out of character for him, and his face was turning a bright red color, as he sat back down.

"James. If you're through celebrating how 'selfless and wonderful' they are, I'll continue." Michael said. He had never seen his brother act anything remotely like this.

James looked as surprised as the rest of them, as he thought, *what just happened to me? Maybe it's all the shocks I've had in the last couple of days. Also, it must have traumatized me, revisiting the scuba dive that scared me so badly. However, I am positive; it has everything to do with having to be around Maggie so much. She's had a terrible effect on my nerves.*

"Sorry, Michael, go ahead with the letter," said a contrite James.

"OK," Michael charged forward again, as he read; *"I've regularly supported them behind the scenes, sending anonymous donations to help them out. I have picked up the phone and swayed as much power as I can wield for them. I've also called in many favors, over the years, on their behalf.*

If you ever do go back to Sea Crest, you ought to look them up. You would both be absolutely amazed by them."

"That's the final straw. What on earth, is Grandma talking about now? I told her repeatedly that I'd never go back to Sea

Crest." yelled James. *Why did she write that in her letter? What is going on?*

"And yet, here we both are, in Sea Crest. Can you believe it?" asked Michael, happily. Then he added the final point, "Not only have we met the girls, but we also are amazed by them, and I fell in love with Kate and married her." *Now it's your turn*, he felt like saying, but he didn't dare.

The ladies all agreed, stating how wonderful and yet ironic, it all was.

Michael finally said, "We're almost finished here. Next, she says; *"That brings me to the end of this important letter. Maggie has some big projects in the works. They are not to benefit herself but to work with the FBI and Coast Guard to help the Sea Crest Community and mainly support work on the Sea Crest Lighthouse and future Museum. She has been assessing possible locations necessary to work this multi-project endeavor. She also needs to conduct surveillance for the FBI and Coast Guard to stop the drug trade along this stretch of coast. Her proposals include feasibility studies to show how this can work.*

One property would be ideal in every way, and it has remained unused for many summers now. You have probably guessed by now that she has shown her greatest interest in and has sent me offers to see if she could lease or buy the Chambers' beach house. It is time for her to go forward with this project.

I need you both to know that I am deeply beholden to Sean O'Hara. I am also very impressed with how My Dear Sweet Maggie has grown up. I would like to be half the woman she's turning out to be, and I would love to honorably pay back her father for saving the lives of my loved ones.

That is why I am leaving Maggie O'Hara, the Chambers' beach house, overlooking the Sea Crest Lighthouse, in my will. I hope you will agree and I know your mother would be very proud to know that the family that saved her son, James, and her husband, will be repaid, in some small way."

"With Much Love,
Grandmother Chambers"

Chapter 53

Kate gave an ecstatic scream, "Maggie, this is terrific!" She jumped up and hugged her.

Maggie in-turn was mumbling something, "So that's why she left it to me. I could not understand why she would do that. I didn't think I'd even met her before."

"What do you mean? You sound like you already knew that she left the beach house to you," said Kate.

"Joe showed that part of the will to me, but I knew it must have been a mistake," said Maggie.

"Well, now you know it wasn't a mistake. She meant to leave it to you." cried Grace enthusiastically.

"No, not yet," said Maggie, as she looked at James and Michael. "I understand that the family is contesting the will. They had no idea that their grandmother was going to do this and they certainly didn't know 'why' she would."

"James, what is she talking about?" asked Michael. "Did you know about this?"

"Of course, I knew about it. That is what I was trying to call you about for the past few days. I needed to tell you that we were contesting that part of the will, immediately."

"Well, this is the first that I've heard anything about the will," said Michael.

"I completely understand why both of you would be confused and want to contest such a shocking action. I did not mention anything because I wanted to give all of us a chance to come to terms with their grandmother's will. Let the dust settle and see if it was the right decision for both the family and for me," said Maggie.

"What, pray tell, is that supposed to mean?" asked James.

"I'm sure this will come as a real shock to you, James, but I'm not in the habit of stepping on other people to get ahead."

"I do hope you realize that just because a person can 'legally' do something, does not mean it is the 'right' thing for that person to do.

In this case, I would have to know if it was ethically and morally, the fair thing to do. That's why I did not say anything. I did not have any facts to show 'why' your grandmother left anything to me. Until I did, I certainly would not go forward. It's just not right."

"Gee, Maggie," said Kate. "I can't believe you didn't tell us."

"Well, if I decided to refuse the beach house, out of respect for the families wishes, I didn't think it would be fair to the family, to talk about it to anyone. Life in these circumstances is hard enough, without everyone having an opinion and judging the decisions that were made during a time of great personal loss."

These words were met with dead silence.

"Anyway, you don't have to make a decision today," Maggie said.

"Could you please explain exactly what you mean?" asked James.

"I think you two brothers should talk over the next few weeks, and come to an agreement, as to what you'd like to happen with the Chambers' beach house," Maggie said.

"But our attorney is drawing up the papers to contest that part of the will, even as we speak," replied James.

"That's not necessary. I'll have Joe draw up an affidavit that I'll sign, which states that I'll not take ownership of your grandmother's beach house until you make that decision and that you both wholeheartedly agree with it," said Maggie.

"Why on earth would you do that?" asked James, as if he couldn't believe it.

"I already told you. However, I have been under the impression that your family was not going to live there even in the summers anymore, for some unknown reason. I also have an offer on the table for your grandmother, or in this case, the family, to lease or buy that same property if you both decide that is what you want to do."

"Man, I don't understand you, Maggie," said James.

"Well, it's very simple. It's still your beach house. If in fact, you would prefer to leave it empty, you certainly can. Maybe you would like to spend summers here now, James. We'd all love that." she joked sarcastically, as they all laughed.

"Maybe Michael would like to live there with Kate," she offered with a warm smile. "I hear he plans to handle the repairs of the lighthouse."

"If you choose to leave it empty, I'd like to lease it and see if we could save a few lives and make some positive changes in the drug smuggling business, in the Sea Crest Coastal area."

"I'm thrilled to pieces that your grandmother knows about Kate. I am sure she's looking down, smiling to see the love that Michael shares with her. She would be so pleased by this."

"So, take some time and decide what you'd like to do," said Maggie, as she got up and started to clear away the brunch things. She loaded up the dumbwaiter for its return trip down to ground level.

James came alongside her and said very quietly, "Yah know, Maggie, you never cease to amaze me."

Maggie smiled up at him with a quiet little laugh, as she arrogantly replied, "I'm sure I don't know what you mean."

"One minute you're making me so mad, I can't see straight," he said. "The next minute you're about the nicest lady, I've ever had the pleasure of meeting." He could not help but smile, as he softly divulged, "You've got me on a roller coaster."

Maggie just stared at him. She turned and smiled secretly to herself as she stepped to the head of the spiral staircase. *Just hold on, James,* she thought. *You ain't seen nothing yet.*

Thanks for reading! If you enjoyed this book, I'd be very grateful if you'd post a short review on Amazon or Goodreads. Your support really does make a difference and I read all the reviews personally.

Thanks again for your support!

Carolyn

Keep reading for an excerpt from *The Lightkeeper's Secret*, the second book in The Sea Crest Lighthouse Series.

By Carolyn Court

Joe thought with delight, *Oh James and Maggie... Tsk, Tsk. That line in the sand, between Love and Hate, is so blurry, isn't it?*

I've seen first-hand the passion with which you have provoked each other. However, when Kate and Michael were finally discovered, unharmed, and the reason for the anger and outrage, was removed, all that pent-up energy crashed together, and the objects helplessly collided. At this point, total indifference is hard to achieve. It's the simple, law of attraction vs. repulsion or something like that.

Her clicking heels slowed and came to rest outside her attorney's office. She hesitated to enter, as she contemplated; *What is the worst thing that can happen?*

She took a deep breath and stepped inside, while the alarming answer was sounding in her head, *Well, my whole life may change forever.*

Today is the day I will finally find out what the Chambers' brothers have decided. Will I inherit the Sea Crest Beach House that had been the summer home of their grandparents for many years according to their grandmother's wishes?

James placed a call to Jeffrey Williams, his attorney in New York.

"Hi Jeff, I need a favor. I'm down here at Sea Crest, and I need you to look into something for me. Time is critical on this. Do we have any detectives or investigators, who can drop everything else and do some research for me? It will be like a needle in a haystack, but I'll make it worth their while.

"What's this all about, James? Are you trying to find a reason to contest your grandmother's will again?"

"Of course not, however, someone abandoned a Great Dane dog, down here in Sea Crest and Maggie has taken it in."

"What? A Great Dane? Do you know how big those dogs are?"

"Yes, Jeff, I've met the dog, and it's heartwarming to see them together. The problem is that she's fallen in love with Misha, and she's afraid someone will return and take her away."

"Well, that sometimes happens if the people feel guilty and go back to retrieve the dog. Sometimes the dog was lost through an honest mistake or misunderstanding. Most often, I believe it is intentional, and the owners feel bad and try to find the dog again," replied Jeff.

"Well, I promised Maggie that I wouldn't let that happen."

"You did what? You're kidding! How are you going to do that?" asked Jeff.

"She had tears in her eyes. I couldn't stand it!" said a desperate James. "I had no choice."

Now the truth behind this strange promise was beginning to dawn on Jeff. "Listen, I'll get my best guy on it, but it's going to be hard to find the person who dropped the dog off and abandoned her."

"Well, I'm sure Joe Lawrence will do all he can from this end but don't involve Maggie. I said I wouldn't let anyone take Misha from her and that's a promise that WE are all going to make happen. I want her to have a legal document that guarantees that in writing. Of course, money is no object. I'll authorize whatever it takes to get this done. The sooner, the better, time is of the essence."

"Okay, James," said Jeff. His next question took James by surprise, "By the way, this Maggie isn't the same Maggie that's an FBI Special Agent; and the same Maggie that put you in jail a few weeks ago, is it?"

"Listen, Jeff," James paused, trying to come up with a logical explanation. He finally admitted as he blasted away, "Of course it's the same, Maggie! So, what if it is? It doesn't matter anyway. That was all a big mix-up when she put me in jail, and you know it."

Jeff laughed out-loud at this strange turn of events. "You've got to be kidding me. Well, now I've heard everything."

"Never mind! You, Jeffrey Williams, have not heard anything! Just make sure she can keep her precious dog, Okay?"

"Sure, I'll be in touch," said Jeff as they hung up. He shook his head, as he chuckled and exclaimed out loud, "Boy, I never saw that coming!"

Acknowledgements

~♥~

My special thanks and appreciation go to those who shared their expertise and time, to ensure the accuracy of this novel.

If errors exist in this book, they are my mistakes alone.

The characters and events in this story are completely fictional, and any resemblance to living persons or events is purely coincidental.

My husband, Paul, has been very, supportive and encouraged me to write this book. He has been great, each step of the way.

I would like to thank my son, Thomas Hickok Jr. for his total support, his generous spirit and his many examples of 'Anonymous Acts of Kindness.' His positive outlook is truly impressive.

My mother knew about the parachute wedding gowns during the war. However, she wore a navy-blue suit, and my dad wore his uniform for their wedding in 1945.

My daughter, Elaine who is a certified scuba diver, helped with some of the details of diving around the shipwreck. She also gave us plenty of time with her precious Great Dane, Misha. Thank you for those special memories.

My sister, Betty Lynn Courtright, has been a source of encouragement from the start. Her reading and advice were always helpful. She also had a terrific sense of humor. Thank you.

I would like to thank my sister, Joan Losier, for showing me around Pensacola, FL. She happily shared her time and knowledge as we visited the National Museum of Naval Aviation at NAS, (Naval Air Station). I was even able to see the US Navy HU-16 Albatross plane, on display there. I was also, privileged to visit the Pensacola Lighthouse with her.

My brothers John and Gary supported my writing and gave me feedback and insightful help on lighthouses in Michigan. Thanks for your enthusiasm and sense of humor.

The pie crust is my maternal grandmother's recipe. Her name was Lela Huff and she was wonderful! I don't think the recipe was ever written down, but as a child, I always watched her make it the same way. I like to think my love of baking came from her. Throughout my life, this is the only pie crust I've made.

Thanks, Grandma.

Joan Brown and Myrle Burnside, thank you for your encouragement, help and commitment to this book from the start. You are each valuable to me and a blessing in my life.

Sandy Wemmerus, you have been a valuable source of help from the beginning. I appreciate your insight and your humorous take on various parts of this book as you reviewed it. You are a joy to work with.

Jeanette Embrey and Sheila May Martin, thank you for your perseverance, positive attitude, and for sharing your talents to get this book into print. Your appreciation of the history that I've woven into the storyline, validated and encouraged my efforts to continue. Your senses of humor and your friendships are the best!

I admire and appreciate each of the fantastic women in my weekly Mah Jongg groups. These include in no particular order: Carla, Sandy, Roxanne, Joanie, Jeanette, Sandra, Sheila, Mary, Linda and Robin.

You have generous spirits and make my life better in many ways. Thank you.

References and Resources

National Mah Jongg League, Inc:
nationalmahjonggleague.org

The United States Lighthouse Society:
uslhs.org

Information on many of the subjects I have included in my book is on Wikipedia:

Lighthouse Traveling Library Box:
en.wikipedia.org/wiki/Traveling-library
michiganlights.com/lhlibrary.htm

Information on the State of Michigan, has 129 lighthouses and many Lighthouse Festivals
Michigan Lighthouse Festival:
michiganlighthousefestival.com
michiganlights.com/Keeperstools.htm

Great Michigan Resource Guide:
michiganlighthouseguide.com

Information on 'A Picture Worth Taking,' references: A SAILOR KISSES A COMPLETE STRANGER, A Nurse, in Times Square in New York City on V-J Day Aug 14, 1945. A picture of, The Kiss, appeared on the front page of the New York Times the next day.

Information about The Parachute Wedding Gowns in World War II, can be found at:
en.wikipedia.org/wiki/ - parachute wedding gowns and scroll down through the options.

Information on the destruction of lighthouses during both the Revolutionary and Civil War by both Union and Confederate troops found at:
en.wikipedia.org/wiki/ Cape-Lookout-Lighthouse:
This is one example, among many, of historical records, recounting destruction of lighthouses during the Civil War.

The disaster relief background was discussed at length during my time as a member of The Caribbean Tourist Board, Washington, D.C.

Samaritan's Purse International Disaster Relief, Clean Water Projects: samaritanspurse.org

Information on American Red Cross; First Aid/CPR/AED certification can be found at:
redcross.org

Information on the Pensacola Lighthouse and the knowledge of the National Museum of Naval Aviation at NAS, (Naval Air Station), in Florida, was from a personal visit. They had the US Navy HU-16 Albatross plane, on display there. It is also documented at:
en.wikipedia.org/wiki/-_US_Navy_HU-16_Albatross_plane

Some of the events in this book are from real events, with the approximate time and location in which each character was living. However, I have taken liberties with many details to weave them into the storyline based on their value to the history of lighthouses and the lives of these fictional characters.

I am a current member of the United States Lighthouse Society. The subjects and events about lighthouses and shipwrecks are from my imagination, not a specific lighthouse. My book reflects my knowledge that I have obtained from my visits to numerous lighthouses in Asia, Europe, The Caribbean, Bermuda, Tahiti, The Galapagos Islands, Canada, and America, including Alaska and Hawaii.

Much of my knowledge of Scotland is due to my travel to Scotland, as well as attending meetings of The Scottish Tourist Board, in Washington DC. The national tourism agency for Scotland currently meets under the name of 'VisitScotland.'

The historical figures, including inventors, in the book, are real along with their inventions. I have woven them into the storyline based on their approximate timeline and their value to the history of lighthouses and the lives of these fictional characters.
These inventors are at:
en.wikipedia.org/wiki

David Brewster, Kaleidoscope, Patent granted 1817

French physicist Augustine Fresnel, Invented the Fresnel Lens in 1822

Alexander Parkes- unveiled the first man-made plastic at 1862 Great International Exhibition in London; also holds first several patents on a plastic material called Parkesine.

GW Ferris- Invention of the Ferris wheel for the 1893 Chicago World's Columbian Exposition
en.wikipedia.org/wiki/George_Washington_Gale_Ferris_Jr.
en.wikipedia.org/wiki/Ferris_wheel

The Biblical passage was quoted from I Corinthians 13:13, which explained Love and ended with, "and now abide faith, hope, love, these three; but the greatest of these is love, (NIV).

Made in the USA
Middletown, DE
08 June 2019